Susan
At 2:00 AM
Read Chapter 25
Try to put book down
Keep Smiling

April, 2008

Donated to Alexis Gardens Book Club in memory of Binny Szychowski

Don & Ruth Smith (daughter)
Riverview, FL

Managed Murders

a mystery by

Thomas Summerill

A Plum Publishing Book

This is a work of fiction. Names, characters, locales and incidents are either the product of the author's imagination or are used fictitiously, and any resemblance to actual persons, living or dead, is entirely coincidental.

Plum Publishing
9522 Silverside Dr., Ste. 300
South Lyon, MI 48178

First edition; 2003

Edit and book layout by Dorrie O'Brien
Book cover design by Margaret Kelly

ISBN 0-9724706-1-1

1 2 3 4 5 6 7 8 9

For Andrew Robert, a wonderful man
who left us too soon. You were a terrific role model.

And for his daughter, Trudy,
who has been my rock through
sickness and health and
for better or worse for
twenty-four years.

To Anne and Stephanie,
thank you for your editorial comments and wisdom.
I value the input.

—Acknowlegements—

For me, the writing was the easy part. Turning that effort into *Managed Murders* involved many individuals. For everyone who said an encouraging word along the way, thank you. Your support was inspirational.

To my reading group friends, particularly Cynthia, Karen, Michelle, Ronda, Sally, Sam, and Wendy, I appreciate and thank you for your ideas, comments and support.

To my editor, Dorrie O'Brien, your professional words of wisdom and diligence made all the difference.

Finally, to my family, Trudy, Drew, and Nichole, your love and consistent support have allowed me to be successful in so many ways.

–Prologue–

It was a picturesque summer day in June that most people would have relished.

But the day was completely lost on Dr. Andrew Albright.

Like so many times before, Andrew had been awake most of the night, though even when he did sleep, it couldn't have been called restful. This time, however, instead of gazing around his bedroom, he'd been staring around the inside of a jail cell.

He was having trouble comprehending the charges he faced. Andrew needed to get a grasp of the devastating future facing him. He could have gone anywhere, but his dilemma brought him to the place he felt most comfortable: the cemetery at St. Patrick's.

Julia Osborn, his love and soul mate, had been buried there for ten months.

Many times since that dark day in September, he had left his house on the south side of Ann Arbor in the pre-dawn hours. After stopping for a cup of coffee to go, he'd head straight for St. Pat's. This particular day, however, he'd come straight from the police station where he'd spent the past two days being detained for a crime he hadn't committed.

Andrew didn't care what others thought about his cemetery visits. He'd lost count of the times he'd been told "to let Julia go." Regardless, he continued to visit and talk to her; sometimes he'd visit an hour and sometimes several hours. Today, he suspected he'd have a lengthy visit. He'd written down his thoughts days before, something he'd learned to do from the psychologists at the clinic. It was supposed to help him deal with his anger.

He began reading to her: "Dearest Julia, this is for you:

Letting Go
When will I stop missing you?
Julia, please tell what I'm supposed to do.
I have given this matter significant thought;
I am sad and confused as if forever caught.

I cannot go forward and I cannot go back,
My memories of you are a constant attack.
It was always so easy to invite you inside.
I cannot escape you and I know I can't hide.

You have never left me off the hook,
To you I was always an open book.
You planted a seed and helped it grow,
Your affect on me you shall never know.

By sharing your soul you allowed me to see
That by giving to others, I could be a better me.
You never told me that this was your plan,
That now I've become a more complete man.

All of a sudden you were just gone.
The angels came and you moved on.

If I close my eyes, I can see your bright smile.
You come and visit me, but just for awhile.

Your earthly shell we can no longer see.
Your spirit now soars forever free.
Your visits leave me feeling so blue.
Julia, my love, what am I supposed to do?

Moving on with my life is where I should go.
It's the right thing to do; you keep telling me so.
Knowing when or how, I simply can't guess.
As for our time together, I am truly blessed.

There are many ways for me to remember you;
Someday I'll start by sharing these gifts anew.
Even then I will cherish and savor our love
As you, my angel, smile from the heavens above."

Andrew Albright had to move on. When he got to his car he saw the newspaper he'd picked up on the way out of jail lying on the front seat of his car. Staring him in the face was the headline: POPULAR PHYSICIAN ARRESTED FOR ANN ARBOR'S MANAGED MURDERS, which certainly ensured that his life was changing course.

—Chapter 1—

It was during the summer of 1995 when Andrew Albright's world first came apart. It had taken Laura Donaldson Albright several weeks to muster up the courage to tell her husband that she wanted a divorce, but she couldn't wait any longer; the guilt about her affair was crushing her. She arranged for friends to watch Drew and took Andrew to the park where they'd often spent lazy, carefree afternoons.

Once she'd set out a picnic, opened a bottle of wine, and filled a glass for him, she started. "Andrew, I've always loved you, but for a long time I have not been *in* love with you."

"I'm a man prone to missing the obvious, but that's been pretty clear for awhile now."

"I need you to know that this is not about you, this is completely about me, and I have to leave you," she said.

Andrew felt like he had been gutted. Although not a wine and roses marriage by any stretch of the imagination, it was functional and safe. "You just want to throw our marriage away? Just like that? Isn't this something we should work on?" He was confident he could fix this–just like he did with his beloved patients.

"Andrew, please listen to me: I can't do that. It would be a waste of your time."

"What are you saying?" he asked, almost willing her *not* to say it, not make it final, unable to be undone.

Crying, she said, "I'm leaving as soon as it's practical for me to do so."

"Please reconsider what you're saying. I need you. We have so much to be thankful for, and we're fighters. What about our son?" Suddenly a light dawned. "Is there someone else?" he asked, staring at the ground, waiting for her betrayal to hit him full force. He wanted to see it in her eyes but couldn't muster the courage to look at her.

"Yes. I'm sorry, but I've fallen in love with someone else," she said, unable to look him in the eyes either.

Andrew waited, thinking she was going to explain where he had gone wrong, why she wanted another guy. After a lengthy wait though, it looked obvious that she wasn't going to add anything, so he asked for the details. "So how long have you been seeing the guy?"

She didn't respond for several minutes. Laura was in pain, but she'd known that how she felt would be nothing compared to how Andrew was going to feel when she explained. "The person in my life is not a man, she's a woman. We've been in love for quite awhile now. That's what makes this breakup about me, not you."

She waited anxiously for his reaction, but Andrew was speechless. A failed marriage was tough enough to live through, God knew, but his wife was going to leave him for another woman! How was he supposed to handle that?

—Chapter 2—

Laura wasted no time filing for divorce. Andrew met Lindsey Resnick, his wife's lover, at the custody hearing for their five-year-old son, Drew. What struck him most was her age: Lindsey was only twenty-five, more than a decade younger than he was. Laura had not only dumped him for a woman, but a younger woman, too. She was the total opposite of Laura, a petite brunette with a dark complexion; Lindsey was tall, blond and fair.

Andrew didn't try to hide how angry he was at the image of his wife being intimate with Lindsey, and the fear that she'd been cheating on him all along. It ate away his self-confidence like he was host to a tapeworm, always there, reducing him from a healthy male to a self-absorbed social recluse. But the worst part, the part that kept his anger stoked, was that Laura and Lindsey were moving to California and planning on taking his son with them.

More by accident than calculation, Andrew chose a female attorney for his custody battle. Beverly McNeil was black, tough as nails and as smart as they came. Her law firm, Harris, Steele, and Washington, was one of the largest and most prominent in Ann Arbor. The only mind in her firm thought to be brighter than hers was that of her partner and husband, Travis Washington.

The courtroom felt cold and sterile to Andrew. It was actually just a hearing room situated in an annexed part of the Washtenaw County Courthouse. Judge Cynthia Parker was hearing the case. She was one of the few female, minority judges on the Southeast Michigan Bench. She was the Family Court's toughest judge on dads. Beverly had sighed when she'd heard the case had been assigned to Judge Parker. She wasn't going to be impressed with Andrew's workaholic ways; she'd probably see it as a short-coming, as opposed to a stable economic environment for the boy.

While waiting for Judge Parker to come in on the final day, Andrew asked Beverly, "How do so many life-altering decisions get made in this cold, windowless room?"

"The law itself possesses neither emotion or passion. People bring that with them. It often either saves them or destroys them," she answered logically. "So, pay more attention to your actions and less to your surroundings."

Great, he thought, a philosopher. Let's hope she's the fighter everybody's told me about.

Judge Parker came in and Laura's attorney, Mark Patterson, started right in. "Your Honor, Ms. Donaldson has every right to follow her own path to happiness. Even though many might question her sexual-preference decisions, that is not our issue today. I would again like to stress that my client is a competent and fit mother. She has accepted a position to teach at California State University in Irvine. Her life partner, Lindsey Resnick, has just graduated from the University of Michigan with a Ph.D. in Sociology. She has been accepted to the faculty at Cypress College. This is a stable relationship. On the other hand, Dr. Albright is a single professional man who works in excess of sixty hours a week. While he believes that he can change that pattern, we see no reason to disrupt Drew's world based upon that promise. The child would absolutely agree if we asked him."

"Let's just stop the bus right there, Mr. Patterson," interjected Judge Parker. "Drew is way too young for this court to ask him how he feels, despite your assurance that he'd want to be with his mother. Please tell this court why we should be so confident that your plea is in the best interest of the youth several years from now? After all, your client is planning on moving two thousand miles away."

"Laura Donaldson is a loving mother. Our testimony over the past two days clearly shows that Drew's development would be better served by having her and Ms. Resnick as custodial parents, rather than an absent father. Ms. Donaldson's choice of life partner, no matter that they're both women, has no bearing on Drew's best interests."

Andrew made a mental note to ask his wife when she'd dropped the "Albright" moniker. Their divorce was nowhere near final.

Beverly had heard enough and said, "Judge Parker, given that the couple are not seeking a legally binding marital relationship, this new environment looks less than stable to me."

"You'll have your turn shortly, Ms. McNeil. Mr. Patterson, why don't you continue your white-washing of our values structure."

Andrew felt a jab of hope. The judge was on his side. What better indication could there be than for the judge to question Laura's morals?

"We've made our relevant points," Mark said. "I'm willing to turn the floor over to Ms. McNeil, as long as you allow me some latitude to rebut when she's done."

The judge turned to Beverly. "You have my complete attention, Ms. McNeil. Are you ready to wow us?"

"Judge Parker, my client is one of the most respected physicians in this town. Besides the humiliation of these events, taking his son that far away is simply wrong. Frankly, we believe that joint custody would be in the best interest of the child." It had taken a great deal of effort for Beverly to convince Andrew that fighting for sole custody was a losing battle. Short of criminal misconduct, no judge would take a child away from a mother.

"Ms. McNeil, you know as well as I do that the State of California has very different child custody laws than we do here in Michigan. How do we reconcile that issue down the road?"

"That, frankly, is a part of the consequences of making the decisions they've made. Doesn't my client also have rights? Of course he does. Rather than argue the subjective benefits of sole custody, we choose to offer the compromise of joint custody. Dr. Albright really wanted sole custody, but we didn't want to totally take the child away from his mother."

After writing a few notes, Judge Parker inquired, "Mr. Patterson, do you have anything further?"

"Not at this time, your Honor."

"Then as the hour is late, I will adjourn this hearing and reconvene it at eleven tomorrow morning."

Beverly and Andrew left the courthouse quickly. They headed back to her office to debrief. Neither was confident of the outcome.

Andrew arose after a fitful night's sleep. He went through the motions of seeing his patients at University Hospital. Most days, he loved to get an early start, but today he simply wanted the morning to be done with as quickly as possible. He hoped for the best, but feared for the worst.

By 10:30, Andrew was in Beverly's office. She had conferred with her colleagues and with her husband, Travis. They all knew that Judge Parker was a liberal judge who strongly supported women's rights. Beverly had used that to her advantage on many previous occasions, but this time it wasn't an advantage. The chance that she would rule in favor of Dr. Albright was not very good and she knew it.

At 11:00, Christopher Cromwell, Andrew's long-time friend and coworker, joined the two of them in the courthouse lobby. A simple hand on Andrew's shoulder as they entered the hearing room as a gesture of quiet support was a much-needed boon. Chris was a powerbroker in town and being his friend had many benefits. Andrew wondered briefly if making Laura disappear was among those perks. As soon as he thought it, he was ashamed of himself.

After dispensing with the preliminaries, Judge Parker began, "These cases are never easy. I see too many couples involved in physical and sexual abuse, drug use and or suffering from mental disorders; it makes decisions regarding how to protect children easier. But this case does not fit that profile. What I cannot do here is call the relationship between Laura Donaldson and Lindsey Resnick wrong, or detrimental to the child's welfare. As much as you want me to, Dr. Albright, I cannot."

Andrew closed his eyes. He stopped listening. He knew the rest was academic.

Judge Parker continued, "While I appreciate the compromise put on the table by your attorney, Dr. Albright, I cannot rule in favor of it. Drew Albright is too young to be shuttled around the country. Ms. Donaldson, are you willing to agree to a two-year trial custody arrangement, at which point this court can re-evaluate how Drew is doing once he has been in school for a few years? Dr. Albright will be granted liberal visitation rights. A visitation plan will be filed with this court within thirty days. You will be required to return to the state of Michigan in two years for an evaluation of Drew's situation and progress. This court will have jurisdiction. Do you understand that?"

Mark Patterson spoke up, "Your Honor, may I have a word with my client?"

"Of course you can."

Mark leaned over and whispered, "Laura, this is a dangerous move in that Drew will be called to testify in two years. In most of the cases I've seen, the child almost always wants to be with the parent he or she spends the *least* amount of time with. It's always a vacation. It's fun, and there's less discipline. As your attorney, I advise against this."

"So what are our options?"

"Well, let's find out." Returning to his feet, Mark addressed the bench. "Your Honor, my client believes that this places the child in the unenviable position of having to choose one parent over the other at the end of two years."

"Mr. Patterson, Ms. McNeil offered a compromise, as did I. Joint custody, which at the distance the parties will live apart, will require the child choosing sooner or later anyway. Does that prospect excite you, Ms. Donaldson? Your other option is the one I outlined."

Laura looked at Lindsey, who simply nodded her head: Take the risk. A bird in the hand was good enough.

"Your Honor," Laura said voice cracking, "We are willing to accept your proposal."

She looked at Andrew, who looked dumbstruck at losing. After the judge whacked her gavel, Laura tried to hug her soon-to-be ex-husband. He turned away from her and spoke to Christopher instead. "What am I going to do now?"

"You're going to go on with your life, man. You're going to continue to be a great doctor. Most importantly, you're going to continue to be my friend and colleague. You'll adjust; it'll just take some time."

They walked out together.

Twenty-four hours later, Beverly came to the clinic with the papers he had to endorse that would sign away his custodial rights. He was so angry at losing his son he practically shredded the paper when he signed his name.

—Chapter 3—

Andrew went on with his life, slowly and painfully. He worked more, not less. He became the President of Partners Medical Group, the youngest in the clinic's history. With that honor came a seat on the Board of the local managed care company, QualityCare where Christopher was the CEO. In both settings, his passion for his patients and upholding the highest standards of care were second to none.

The only time he took away from his work was for the occasional golf outing and time with Drew. He traveled to Huntington Beach, California, once a month to spend a long weekend with his son.

Andrew went on many first and a few second dates, but his heart wasn't in them; any possible relationships died before they had a chance to start. He was at a summer picnic when he overheard Chris and his most trusted nurse, Amy, discussing a betting pool–the winner being the person who set him up with a woman who dated him for at least a month.

Amy and Christopher were sitting beneath an old ginkgo tree; they thought they were alone. Andrew was about to join them when he heard Amy say, "Well, if our little Andrew Albright dating pool continues to grow, one of us'll be able to retire with the proceeds."

Amy was the odds-on favorite to win; she spent the most time with Andrew; she knew him best and had his trust. She always wondered why none of her dates ever lasted.

"At last count the total's up to over three grand," Christopher said with a hint of disgust. "This is getting ridiculous. Twenty-four months is long enough. How long can it take for a man to get back on the damn horse?"

Christopher stopped as soon as he saw his friend come from behind the tree. Andrew hadn't intended to spy on his friends, but was glad that he had. He sat down at the picnic table. After a minute of awkward silence, he said, "Hot day, don't you think, Amy?"

"Yup," she said, attempting not to giggle.

He waited for them to confess. "By all means go on. I believe you were discussing a betting pool about my social life." He tried to keep a straight face, but he had to put a hand in front of his mouth to hide his telltale smile.

Christopher said, "His 'social life,' he calls it. If it weren't for the money involved, do you think any of us would care about your so-called social life?"

"That's really low. Money is more important to you people than my happiness?"

"No doubt about it." Christopher cracked a smile.

Andrew couldn't hold back any longer. He laughed harder than he had in a long time. "I guess two years is a long time. I'll see what I can do."

As they were walking back to the crowd, Chris commented, "You know, you could start by not boring your dates to death."

Andrew kept walking; he was used to Chris having to get in the last word.

In the fall, he made two important decisions. The first came during a visit with Drew. It was time to get more aggressive with his ex-wife. He had just lost another court outing with Laura. Judge Parker had determined that Drew would stay with his mother. They would go through the evaluation process one more time in May, 1999. His son was beginning to struggle with the realities of his mother's choice, and it was hurting him in school. The second decision wasn't actually a decision: he felt a growing need to find another life partner.

That Thanksgiving it happened when he least expected it. While visiting his sister he was introduced to Julia Osborn. Many of the pool participants had stopped egging him on–they'd honestly come to believe that Andrew simply hated women.

Andrew was very close to his Sissy. She'd been the rock of his childhood and they'd remained close throughout the years. She lived just down the road in Ft. Wayne, Indiana. She was a key figure in state politics and was currently preparing to run for a seat in the U.S. Congress.

Carol called him often, concerned about her baby brother. "Hey, little brother," she said on one of her calls, "you *are* planning on doing Thanksgiving dinner down here with me this year, aren't you?"

"As always, of course. I've had enough of both my own cooking and hospital food."

"Great. I think I'll hold it later in the evening this year–I'm tired of competing with football games. And I've got a slew of my backers coming over–no rest for us politicians–any chance to spread the word is a good one."

No reason to mention the lovely Julia Osborn, she thought. Thirty-four, divorced, and no children.

"Yes, I'm sure. That fat-headed Zeller gonna be there again this year?"

"Not a chance. He deserted me for another last summer on a bill I wanted passed. He's off my list."

"Good. He was a jackass anyway. How later in the evening? Should I dress up or is this gonna be an old-fashioned gather-around-the-food-and-gobble-it-up kind of dinner?"

"Oh, comfortable, I think. You'll know most everybody, and I'm going to do a buffet, so there's not going to be selected seating and you can gobble-it-up as you please. Come as early as you like. The rest of the crew will arrive around six. Plan on staying over, if you can. Okay?"

Thanksgiving Day arrived; he made his usual rounds at the hospital, caught enough of the Detroit/Dallas game to know that it wasn't likely Detroit was going to get out of its losing slump, checked his answering service–no emergencies–and drove down to Ft. Wayne.

Carol lived in a quiet community on the northeast side of town. She and her husband Bob, an orthopedic surgeon, had built a home designed specifically for entertaining. When Andrew arrived, she gave him a giant hug, then began introducing him–or re-introducing in some cases–to the guests who'd arrived early. Walt, Maureen, Shirley, Grover, Peter . . . the names slid past his ears, but then she said, "And this is my good friend Julia Osborn; I don't think the two of you have met, have you?"

If he'd been sucker-punched he didn't think his stomach would've reacted as strongly as it did when he looked at Julia. She was petite, with shoulder-length, auburn-colored hair. Her eyes flashed and twinkled with an energy that pulled him to her. She had well-formed legs, and her shoulders and arms exuded strength without making her seem the least bit masculine.

"Uh, no," he answered lamely.

"This is my brother the doctor," Carol said. "He's used to mumbling things like 'mm-hm,' more than making small talk." The two women smiled at each other, nodded like they'd just formed a cabal, and Andrew grinned–he'd been set up. Not a problem.

"Can I get you a drink?" he asked. "I'm used to doing that."

"Sure," Julia said. "A white wine would be nice."

He got their drinks; they talked. Andrew spent time with other guests, but somehow he kept making his way back to her. Carol even teased him that he was ignoring all her loyal subjects. Not a problem. Maybe it was her smile and maybe it was her humor. Whatever it was he didn't care. A brief touch of skin at the buffet sent an electric shock up his arm. First time since he'd met Laura that he'd felt anything like that.

Before he realized it, the time had come to head back home; he couldn't stay over like his sister had asked.

"Sis, I gotta go. I'm on duty at the clinic tomorrow. I traded some time so that I would have Christmas off to spend with Drew." He looked at Bob. "We internists have to work holidays. I doubt you surgeons will see the hospital tomorrow." Bob just brushed him off, mumbling something about internists being soft.

Carol had to act fast. "Andy, why don't you let Julia give you some golf lessons? It would be good for your image to stop embarrassing yourself on the golf course." Bob nodded his head sadly; he was used to taking Andrew's money; if Andrew got better, it'd be Bob's loss.

Andrew thought for a moment before finding an escape hatch. "Well, Sissy, I already have one long-distance relationship in my life with Drew in California. I don't need another one. No offense," he said looking toward Julia.

"None taken, softie," Julia said as they all laughed. "Would taking lessons from a woman damage your ego?"

"Honestly, I do live in Ann Arbor–another area code. Hell, the last I checked my geography, it's in a whole different state. If it weren't for that, I could take you up on my sister's offer."

"Well, little brother, you're in luck. If she hasn't told you yet, Julia only *used* to live here in Fort Wayne. Now she lives in Brighton, Michigan. Now, that's another area code, of course, but it's close enough for you to stop making excuses."

"Well, you have me there. I think, however, that you, Ms. Osborn, withheld a not-so-small-point all evening long."

"What small point would that be?" she asked, looking at Carol with a slight grin.

"Like where you live."

"Oh, that. You just assumed that I lived here in Ft. Wayne, huh?"

"Well, yes. But okay, since you live close to me, I'd be glad to let you work on my golf game. Isn't it fortunate for me that I have five months of winter snow to separate me from that day?"

Julia smiled, looked back at Carol and said, "Your luck just ran out. I give lessons all year round at an indoor facility in Pinckney. Teachers aren't paid anywhere near what you doctors make, and a girl's got to live. How about a week from Saturday? I'll call you with the details."

Throwing a quick glare at his sister, he replied to Julia, "I'll be there with bells on." Not only set up, but trapped into self-improvement, as well. Not a problem.

After saying a reluctant goodnight to Julia, who was staying with friends in Ft. Wayne for the weekend, Carol walked him to his car. Before getting in, he turned to her and said, "You set me up. You two planned this all along, didn't you?"

"Oh yeah. Good idea, huh? Julia and I go way back. I have no idea why I didn't recommend her earlier." She kissed him goodnight. "Drive safe and be sure to send me reports."

"Sure you don't want to come watch me humiliate myself?"

"Not a chance. My work here is done. But you heard it here first: I'm gonna win that Andrew Albright betting pool with this one. I need the money for my campaign fund next year."

"I can't believe you're in on that, too. You heard it here first, as well: I hope you're right."

The next morning, Julia called Carol to thank her for the dinner invitation and added, "Andrew is everything you said. I'm even looking forward to cracking his shell like we talked about. He does seem to want to get out of his black box. That's good, I think."

"You read him right, but read me right as well: If you hurt him, I'll personally track you down and punish you." Julia giggled as if she thought Carol was making a joke. "I'm not kidding, don't hurt my little brother."

Julia caught her drift and responded, "So where were you when I needed help with that man known only as my ex-husband? I know what hurt is, and I could have used your muscle."

"I hear you, sister." They laughed and agreed to get together the next time Carol was in Michigan. She also made Julia promise to share progress updates. It was unlikely she'd learn anything from her brother.

Julia smiled to herself as she hung up the phone. Originally, Julia had been very nervous about moving to Michigan. But she'd needed a fresh start. Her adoptive parents had moved to Arizona years before and both had died while she was still in her twenties. Her ex-husband had proven not only to be a bad spouse but also a bad father to the two kids from his first marriage. There was nothing to hold her in Indiana. Now maybe there was something to hold her in Michigan.

—Chapter 4—

On December 7th, Andrew took his first golf lesson from Julia. Andrew had played golf at Whispering Pines before, but had never run into her. He'd been looking forward to their meeting ever since Thanksgiving. The game of golf was something he'd tolerated, until now. Playing it had felt like a necessary evil that doctors did as a rite of passage, until now. He found her in the pro shop. She was dressed in black slacks and white turtleneck sweater, with a waterproof jacket hanging off her clubs.

"Hi," she said. "Ready for a whole new way of playing?"

"As I'll ever be, I guess."

It took him twenty minutes before his nerves calmed down. His first dozen shots looked as if he'd never picked up a club in his life.

During a break in her training session, he asked, "How come I've never seen you out here before?"

"Easy. While you doctors rule the golf course on your leisurely Wednesday afternoons off, I'm busy teaching America's future leaders in the classroom. You guys really are soft."

Andrew paused and laughed. "What a horrible stereotype of my colleagues. I expected more respect from you than that, young lady."

"When you prove me wrong, I'll offer you my sincerest apology. Until then, let's get on with this, shall we? When we get done in here, we're heading to the course to see if you learned anything. We don't get many fifty-degree days this late in the season." She picked up a club and took a practice swing. "By the way, I almost forgot–there will be the small matter of a wager on the outcome. The loser buys dinner. You up for that?"

"Do I get a handicap? Otherwise, I might think I'd been set up here."

"I'll consider it, but it won't matter," she said shoving him back toward the practice tee.

The golf lesson ended well. The nine-hole torture test was another story. Andrew was nervous, but it wasn't his golf game that created it. It had just been too long since he'd felt comfortable around a woman. Julia tried to make it easy on him: She offered him a stroke-a-hole advantage, and then played cat-and-mouse with him. She birdied the first hole; he struggled with a double-bogey. She kept him in the game by letting him win a hole now and then. She didn't have to, but it made the bet and teasing more fun. In the end, she won, but so, of course, did he.

They agreed to meet in Ann Arbor for dinner. He made reservations at the trendy Gandy Dancer–always a safe first date spot. He arrived early and was in the bar when Christopher Cromwell and his wife, Roxanne, came in.

Chris teased him, "Why, Andrew Albright, what are you doing hanging out in a bar by yourself? If you're looking for women, might I suggest you try another spot? Not too many women come in here alone and even less are going to dump their boyfriend at the first sight of you."

Roxanne came to his defense. "Pay no attention to this bore. He's just jealous that you're single and available. Plus, he knows you're meeting a date and he's poised to run her off he wants to win the money in the betting pool. This guy would turn his mother out if there was money to be made on seventy-three-year-old hookers."

Roxanne could be a sweetheart, but she was better known as being high-maintenance and expensive. She ran in the highest political circles, lunches with the mayor and fund-raising for the governor. She loved the glamour, but when it came to rolling up her sleeves and getting her hands dirty with civic work, she was seldom around. She liked the fact that Chris was a CEO, even if it was for a managed care organization, those organizations having such a dreadful reputation around the country. It bothered her that the American public ranked Health Maintenance Organizations just one notch above tobacco companies. The good news was that QualityCare was actually owned by the doctors in town, and it was well respected because its owners refused to cut corners on the quality of health care it delivered to its members.

Julia arrived right on time, dressed in the staple of every woman's wardrobe: the understated black cocktail dress. It may have looked simple on the rack at the store, but Julia made it look elegant. Somewhere between the ninth hole and dinner she'd done up her hair, leaving wisps to fall down by the sides of her face; they framed her emerald earrings and necklace perfectly.

Andrew caught himself staring at Julia and then blushing as Christopher asked if he was going to introduce his date. After the introductions, Chris invited the new couple to join them for dinner.

"Thanks, but no thanks; this is a first date and we're just getting to know each other. Besides, I'd hate to subject Julia to your boorish behavior; it might reflect poorly on me."

Christopher wasn't going to let Andrew have the last word; a Harvard man could hardly let a Florida man get the better of him. "Well, Ms. Osborn, rest assured that you are likely to be sleeping in your soup. Dr. Albright here isn't exactly known for keeping his dates awake."

"I'll take my chances. An internist knows more about the entire body than you cardiologists do. You may know your hearts, but Andrew here is working on my head. No need for a heart man just yet."

Christopher had no comeback. A woman had just bested him. Roxanne just smiled. Andrew led his date to their table, grinning back at Chris.

Dinner was much more relaxing than Andrew expected. The two of them talked leisurely about what was going on in their lives. She talked about children and education, and he talked about the clinic and his duties there. They drank a bottle of 1995 French Malesan Bordeaux, a favorite for both, which was a pleasant surprise: It was very hard to find in restaurants around Ann Arbor and they both marveled at the thought they each had found something so rare; it felt like an omen of good luck. They shared and experimented with dishes of elk and caribou, and they joked about how they were taking a risk, albeit only a culinary one. The time passed so quickly, Julia was surprised to see that it was going on ten when she glanced at her watch.

"Andrew, I really want to stay but I should be going. This has been delightful, but I do have other obligations to tend to."

Without even thinking, he asked, "Julia, do you trust me?"

"Is there a reason why I shouldn't? Your sister vouches for you, which is good enough for me. For now."

"Well, I'm a doctor who occasionally plays golf on Wednesdays, does that count?"

"Are you kidding? I'm a teacher who'd be playing golf on Wednesdays too, if I could."

"Here's my proposal: Leave your car here; we'll take my car into town and stop for coffee and dessert at another restaurant I know. You can spend the night at my place, in the guest bedroom."

"Do you think that's a good idea? What will people say? No one has even won the pool of money yet." Carol had told her that the pool had grown to over three grand.

"I think it's the best idea I've had in years. I'm in no hurry to rush our relationship, and I can assure you that my intentions are honorable."

"Can I modify your proposal? I do have to check your flexibility."

"I'm listening."

"Let's leave my car here and stop by and pick up dessert. I assume that you have coffee at your place. If not, there's no chance this Irish girl is going home with you."

Andrew felt his heart race. "Well, little Miss Ireland, I've even got some dessert at home to go with your Irish coffee, if you want it."

"Wow, this is a spontaneous offer, right? I'd hate to think you'd planned to take me home with you all along."

"Now I'm hurt," he said as they walked out the door.

They stopped by her car. Andrew was shocked when he saw an overnight bag in her hand as she got in his car. "Why, Ms. Osborn, I hope you carry that ditty bag in your car all the time. I'd certainly hate to think you'd set me up twice in one day."

"Men. I was planning on spending the night at my girlfriend's here in Ann Arbor to avoid the drive home. She is my snow emergency stopover. Besides, you only *wish* I was that easy."

"Hmm, left that fact out of the dinner conversation didn't you? This is becoming a pattern with you. Well, you'd better call her and let her know not to expect you. Will she be disappointed, do you think?"

"No. She's actually out of town 'til tomorrow afternoon. We're having dinner tomorrow night when she gets back."

She couldn't wait to share the news with Carol about how well their plan was working.

When they got to Andrew's house, situated on the fifth hole of Stonebridge Golf Course, she couldn't resist saying, "For a guy who lives on a golf course, you sure are an atrocious golfer."

"Let's thank God then that I'm a better doctor than golfer."

"You take care of me, Dr. Albright, and I'll take care of your golf game."

"Deal."

Andrew's colonial style home was decorated in soft-toned fabric and elegant dark wood that surprised and concerned her. It didn't have the look of a male-dominated place; it clearly still had Laura's influence. As he was making Irish coffee and serving up Zingerman's cheesecake, she looked at the pictures of Drew in the family room. When he came in, she asked him more about his son since he hadn't said much about him at dinner.

It was painful for him, but he told her about Laura, Lindsey and Drew. Halfway into the story, Julia told Andrew that it was okay to save the rest for another day. She could tell that it was taking its toll on him. As Andrew paused, she asked him if he was ready to date *any* woman after that experience. He did the second thing that night without thinking: He reached over and stroked her face with his fingers.

As he looked into her eyes, it was she who said, "Can we get this kiss over with?"

Andrew drew his lips ever so gently across hers. His breathing quickened as he brought her closer to him. Their kiss was what he'd always thought a first kiss should be, soft but passionate. It did what it was supposed to do: stopped the world, if only for a moment. As they looked at each other, they laughed to lighten the moment. Julia was afraid she was taking advantage of Andrew's vulnerability, but it also crossed her mind to worry about her own.

Andrew did the smart thing. As easily as this could turn into a night of incredible passion, that was not what he wanted. He cleaned up the dishes while Julia changed her clothes. He prepared the spare bedroom and they figured out what time they needed to be up for breakfast. Andrew hadn't thought about what to do with Sunday church services, but he could worry about that in the morning.

He kissed her goodnight. As he lay awake in bed, hands cupped under his head, staring at the ceiling, a feeling of calm settled over him and suddenly he was tearing up. Not tears of pain or anger, but for regret for the lost time in his life.

He was startled by a quiet knock on his door. He was embarrassed when Julia came in and saw a tear on his cheek.

"What's the matter?" she asked, forgetting for a second why she'd come.

"I've spilled enough of the Andrew Albright story for one night. Do you need something? Another blanket or something?"

"No. Uh, can I test your flexibility one more time?"

"I don't know. You're starting to become a pushy broad, but go ahead."

"I just want to be near you. Would you hold me?"

"Not a problem."

She fell asleep in his arms, still wearing her makeup. He fell asleep watching her breathe. Sometime in the middle of the night, he came awake, astounded for a brief moment to find someone in his bed. He rose and sat at his desk to write down his thoughts. When he was done, he climbed back into bed, careful not to wake the Irish girl.

Julia woke to the smell of fresh coffee, but no Andrew. She wondered if he was coming back. Feeling a little self-conscious, she sat up in bed and she saw a handwritten note propped up on the bedside table. Picking it up, she read:

Julia,

Grace

Some people I know can simply never be free
To look in their soul and accept what they see.
There was a time when I thought that was me,
But you've come into my life and filled it with glee.

While our union is yet quite early and new,
And the time together are moments too few,
We're building our bridge between lost hearts,
Its beauty clear, right from the very start.

Those soft, blue-green eyes are so full of trust
It gives me confidence, which I think is a must.
But only to hold you; I would feel so secure.
It is an emotion I cherish, so needed and pure.

You say we are different, but I think, the same.
I am bursting with joy and you are to blame.
I see in your smile that you're in the same place.
It can be a bright future under God's shining grace.

She put on her robe and went looking for her host. She found him sitting on the porch. She sat on his lap and hugged him. She filed away the questions she wanted to ask; it was too early to try to interpret the poem.

—Chapter 5—

After a minute, as if she'd been caught being naughty, Julia whispered, "Thank you for a wonderful evening last night. And thank you for the stealth poem. I'm glad it wasn't a 'gone to work, be home soon' note."

"I often write down my feelings. Sometimes they're just journal notes and sometimes it's poetry. I don't know, it just frees my soul, I guess."

Julia, being the direct Irish girl that she was, asked, "I'm curious as to why we weren't more intimate last night?"

"It's been a long time; I wasn't sure I could carry it off. And besides, I didn't want you to think I'd just *presumed* you were okay with it."

"Well, that was good, but I make my own decisions. At least you could have asked me so I could say no."

"I'll know better next time," he said, wondering when the next time might occur.

"Who said there was going to be any next time?"

"My God, did I miss my only chance?"

"Maybe, and maybe not." She was baiting him, which wasn't really her style, and she wondered what it was about Andrew Albright that brought it out in her. She was also wondering why she was about to do what she was about to do. "I could really use some coffee, but I could also really use a shower. Would you mind bringing me a cup of coffee upstairs while I take Lucifer's painting off my face?" He looked a question at her. "You know, makeup. Men, they're so slow on the uptake." She pecked him on the forehead and went inside.

He came with the coffee, and some fruit. She thanked him and asked, "Do you want to help undo Lucifer's work?"

He was going to answer, but the phone rang. "Saved by the bell." Heading toward the phone, Julia called him a chicken.

It was Carol, calling for her update. She had already called Julia's house and gotten her voice mail. She left a message saying that she hoped Andrew had kidnapped her. "So, little brother, how did your date go?"

"Terrific. You may have started something good here." He told her about their dinner at the Gandy Dancer.

Apparently Carol could hear water running because she asked, "Are you taking a shower? I can call back later."

As though it was no big deal, he said, "No, that's just Julia taking a shower."

"Oh. Well, I guess you did have a terrific date. Can I count on collecting the money in the pool?"

"Sissy, nothing happened, and you might want to wait on looking for the money."

"Little brother, try thinking like a prison inmate who hasn't had sex in two years. You have a beautiful naked woman in your shower, and you're on the phone with me? What the hell is your problem? If she didn't want you in the shower with her, she'd've taken one at home. I hope she hasn't shampooed her hair yet. You're offending this girl; get in there. 'Bye."

Andrew thought Carol might have read one too many trashy novels, but then again, she was usually right about things like this. He wasted no more time joining Julia in the shower. "I really didn't want to offend you," was all he could think to say.

"So you say. You can prove it by washing my hair."

That convinced him: He was in a conspiracy of the highest magnitude.

Although he managed to get the shampoo in her hair, he made a mess of it by being too busy looking at the rest of her. Her legs were long and slender and her shoulders broad. Her breasts were the perfect size to him, although she appeared to be self-conscience about them; she used a washcloth to hide their small size. He finished her hair and they washed each other much longer than just getting clean would dictate. They were exploring. Their second kiss was even more passionate than the first, but given the circumstances, neither was surprised. They took turns drying each other and he offered her a robe, which she reluctantly took to stave off the cold air. He led her back into the bedroom.

"Can we negotiate?" she asked.

"What exactly would you like to negotiate, Irish Girl?"

"I want you to take your time; I want this to be special. I want to remember this always. I'd like you to make it memorable."

"Well, I could do without the performance anxiety associated with making it memorable, but I'm willing to follow your lead."

"Andrew, I want you to want me."

No problem. He spent the next hour pleasing his Irish Girl in ways that surprised them both. He made her the center of his universe. Her skin was every bit as soft as he'd imagined. And he was anything but Mr. Softie now. As she commented about that they both smiled, which only made the moment better.

When they were done and almost finished dressing, she asked, "Where are you taking me now that you've ravaged me?"

"Why, to breakfast at Angelos, a favorite of the truly knowledgeable Ann Arborite or anyone who has spent more than two days on the University of Michigan campus."

"You, Scottish Boy, just failed my first test. No, I take that back. You passed test number one with flying colors. Thank you for the memory. But now, what do good Catholic boys normally do on Sundays in Scotland?" Where they went that morning was important to her; it would tell her something about where their relationship might go.

"They go to church, which, under the circumstances, would be inappropriate. I'd hate to leave you here."

"Typical man you are, Scottish Boy. Hello, I'm an Osborn, and I'm Irish, so I just might be Catholic, don't you think? More importantly, I might be a *good* Catholic girl who needs to go to church to confess this horrible sin I just committed."

"I hope not," he said with a twinge of guilt in his voice.

"You hope I'm not Catholic, or you hope I didn't just punch your ticket to hell?"

"I'm going to take a chance and suggest we head to St. Patrick's for eleven o'clock Mass."

"You're getting smarter. For a minute I thought you might be totally stupid. You saved yourself in the shower, and now you've redeemed yourself here. But boy, I gotta say it again: slow, slow, slow."

Julia had never been to the old St. Patrick's on the northernmost edge of Ann Arbor. Andrew cherished its age and beauty. The Gothic arches throughout the church reminded him of the small churches of Europe. The floors and pews were made of carved wood that had aged gracefully over the hundred and thirty years the church had stood. The chapel was just small enough to feel intimate. Julia immediately fell in love with the many stained-glass windows, and the two oil paintings between each window that made up the Stations of the Cross.

After the service was over, they stayed around so that she could admire her surroundings. She was used to attending St. Patrick's in Brighton, one of the largest Catholic parishes in the state. This small place of worship, however, took her back to her own childhood when she and her parents had attended a similar church, near Lansing. Andrew admired her as she admired the beauty. They left holding each other. It crossed his mind that although it was still too early to tell, he just might be falling in love.

—Chapter 6—

Six months into their relationship summer came, as did a spontaneous vacation to London. Julia had summers off and Andrew had not taken any time away from the clinic in two years, other than to visit Drew in California. They settled into their seats as best they could, got through take-off, and the obligatory round of drinks, and were waiting for dinner to be served when Julia asked, "I'm really happy that Carol introduced us; she certainly was confident we'd be good for each other. Why do you think that is?"

"Probably because my sister knows me better than anyone else. We've been protecting each other since we were kids. I think she understands my deepest insecurities and must have seen something in you that would make me more secure."

Julia was quiet for a moment, thinking. "Okay, I can buy that, but what do *you* see in me?"

He chuckled. "Now that's an easier question to answer. You're everything I'm not. You have an aura around you that glows with confidence. You are everything the women in my life haven't been. You focus on others, not yourself."

She stopped him before he could go on. "Do you want to have more children?" It felt impetuous to ask, but she needed to know before things got any more serious.

"That's a harder question. I don't need children to make me feel whole, but I'd like to have a couple more, I think. The hang-up is that I'd need to feel incredibly secure. Being a parent to Drew at this distance is the hardest thing I've ever had to do. All because of a stinking lack of commitment to a relationship."

Julia stared out the window. What she wanted to hear was a raving endorsement for wanting to have children with her. She wanted to hear him tell her how much he loved her. Unlike Andrew, children were the one thing she needed to feel whole, to feel secure.

"There's something I need to tell you–I'm sorry I didn't tell you earlier," she started.

"Julia, whatever it is, it'll be okay. Your strength and confidence are what I admire most about you."

"That's the problem. That strength and confidence is just a cover up for my own fear of abandonment. My parents did not want me. I've never really gotten over the fear that I'll get left again."

"I don't understand."

"My birth parents left me with relatives when I was one. My relatives left me as a ward of the state at three. I was five before my adoptive parents saved me from orphan hell." She paused until his touch calmed her. "I, uh, I'm scared you'll leave me."

"Not a chance. I'm the one who should be afraid you'll leave me, because I don't deserve you. And I have my own secret family problem, too, so don't feel like you're the only one with an embarrassing past."

He held her hand as she leaned her head against his shoulder, listening to his story, his words comforting her, for she could believe now that indeed she wasn't the only one with family problems. Julia drifted off to sleep. Andrew took out his notepad and collected his thoughts, mainly concerning how hard he had fallen for Julia. His thought drifted into a poem, written and filed away for delivery at a later date.

London felt like a honeymoon. They stayed in a cozy little hotel, 22 Jermyn Street, went to Mass at both Westminster Abbey and St. Paul's Cathedral, attended various theaters at night and had breakfast in bed in the morning. Although it was summer, the weather was cool, which made for a romantic evening carriage ride through St. James Park.

The night before they left London, they giggled in a pub in Mayfair. Here they were, the good Irish Girl and Scottish Boy, hanging out in an English pub telling stories with the locals. They decided they'd travel next to Ireland and Scotland to play golf on the links courses and mingle with the locals there. They would also take the advice of their newfound pub friends and try to track their roots. It would make their stories even better.

On their last day in London, room service arrived with a breakfast tray that had a special treat. In addition to a single yellow rose, Julia found an envelope with "For the Irish Girl" written on it. Andrew was in the shower down the hall. She briefly thought about waiting for him to finish his shower before she read the note, but curiosity got the better of her and she opened it.

Dearest Julia:

Falling
I cannot believe what
Has happened to me.
While I was not looking
I woke up to see
That who I am today
And who I want to be,
Are so incredibly close

As we move toward "WE."

I am not quite so sure
Why this gift was you, and
There are things in my life
For which I haven't a clue.
The future is bright and
I am enjoying the view.
I love how I feel, and
Pray that you do, too.

I am thankful you aligned
The horse with the cart.
I now look at our union
As God's work of art.
I truly believe that my
Head is with my heart,
For I am falling in love;
Oh, what a beautiful start.

Love always, Andrew

Andrew emerged from his shower to a babbling Julia. "You're such a sweet man and I love you so much. Is there any chance you'll keep writing me poems and sonnets for the rest of my life?"

He paused before answering, giving her cause for concern. "I'm the one who thanks God for bringing you into my life. You've made my world a complete joy. I'm absolutely sure that we can negotiate an arrangement to keep you supplied in poor poetry and lasting love. To quote a good friend of mine, I want you to want me, too. I love you."

On the plane on the way home, Andrew thought about when and how to ask the Irish girl to share her life with a Scottish boy. He played around with a few ideas, threw them out, started over, came up with other scenarios, happily passing the flight time with daydreams.

The only blemish on the summer was Drew's continual struggle to make sense out of his world.

He would enter the second grade in the fall. He was starting to comment on the negative things in his life. He was having problems in his summer school and was acting up with his mother. He was getting teased for having two mothers and it was affecting his confidence. Although he was only seven, he was starting to react to the lack of a male parent. Andrew's level of contempt and animosity for Laura and now for Judge Parker, grew increasingly vicious.

Julia worried about it so much that she finally confronted Andrew. "Can we talk about this custody thing? I'm very concerned about how you're reacting to it."

"What's that supposed to mean, 'concerned'?"

"Sweetheart, you clearly hate the woman, and you hate it that she and Lindsey have Drew."

"Well, of course I do. If someone came and took your child away, wouldn't you hate the ones who took him?"

"I don't know how I'd act or react, but I'm concerned that your fury isn't healthy and is going way beyond just mad. I want to help. Tell me how, please. We need to put this behind us so that we can move on with *us*."

"You could start by eliminating the problem for me. That woman is going to burn in hell. The sooner she gets the chance, the better off we'll all be. Now that would help." He regretted it as soon as he said it.

Julia let the comment drop. She had already learned that conflict was something Andrew didn't handle well when it involved him personally. When the situation revolved around his work or patients, he was a pro, but personal conflict brought out the worst in him.

Julia returned to the classroom at the end of the summer, but moved from the Brighton school district to a private school, Greenhills, in Ann Arbor. She was spending so much time with Andrew that the forty-five-minute drive had become a chore. She missed Brighton, but Greenhills offered her the opportunity to teach different subjects to a variety of age groups. She thought about enrolling at Eastern Michigan University to finish her second graduate degree in Education Administration. She badly wanted the credentials that would allow her to create environments where children could be offered higher-quality education. But she put it off for a year. She did, though, quit her part-time golf lesson gig, in favor of working on her growing relationship with Andrew.

Andrew spent the fall helping Partners Medical Group restructure their contract with QualityCare which was to expire at year-end. Improving the environment for patient care in the face of constant insurance cutbacks was always the goal, even in contract talks. It was always awkward to negotiate business deals with QualityCare. Andrew was on the Board of Directors; Christopher was not only the CEO, but also his friend. Andrew had an obligation, however, to his clinic partners to create that better environment through a fundamental change in their contract regardless of personal friendships.

Partners had a rich history that Andrew clearly understood, and he believed it was his responsibility to uphold the original principles of the founders. Three physicians who'd wanted to share the coverage duties of house calls had established Partners Medical Group in 1952. Medicine was a noble profession then and seeing infirm patients in their homes was an honor, but it was also time-consuming. The clinic grew steadily; by 1980, it had 72 physicians, all of them practicing primary care. In 1984, PMG made its first major organizational change by diversifying its practice by adding several specialist physicians. Given their proximity to the University of Michigan Medical School, recruiting physicians had never been a problem.

That same year, many of the physicians in Ann Arbor came together to discuss the impact that the emergence of managed care was having on their lives. The Detroit auto manufacturers were pushing for managed care as a panacea for the rising cost of insurance premiums. Many saw it as an intrusion in their practices, but some saw it as an opportunity to control their destiny. Their rallying cry was "We can do it better than they can." Few trusted the insurance companies or the federal government when it came to doing what was in the best interest of patient care. After a series of planning meetings, the physicians came to the conclusion that if managed care was in fact coming, then they should start their own HMO. And so QualityCare was born in 1985; each physician put up $10,000 to fund the start-up of the company.

Things actually went better than expected. QualityCare broke even financially in 1989. The organization was well ahead of schedule on that front. That same year, two major events occurred that altered QualityCare's future. The first was hiring Christopher Cromwell as their CEO. The second was the advent of capitation as a payment methodology.

Christopher Cromwell had grown up in Michigan. He attended Michigan State University and went on to Harvard Medical School. He specialized in cardiology and went to work for a managed care company in Boston. After a stellar career as a cardiologist, he worked his way up to Chief Medical Officer of the HMO he worked for. In 1990, Christopher decided he wanted to run his own show and QualityCare was in need of a CEO. Many touted him as a talented physician, while others saw Christopher as a greedy and egotistical pain in the ass.

The risk-takers, or greedy, as some would later say, won out and Christopher took over the reins of QualityCare on January 1, 1991. It didn't take Christopher long to approach the Board with the idea of capitation. Essentially, the physicians would get a fixed amount of money based upon the age and sex of each member of the health plan. Under traditional insurance models, physicians got paid more money for doing more procedural work. Under capitation, physicians would own all the money, thereby cutting out the insurance company profit. The theory was that physicians would have a bigger incentive to do only the necessary work, otherwise they'd be taking money out of their pockets every time they did an inappropriate procedure. Employers buying healthcare benefits liked how this would eliminate the waste in healthcare that was eating at their bottom line.

In the beginning, capitation worked relatively well. Both the physicians' risk pool and the HMO were financially successful. Toward the late 1990s, Chris' model began to fall apart, the incentives were no longer working, patients were revolting, and it was Andrew's job to fix it. His goal was to transfer the majority of the risk back to QualityCare, arguing that the doctors should focus on taking care of patients and not on managing the insurance company's money. There were too many conflicts playing both provider and insurer. Providing less care was inconsistent with the vision of PMG's forefathers.

Andrew had the support of his partners, the business community and most of QualityCare's Board members. The HMO was the largest insurance company in Ann Arbor, generating nearly a billion dollars in revenue per year. PMG was growing, too. It represented 55% of QualityCare's business. It was now a multi-specialty medical group representing over 250 physicians.

While Christopher was the powerbroker on the Board, he knew that PMG, and Andrew, held the aces in this poker game. Without PMG, QualityCare was nothing. There had been growing tension within the organization, and especially between Chris and Andrew. Many people tried and failed to figure out why Christopher was so opposed to Andrew's new business proposal.

At the December 7, 1998, Board meeting, after the minutes of the last meeting had been read, and old business covered, Christopher opened the discussion of new business by stating flatly, "Dr. Albright's contract proposal plan is not in QualityCare's best interest. His position is antithetical to our goals and his obvious conflict of interest cannot be ignored. I can assure you that we are ill-prepared to accept the amount of financial risk that it suggests we take. As CEO, I simply must recommend against it."

Phil Kunkle, who was a banking executive in town and Chair of the Finance Committee, said, "First, Dr. Cromwell, since the day we started this organization, we have negotiated contracts with our physician owners." Chris looked away in disgust. He was initially certain that he could count on Philip, but now he wasn't so sure. "Secondly, our balance sheet indicates that we have three times the amount of cash reserves required by the state. What is it that indicates to you that we should not take back some of this financial risk?" Phil was a hulking man who commanded respect, not only for his size but also for his financial prowess.

"We're looking at a changing industry, Phil. Surely you know from the business side that employers are asking us to reduce our premiums. You heard earlier this evening that our pharmacy costs have been going up by fifteen percent a year. This is a bad scenario for our business."

Martha Goodwin, the CEO of University Hospital, spoke up. "Dr. Cromwell, are you suggesting that this deteriorating business scenario be made the physicians' responsibility to fix?" She knew very well that PMG had a contract with a competitive HMO, Security Care, and her hospital wasn't part of Security Care's provider network. If PMG felt it was better served by moving its HMO business to Security Care, it would cost her hospital a considerable amount of admissions. This was completely unacceptable for her organization. She needed Andrew and PMG to be happy with their QualityCare deal.

"No, it is not the physicians's fault or problem. Truth be told, we must stick together. If we let the market dynamics pull us apart, then we're no better than the big insurance companies that have attempted to divide and conquer us for so long. There is a reason why the providers in Ann Arbor have avoided working with them."

"I've been on this Board since its inception," said Phil. "I have always found that when business conditions dictate fundamental changes, the issue is less about the good ol' boys than it is about fairness among the partners. I ask the Board to focus on being fair and put aside politics."

Other Board members nodded their heads in support.

One of the newest Board members, Bill Bronner, didn't get it, but was afraid to ask a question right out in the open. So he leaned over to Philip and whispered, "What's the big deal? This sounds like we're makin' more out of this than ought to be made."

Phil responded with his hand over his mouth. "It's about the money. The docs want Chris to eat any financial losses."

"Okay, but I still don't get it. If I wreck my car, it's the insurance company that pays, not the repair shop. So, why should the docs pay when people get sick? Isn't their job simply to treat the sick?"

"Ah, you do get it," Phil said, with a positive nod of his head.

Martha smelled a rat, and went after it to safeguard her own self-interests. "Dr. Cromwell, are there strategic factors that impact this decision that we are unaware of?"

Christopher looked away before responding. "None that I can think of," he lied.

Another Board member, Dr. Bruce Meyers, could remain silent no longer. "Andrew, what are PMG's options?" He was Andrew's designated "plant"; he already knew the answer. Bruce was the Chief Medical Officer of PMG, a young and ambitious surgeon from the University of Michigan, fiercely loyal to Andrew.

Andrew replied quickly, "Bruce, and members of the Board, I mean no disrespect to QualityCare, but we need to either move in the direction of this contract or Partners Medical Group will need to achieve a better balance in its overall membership distribution with Security Care."

Martha Goodwin sighed. There it was–the threat. Exactly what she didn't want the clinic to do: move its members to the competition and away from her.

After about an hour of niggling legal mumbo-jumbo and risk-factor scenarios and carping back and forth, Phil Kunkle finally spoke up. "The hour is getting late, and I wish to call for the question. I move that we adopt and accept Dr. Albright's proposed contract modifications with the following amendment: The implementation of that contract will occur in two phases, the first phase to occur on January first, 'ninety-nine and the second to occur on September first, nineteen ninety-nine."

"What's the specific purpose of your amendment?" Chris asked.

"To allow you time to build the appropriate infrastructure to take and manage the risk that PMG is sending our way. I'm buying you time. I'm offering a compromise."

The compromise and Andrew's threat were the kiss of death to Christopher. The Board voted ten in favor of the motion and five against.

Andrew went home to Julia with a bottle of wine to celebrate his victory and the anniversary of their first date. He thoroughly believed that this was a victory not just for PMG, but also for the patients it served. Christopher went home to Roxanne and drank away his misery. Roxanne contributed condolences: she called him a horse's ass for losing the vote, and stupid, to boot. He drank some more.

—Chapter 7—

Andrew, and to a lesser extent, Bruce Meyers, returned to PMG the next morning as heroes. It was going to be a great holiday season. The clinic Christmas party was that weekend, Julia would be off from school, and Drew was coming to visit the following Monday.

Andrew hadn't seen Drew for two months because he'd traded his time in November for a longer visit around the holidays. They talked on the phone nearly every day. Laura disliked these "conversations with dad" because they always left Drew wondering out loud why he had to live so far away; sometimes she'd simply tell her ex-husband that Drew wasn't home to avoid the questions before they got started.

Julia went over to Andrew's house an hour early on Saturday, so she had extra time to spend putting herself together for the party at the clinic–this was her first big public function.

When she was done, Andrew stood back and said, "You look both elegant and exquisite; you're sure to be the most beautiful woman at the party." She looked festive in a Christmas-green dress that highlighted her features.

He'd chosen to wear his traditional Scottish garb–a kilt in his family tartan colors of sapphire-blue and forest-green, a white silk shirt, a blue V-neck sweater, long white socks with green tassels and black dress shoes. His outfit was far from the starched white lab coat that he usually wore during the day. It was always the hit of the party.

Julia posed like a runway model. "Thank you. I am pleased that you're pleased. But we have a problem." She paused, then continued with her hands on her hips. "I'm not sure I can go out in public with a man wearing a skirt. If you'd told me that it was role-reversal night, I would've rented a tux."

"We can save that for another day. What would you expect a good Scotsman to wear for dress-up?" She shrugged her shoulders. Truth be told, she liked it when Andrew stepped outside the traditional role of physician and executive. "But you're right; we do have a problem that needs to be corrected."

"And what would that be?"

"You're missing something." He handed her two boxes and kissed her. "These gifts are simply a reflection of the bright light that you are in my life."

"Should I open them now?"

"Absolutely. Start with the smaller box."

She tore the paper off the box like a two-year-old faced with her first holiday present. Inside was a pair of exquisite teardrop diamond earrings. She smiled, not only because she loved the earrings, but also because he had inadvertently corrected her mistake: she'd brought emerald earrings instead of pearl, which she thought was too much green for one night. She put the diamonds on and admired them. He handed her the second box.

Hugging him she said, "You mean there is more than these?"

"I'd be happy to donate the next gift to one of clinic's silent auctions if you can't handle so much booty," he said in his most serious voice.

"What if I tell you in a minute?"

"Nope, not an option, Irish girl." She was testing his patience; it had been difficult enough for him to keep the presents a secret this long without her prolonging it.

Inside the second box was a piece of paper; she unfolded it and read out loud. "Diamonds: forever and bright; very similar to your place in my life. I wish you a Merry Christmas and I promise you a memorable New Year." Inside the box was a heart-shaped diamond-and-emerald necklace.

Julia hesitated before saying, "Thank you, my Scottish man of honor. Next time, try surprising me before I put my mascara on, tears just wreak havoc with makeup. Please help me put this on." Her hands were shaking.

In his best Irish brogue, Andrew said, "My, you were a cute lassie before, and now you're just plain irresistible." He kissed her on the cheek.

Julia fixed her makeup and grabbed her coat and purse. As they were walking out the door, she asked, "Scottish boy, exactly what are you wearing underneath that kilt?"

"If you're lucky, I may let you find out later."

"Hmm, and here I was thinking that it was you who might be lucky enough to find out what lies beneath this green dress." She pulled up her dress just far enough for him to see her garter belt and stockings.

It was going to be quite an evening.

The Christmas party was especially upbeat that year. PMG was expanding in southeast Michigan, it had been rated the benchmark quality provider in the community, its finances were healthy, its administration was solid, and it had no problem recruiting nurses or doctors. The new QualityCare contract would make 1999 just as good a year, if not better–a significant story in that health care providers everywhere were struggling.

Just prior to dinner being served, Andrew offered his traditional toast to the group of 300 PMG employees and family members. "Today I stand before you prepared to share my state of the union address." The crowd booed and hissed, but they did that every year. Andrew continued, "Okay, I get the message. I'll keep this brief. More than ever, I am proud to be a member of this team. We're setting the standard for how healthcare should be delivered in our community. We have just completed a deal with QualityCare to do exactly what our founding fathers intended, focus on the quality of care for our patients. You are doing excellent work that stands for something. I wish you all a Happy Holiday season, and I urge you to keep the reason for the season in your heart. I also wish you a joyous New Year. New beginnings are always special and I hope yours are special, too."

From the back of the room, someone shouted, "Dr. Albright for President."

"Someone get that gentleman another drink." When the laughter died down, he said, "I too look forward to ninety-nine. This is the last year of a millennium. A finish and a start, and we will end and begin a millennium a winner. Isn't success awesome?" The crowd broke out in cheers. "Even more important than success here at the clinic, I'd like you to strive to keep balance in your life. If you don't have it, find it. If you do have it, cherish it." And then, surprising everyone, including himself, he said, "Lastly, I need to publicly thank the person who's brought total balance to my life, Julia Osborn. She's also responsible for making me the pussycat that I am at work. It doesn't matter what you do to me–she's there to tend my wounds at day's end. Thank you, Julia, for being my partner. Thank you for being the balance in my life. Thank you for being the bright sunshine that warms my heart. I love you."

The women in the audience looked at each other and then at their husbands and dates, waiting for similar affirmation. Julia smiled, thinking she was going to have to repair her mascara again.

The party continued into the early morning hours. While on the dance floor, Andrew whispered in his date's ear what he had in store for her when they got home. The Irish girl and Scottish boy left before things got out of hand. The drive home felt as if it took forever.

Julia kept saying, "Come on, Scottish Boy, hike up your skirt and show me what you got under the kilt." She tried to lift the hem of his kilt but got her hand slapped.

"How would you like to drive while I check what's under your dress, my dear?" It was a rhetorical question; Andrew had already reached his street. He was driving slowly, partly to admire the festive holiday lights adorning house after house, and partly because he liked the attention he was getting.

"Sorry lover, but we Irish girls thrive on being in control and right now that's exactly where I am." She slid her hand farther up his leg before kissing his neck.

Andrew pulled up short of his driveway and said, "I'm a self-respecting man in a skirt, for God's sake; I can't let you treat me this way. You need to get out and walk the rest of the way home."

Julia did as she was told, which took her less time than it did him to get the car in the garage. By the time Andrew made it into the house, Julia was nowhere to be seen. He took his time in the kitchen, waiting for her to reappear. Finally, he saw her note on the counter: *You've been such a good boy tonight that I'm making your job easy. Come and find me; I'll be the one without the green dress on.*

It didn't take him long to pour two glasses of eggnog and brandy. He found her in the bedroom with candles lit, and dress and shoes strewn on the floor. He sat beside her, feeling her skin, warm to the touch and smooth as silk. He kissed her, gently at first and then harder. Her bra and panties were as green as her dress.

"Do you like it?" she asked.

"There's not much about you I don't like, and looking like you do here and now, I'd have a damn hard time being very objective."

"Jeez, we need to work on your responses, but we'll save that for later. For now, I want you to make me feel like a complete woman. Andrew Albright, I want you to want me." It was her standard line. She and Andrew both knew their relationship wasn't based on just physical need. "Want" had as much to do with the acceptance they needed from each other as the sexual side.

"Julia Osborn, I want you to want me, too." There was still a part of Andrew that feared that she would abandon him. It was the only thing standing in the way of a marriage proposal.

They fell into a quiet rhythm at first, exploring as they went along. Both their heartbeats and their pace quickened. What they had both only imagined earlier was now just perfectly fitting puzzle pieces of intertwining bodies. Finally, they looked deeply into each other's eyes as they drifted off into a heaven of passionate release.

They slept peacefully and soundly. They awoke early, before the sun rose, simply lying there, wishing the world would always be as simple as it was at that exact moment. Since Andrew had surprised her with an early Christmas gift, Julia felt it was high time she gave him one of his presents. She walked to the closet and removed a square box.

Andrew looked at it and asked, "Can I open it now and do I want what's inside? Can I trade it for what's behind door number two?"

"Listen, Scotty," she said, acting hurt, "you open the present, take a peek and if you don't want it, I'll trade it in for whatever's behind door two, three or four."

He curiously, quickly opened the box; it contained a large

crystal jar. He looked her a question, and she nodded her head for him to look inside. He found fifty-three identical slips of parchment, one for each week of the year. Then he read her note.

Inside are my hopes and dreams. Inside are fifty-three things that I want to share with you. Inside are things that I want to do with you. I look forward to sharing each of the weeks of 1999– My love always, Julia

"I don't get the fifty-three part if there is one for each week."

"It's the slow uptake gene again. You get one sample now; the rest have to wait for the New Year. Keep in mind that I will limit you to one a week. This is not the candy store."

Andrew removed one of the slips of paper and read it. *You are entitled to breakfast in bed at the time of your choice followed by the treat of your choice.*

Showing Julia the note, he asked, "Can I choose to collect on this one right now?"

She got up kissed him on the cheek and said, "As you wish. Are you sure you don't want to trade it for door number two?"

"You did it just right. Thank you."

Twenty-five minutes later, she returned with a spinach and cheese omelet, wheat toast, orange juice and hazelnut coffee. They ate; when Andrew was done he collected the treat of his choice. They made one more passionate puzzle.

They showered and dressed. It started to snow on their way to church. It was the kind of snow that made the world look peaceful–big snowflakes silently falling from the sky. They paused in the church courtyard together, letting the winter weather swirl around them, then held hands walking into the church. Julia wondered when they would walk hand in hand up the isle of old St. Patrick's as husband and wife. Andrew was wondering the exact same thing. It was time.

—Chapter 8—

Drew was supposed to arrive in Detroit the evening of December 19th. The plan was to spend Christmas in Ann Arbor and then go to Orlando for a week. Laura was less than thrilled that Andrew was taking her son to Florida for a week. Andrew couldn't have cared less if she was thrilled or not.

Drew was right on time. He was now of the age that he could travel by himself on direct flights. He was increasingly happy to get away from his deteriorating west-coast world. Boys at school were still teasing him. They kept calling Lindsey "Butch." It was not that he cared much what they thought of her. It was the rejection he felt that bothered him. Even at a young age, he was exhibiting many of the same traits of insecurity that plagued his father. Other than the beach and the sunshine, there wasn't much in California that Drew wanted to hold on to.

Andrew hugged him and asked, "How's my little man?"

Drew smiled when his dad called him that. It made him feel grown up. His mother and Lindsey were more prone to baby him. The older he got the more difficult it became. He liked being around Julia because she treated him like a real person, too. She was always interested in what he thought. It was the same way she taught her class of second-graders.

"I'm doing real good. I got to visit the cockpit before we took off. We saw lots of big cities from the air. They looked like Christmas tree lights. It was way cool."

Julia hugged Drew and said, "You sure are growing up fast. Are you taking magic growth pills?"

"No. Do vitamins count? I have to take those every day. Are there really such things as magic growth pills? I sure wish I'd grow up so that I can make my own decisions." Drew often made comments about wanting more control in his life. Julia later pointed out to Andrew that control was something growing children often sought, though not usually as early as seven or eight. Drew's life seemed to have hastened the need.

They both thought he was growing up way too fast, getting into trouble at school, bored with it and not getting the kind of male attention he needed in California. By creating trouble, he got to see plenty of men in positions of authority. Not that Laura discussed Drew with her ex-husband–the only way Andrew could get a good picture of how his son was doing was to call the school directly and by visiting his son's teachers whenever he was in town.

Drew raked in the electronics for Christmas. He was computer savvy and Andrew and Julia carefully steered him toward the more educational materials. After opening their presents, they all went to church, which Drew especially liked. The only time he attended church services was when he was in Michigan. If he'd known the words he could've identified why he liked it: It gave him a sense of belonging and acceptance. His mother avoided going to church; she always felt like she was being judged and found wanting.

After church, the three played for hours in the Christmas snowstorm. They made a snowman, per Drew's specifications. They threw snowballs. They rode the sled down the neighborhood hill where at the bottom they would always fall off, howling with laughter.

On Christmas night, Andrew had one more surprise for Drew and Julia. Actually, it had been a bit of a surprise to him, as well. He played coy by asking, "Did I happen to mention that we're flying to Orlando on a private jet?"

Drew was the first to respond, "Wow, Dad, when did you get your own jet?"

Julia's expression clearly asked the same thing.

"Chris Cromwell pulled some strings and invited us to join him on his vacation flight to Florida."

"So when did *Chris* get his own jet?" Julia asked.

"Haven't a clue. He just phoned me up and asked if I'd like to fly down with them."

The flight to Orlando was a thrill for all. Drew got his cockpit tour in-flight this time, played with his new games, and fell asleep somewhere over Georgia.

Chris played the polite host although he never really answered where the plane came from. Roxanne did what she did best, talk about her latest encounter with some social butterfly.

Disney World was action-packed. Andrew and Julia let Drew call all the shots; he certainly had more energy for it than either of the two older members of his posse–he was also typically dead asleep by nine. The only night he was up later than that was the night they stayed up to see the electric light parade through the park. Surprisingly, the place that thrilled Drew the most was Disney's animation studios. He was completely enamored with the way Disney made animated films. He went back to the demonstration room twice.

The ride home was also courtesy of Chris Cromwell, except this time there was an additional passenger on board: Arthur Bishop, CEO of the British Insurance Group and owner of their ride. Arthur explained to Andrew and Julia that he was in the

States studying American healthcare systems. He and Andrew discussed the differences between the socialistic European healthcare models and the more pluralistic structure in the United States. It was Arthur's intent to incorporate some of the concepts he was learning into his insurance company in England.

Drew slept most of the way home. As the plane approached the Ann Arbor airport, Drew came awake.

One look at his face and Andrew knew something was wrong. "You okay, little man?"

"Yeah, Dad, I'm fine."

"You don't look fine. Talk to me."

Drew was uncharacteristically rude. "Dad, I said I was okay. Are you listening to me?"

"Are you sad that we've come back and you have to go home?" Julia asked, perceptively.

The fact that she knew what was bothering him made it hard to blow it off, but he stared stoically out the airplane window. Julia asked again, "Drew, are you ready to go home?"

"No," he blurted out. "I don't wanna go home." The floodgates opened. Through a river of tears and sniffles, Drew asked, "Daddy, do I *have* to go back? I want to stay with you." Drew did love his mother, but he certainly didn't love living with her.

"I want you to stay with us, too, Drew. But right now, you have to live with your mother and Lindsey."

"Lindsey doesn't like me, and she wants to have a baby of her own. She's going to some bank to get a baby."

"Drew, I promise that things will get better. I'm always here for you. I love you, but right now, you have to live in California."

Drew nodded his head as if he understood, but it was obvious he didn't. The rest of the plane ride was a silent one.

The next day, Andrew and Julia took Drew to the airport to catch his flight home. He looked sad and was very quiet. Andrew reminded him that he loved him and would be there for him. Then Drew was gone.

Julia and Andrew drove back to Saline without a word spoken. Andrew was furious and once again wallowing in bitterness. As soon as he got home he called his ex-wife as he always did to let her know that Drew's flight had left on time. Laura wasn't home. He left a message. "I just got back from the airport. Drew is on time. But I believe Drew belongs here, with me. I swear to God, nineteen ninety-nine will be different for him. If you and your girlfriend want to have a baby, that's a decision you can make, but you probably haven't even thought about what that'll do to our son. You don't want him; I do. I'm going to get him."

Once he and Julia were married he figured he wouldn't have any trouble making his promise good.

—Chapter 9—

Andrew kept twiddling and changing and thinking about his proposal plans. He thought first that Valentine's Day was best, then it struck him that St. Patrick's Day would be the perfect day to ask an Irish girl to marry a Scottish boy. He started his search for a ring in January, but couldn't find that perfect "something special," so he had it custom-made: a two-carat emerald-cut diamond, surrounded by fifteen baguette diamonds. The jeweler finished the ring just before Valentine's Day and Andrew almost changed his mind to giving it to her right then and there, patience not being his strong suit. But he held firm, and on March 17th, he was ready.

Andrew sent two dozen yellow roses to Julia's condominium before she went to school on the morning of St. Patrick's Day. He had specifically worked it out so that she would be at her place rather than his that morning. The card said "In hopes of a wondrous day for a wondrous woman. Love, Andrew."

When she got to work, she received another note, which contained specific instructions for the evening. Julia opened it with her friends and colleagues during lunch. She first read the instructions to herself, giggled, and then she read them aloud. "Andrew has the following instructions for me tonight. One: wear the emerald colored dress; two, wear waterproof mascara; three, a limo will pick me up at seven-ten and I won't need my car; four, the driver will know where to go; five, I'm to bring my heart and my head; and six–I wonder what this means?–his sister and brother-in-law are going to be there."

"So, Julia, you think maybe tonight's the night?" one of her friends asked.

"Oh my God I hope so," she replied.

There was more to the surprise. Inside the envelope was another of Andrew's poems. This time she didn't bother to read it to herself first, but started reading out loud immediately.

"Dearest Julia:

Senses

I once was so blind,
But now I can see
You're deep in my heart,
And now I am free.

I once was so deaf,
But now I may hear.
You have opened my soul
Because you came near.

I once was so dumb,
But now I shall speak.
You're the words off my lips;
I am no longer weak.

I once was afraid,
But 'tis no longer true.
I am absent of fear.
My security is you.

I once could not feel,

But now I can touch,
You gave me that gift,
And I love you so much.

How shall I repay you?
I'm not sure that I know.
Shall I spend forever
Keeping your heart aglow?

So, how do I thank you?
I can't say here and now,
But I will never stop trying,
This is my solemn vow.

"Yeah," another friend commented, "I'd say *for sure* tonight's the night, all right."

Her friends convinced her to leave early and get the full treatment. She took their advice and had her nails done and her hair put up exactly the same way she'd done it on their first date. She put on the emerald cocktail dress, did her makeup and was ready for her big night. At precisely 7:10, there was a knock on the door. It was her chauffeur. She climbed into the limousine where there were more flowers, a bouquet of lilies. She took in the smell and tried to stay calm.

It was exactly 7:30 when Julia walked into the dining room at the restaurant. The hostess, whom she knew, greeted her with a hug and said that Dr. Albright and his guests were expecting her. Andrew, always the gentleman, stood, hugged her, whispered that she was a princess, and held her chair for her. Carol and Bob were all smiles.

They had drinks and salads. There was a lull in the conversation when Andrew reached into his inside coat pocket. Julia's heart skipped a beat, but it immediately got right again when

Andrew just pulled out a thick sheaf of legal paper. He spent a few minutes explaining the drafted documents seeking legal custody of Drew.

So that's what we're here for? Julia thought. A celebration because he's going to go to court? Of course that was good, but . . . Dinner came and went and Julia felt very foolish. Had she missed all the signals? She was wearing waterproof mascara–she hoped it was for the right reason.

It was time for dessert and the waitress brought a cart with an assortment of confections. Andrew suddenly stood and walked to the cart.

"You really must have the chef's special, Julia," he said. "It's really fabulous."

He picked up the covered silver tray and placed it in front of her. She just stared at it, then stared at Andrew, then back at the tray. She removed the cover and saw an open, maroon ring box. She started to pick it up, but Andrew stopped her.

With the ring now in his hand, he got down on one knee and said loud enough for everyone in the room to hear, "Julia, it's appropriate that we sit here in this restaurant tonight. It's where we started as a couple. Likewise, it's appropriate that Carol and Bob are here to witness this, since Carol was our matchmaker. Julia, you are the path I have chosen in life, you are my guiding star, and you are the woman I want to spend the rest of my life with. Is it in your heart, as well as your head, to be my wife forevermore? Julia Osborn, will you marry me?"

Julia was now testing the mascara full force. She looked into his eyes and said, "Andrew Albright, I have told you too many times to count that I want you to want me. You finally want me the way I want you. I would be honored to be your wife."

The roomful of fellow diners all applauded.

Andrew placed the ring on her finger.

Was it any wonder that it fit perfectly?

—Chapter 10—

It took Julia several weeks to adjust to the fact that she was going to be Mrs. Andrew Albright. She often told her friends that there was but one missing piece: her adoptive parents, who had moved to Arizona when she went to college. Both had perished in a ballooning accident over a desolate tract of desert. Their death was followed by a bad marriage entered into for the wrong reasons, with the predictable outcome: divorce. This time it would be different.

She had a difficult time concentrating on her classroom work and caught herself daydreaming constantly. Of course, it wasn't only the fact that she was going to marry Andrew that had her 'twixt and 'tween. She could now daydream about what their children might look like.

It was the time of year when most Michiganders tried to convince themselves that April showers really would bring May flowers—a winter survival technique. A bright spot for Andrew and Julia was that QualityCare would be holding their annual meeting at the Ritz Carlton in Naples, Florida. Christopher and Roxanne insisted that the newly engaged couple stay with them at their condominium, which was less than a mile away from their meeting. Both had mixed feelings about staying with them, but Andrew thought that it would be unwise to reject their offer. He and Christopher had not yet overcome the tension that remained after the December QualityCare Board meeting where Christopher had been soundly beaten and embarrassed; maybe this would patch things up.

Just before leaving for Florida, Laura called Andrew.

She said, "I need to talk to you about my son." She never referred to Drew as anything but her son; he thought she did it just to spite him.

"What's wrong? Is Drew all right?"

"No, he's not all right. He's having a hard time. I finally had to take him to a child psychologist."

"What did the doctor say? Who the hell is the doctor? I'll call him first thing–"

"Oh calm down. I called to let you know what's going on. If you'll just listen, I'll tell you. If you can't listen, or get all judgmental, this'll be a very short conversation."

"Fine. I'm listening." He cursed her under his breath. Damn woman. He put her on the speakerphone so that Julia could hear what was going on as well. They sat together at the kitchen counter.

"Drew has been acting out in class the past few weeks. At first he responded to some motherly discipline. This week he had another episode at school and was yelling at Ms. Hockenberry, his teacher. She's been exceedingly patient with him, and we talk about his progress often. But yesterday, Ms. Hockenberry had to remove him from the classroom. I was called to come pick him up. I was tied up at school so I asked Lindsey, who was done for the day, to go get him. When she got to the office, Drew flipped out. He said he was *not* going anywhere with *her*. He made quite a scene. It took the school psychologist about fifteen minutes to get him to calm down. They called me again and insisted I come get my son immediately; I did and we all came home. By dinner time, Drew was totally out of control, screaming that he did not want to live with Lindsey anymore and that she wasn't his father."

Julia held Andrew's hand as he responded, "How is he now? What do you suggest we do next?" His answer was to get on a plane and bring his son home that very minute.

"Drew is fine for now, but I'm sure that his behavior has everything to do with the upcoming custody hearing. I hold you completely responsible for his attitude toward Lindsey. Will you spend some time with him on the phone to help him understand he needs to be respectful to all adults, but Lindsey in particular? It's the least you can do."

Andrew was incredulous: Lindsey thought Drew was nothing but a nuisance. He spoke without thinking. "I'm not going to tell him that he has to respect Lindsey. I can't do that. If she treated him better, maybe. Nope, won't do it."

"Well, thanks a lot for nothing." Laura slammed down the phone, regretting her impulse to ask Andrew for help. Given his reaction, Laura certainly didn't want him to talk to Drew about it. Andrew tried to call his son several times that day. He got nothing but voice mail. Damn the woman; ask him to call and then pretend not be home.

The May 10th court date couldn't come fast enough for Andrew.

Julia's heart ached for both son and father. She wondered how Drew would react to her plans to be a mother. Would it be the same as with Lindsey?

Andrew was quiet and distant that night. He got out of bed in the same mood. He was up early, because he wanted to do hospital rounds and clean up a few things at the office before he and Julia left for the annual meeting. Two days ago he'd been looking forward to getting away for some quiet time with Julia, but now all he could think about was that "evil couple" two thousand miles away tormenting his son.

Before they left at noon for their two PM flight, Andrew tried again to reach Drew. Lindsey answered the phone and told him that Drew was out of the house. Andrew reminded her that it was Laura who'd asked him to call. Andrew told her he would call back in thirty minutes and to have Drew near the phone.

Andrew had Julia drive while he called his son from the car. Drew came on the phone. "Is that you, Daddy?"

"Yes, little man, it's daddy. How you doing? You haven't sent me an e-mail in days. Somebody break your fingers?"

"Nah, I've just been busy," he lied. He didn't have anything good to say and he was tired of complaining.

"I hear you're having some problems in school. Is that true?"

"Come on, Dad, it's not that bad. *She* just makes it worse."

"You're talking about mommy?"

"No."

"Lindsey?"

"Yeah."

"Is she in the room with you right now?"

"Yup."

"Well, listen to me. I know you can't tell me how you feel, but I think I know, and that things are difficult. I need you to do something for me, little man. Can you do something for me?"

"Sure."

"I need you to hang in there. I need you to behave yourself. A month from now we'll have our next court hearing with Judge Parker. Do you remember Judge Parker?"

Drew had to pause for a moment before responding. "Yeah, I think so. She was the pretty lady in the black robe at court."

"That's right. We'll see her in May and she'll decide if you can come live with us in Michigan. I can't promise that she will, but we have a better chance of her saying yes if you stay out of trouble."

"Daddy," Drew said, starting to cry, "I don't *mean* to get in trouble. The doctor guy says that I have anger in me."

"It's okay, everything is going to be fine. I love you and I'll take care of you. I'll call you again soon. In the meantime, little man, I need you to be a good boy."

"I will, Daddy. I love you too. 'Bye."

Julia gave Andrew's shoulder a supportive squeeze. His mood lifted and the darkness faded, but was he still angry. Damn evil couple.

—Chapter 11—

Andrew and Julia arrived at the Cromwell condominium at 5:30, just in time to jump back in the car and head down to the beach to watch the sunset. Andrew had spent a fair share of his time at the beach while attending college and medical school. The rhythm of the ocean and sunsets in particular always gave him a sense of calm. The air felt warm to the snowbirds from Michigan, but the locals were all wearing jackets to stave off the freshening Gulf breeze.

After a few minutes, he said, "You know, this sky is barely matched by your beauty. The natives call it the Gator sky."

"Well, that sure was smooth, comparing me to some ugly alligator. I think I should be offended."

"I guess I deserve that. I'm sorry. So, let me back the bus up. Julia, only your beauty matches the splendor of this sky. I am a very lucky guy to be with someone who rivals the beauty of nature."

"You, my sweet man, are so sweet. Will you charm me like this after we get married, or do I need to carry a tape recorder to catch all of this to play back after you forget just how damn lucky you are to have me?"

With a boyish smile Andrew answered, "You should bank on the tape recorder, but you'll only need it to record how happy I make you every day."

"I'll take that as a promise. But, I don't need a tape recorder. I keep a journal. So how is it I remind you of alligators?"

"Journal? I didn't know that." He made a note to come back to this new revelation. "Just look at this sky. What makes it so beautiful?"

"The colors, of course," she said.

"What colors do you see?"

"Breathtaking shades of orange, blue and green."

"I give you orange and blue, but only an Irish snob could add green to this picture."

"Well, I can see the orange and blue. As for the green, you'll just have to get used to that. You don't seem to mind the color green when it comes to lingerie."

"Guilty as charged, though you make all the colors of the spectrum special." After pausing, he added, "Especially when it comes to lingerie."

"Thank you, sweetheart. Now tell me about the alligators and the sky. Pretty please?"

"Well, we agree that the orange and blue colors are the reason for the beauty of the spring sky. So what are the University of Florida's colors?"

"Why, I think they're gold and black, right?" She knew full well that they were orange and blue.

"Wrong, and five demerit points for you, which I'll collect later."

"I knew that your beloved Florida Gators wear orange and blue. So this type of sunset is called a Gator sky because of the orange and blue, right? So what's the big deal?"

"Ha! If you knew the colors, you lied to me. Ten more demerit points for you. And, it's called the Gator sky because there are so many Gators in heaven that the sky is painted orange and blue. All Gators go to heaven, and so shall I someday."

"Do I at least get credit for being right about the colors and do you do realize that when you marry me, you will already have entered heaven?"

"Not a chance to the first and absolutely to the second."

"Here I thought that the only way you graduated from medical school was to have bought your medical degree or at least had some nasty secret on the dean of the school. Today, you proved that you really are a smart boy." She gave him a butterfly kiss and changed the subject. "So, when are we going to get married?"

"I'm thinking we ought to get married right after Drew comes to live with us. What with this latest screw-up with Laura and Lindsey, Judge Parker has gotta figure it's in Drew's best interest to change the custody arrangements."

"So, what? September?"

"I was thinking more like August. That would give Drew some time to meet some kids in the area. Get him situated before he starts school."

"How about the end of August?" She pulled a pocket calendar out of her purse. "August twenty-eighth is a Saturday. That'd be good."

"So what about a honeymoon? If we wait until the end of August, we wouldn't have time if Drew is moving in at the same time."

"How about we have the honeymoon first? We could go after the hearing but before the wedding, and we'd know how much time we can be gone. Have our cake and eat it, too."

"You're still thinking about going to Ireland and Scotland?"

"Absolutely. That's what we talked about. Is that what you want?"

"I want."

The couple stood hand in hand in the growing darkness with the last hint of sunshine beaming off the ocean.

They looked at each other and Andrew stole Julia's line. "My dearest Julia, I can honestly say that I want you to want me. Always. Thank you for loving me."

"Ditto, Scotty. I love you so much."

"Ditto back, Mrs. Albright."

She smiled as they headed to the car. She liked the sound of "Julia Albright."

At dinner that evening at the St. George and Dragon, the Cromwells celebrated Andrew and Julia's engagement. Chris was still upset with his friend about the Board's decision to accept the Partners new contract, but that had been four months ago and it didn't appear it was going to hurt QualityCare's balance sheet or his long-term plans anytime soon.

Andrew dropped the news over appetizers and wine. "Julia and I just set the date. The wedding will be on August twenty-eighth."

"Oh goody, a summer social event. I do love planning weddings," Roxanne said. Julia avoided asking her to clarify what she meant. She could plan around her later.

"That's terrific," Chris said. "Here's a toast to your continued happiness." He let his comment sink in, then said, "But, I'm afraid Roxy and I won't be able to make it."

"What? Where are we going to be? Wherever it is, it can't be more important than this," Roxanne said.

Waiting a painful minute, Chris said, "Well, I'm not sure where we will be; I have yet to plan that far ahead. It's enough to know that we will be gone."

Julia didn't know if he was kidding or not.

Andrew, taking no chances, retorted, "Not a problem. You're not invited anyway." He whispered to Julia, "Take them off the list." Looking at his friend he said, "As I recall, it was you who said that we wouldn't make it through the soup on our first date. You don't deserve an invitation."

Roxanne laughed. "Don't mind Chris. He was just upset that he lost the dating pool to your sister, of all people."

They all laughed, enjoyed dinner, put the past behind them, and looked toward to the future. There was purpose and therefore optimism in the future.

Sunday's agenda was to begin with a Board meeting during which Christopher would kick off the annual planning cycle for 2000 with a State of the Organization address. He'd outline the plans for the upcoming year. The Board would bless these strategies and then monitor the planning process to put them in place.

On Monday, after a brief Board session in the morning, all the Board members, and the senior staff and their spouses, would participate in a celebrity golf game, if they wanted. No one had ever known how Chris pulled off getting twenty celebrities every year to fill out the twenty foursomes at the outing, or how much the event cost, and Chris saw no reason to tell them that the social coordinator every year was his wife. She knew everybody, or so it seemed. Besides the thirty members in their QualityCare group, Roxanne invited thirty other prominent people from Ann Arbor and Naples to play in the event. The guests donated $1,000 to charity for the opportunity to play in the outing.

After the golf tournament, there was always a silent auction that also raised money for one of the three foundations that QualityCare supported each year. The Board looked at the event as a worthy cause and did not think twice regarding how much of the corporation's money was being used to pay for this annual boondoggle.

On Sunday morning, Julia and Andrew got up with the sun. They spent some quiet time on the balcony overlooking the Gulf of Mexico before heading off to 8:30 Mass at St. John's Catholic Church. Energized by the church service, and the bright spring sun, they felt ready to take on the day's events.

Brunch was a low-key event, but generally everyone ate too much, which made sitting through Christopher's State of the Organization presentation painful. Many a board member accused Chris of planning it that way so that he could sneak all his pet projects past them.

This year they were right on the money. He and Arthur Bishop were setting the table with some new plans.

Christopher opened the meeting with, "I am pleased to stand before you on this bright and glorious day. As is our tradition, we will start with introductions and statements of purpose."

The statements of purpose gave each individual an opportunity to indicate what they wanted to get out of the meeting. It helped Christopher engage each person around the table.

"While you are contemplating that, I'd like to introduce a new member of our family."

He asked Julia and Andrew to come forward. "While it is not our tradition to allow non-spouses to our strategic planning session, I have made an exception in this case. I present to you the future Mrs. Andrew–Julia–Albright." The room broke out in warm applause. "Had the happy couple not informed me last night that they have set a date of August twenty-eight, nineteen ninety-nine, I would never have believed that they would get this over with."

Julia smiled and blushed. Once again, she liked the sound of being called Mrs. Albright and Christopher's choice of words. She recalled her own words to her future husband right before their first kiss. She leaned over and whispered, "Well, Scotty can we get this over with?"

He grinned and kissed her.

They received congratulations from all around.

—Chapter 12—

As the Board settled into its meeting, Philip Kunkle offered up his statement of purpose in his usual authoritative tone. "Dr. Cromwell, I desire to know how we are going to capitalize on the strength of QualityCare's balance sheet. I am not convinced that we are wisely reinvesting our profits back into the community."

"Excellent question, Phil," Chris said. "Keep your knickers on and I will answer that question for you in a few minutes." Chris was pleased with the question. It would make his presentation look less self-serving.

Martha Goodwin, from University Hospital, asked, "How will we protect our turf from other insurance companies that want a piece of our success pie?"

"Because we're *already* partners. Have been for a dozen years, long before you and I came on the scene." He looked directly at Andrew. "We will continue to dance with them that brought us to the dance. That's what partners do. Right, Dr. Albright?" Andrew nodded his head in agreement but knew that this was no idle comment. The rest of the Board made their purpose statements with hardly any fanfare.

Christopher launched into his State of the Organization presentation, quickly covering the basics. He wanted his audience to know that the organization was in better financial shape than a year ago—the fifth consecutive year of earnings growth.

It took the CEO but one slide to paint the picture. "Our balance sheet, as you can see, at year end nineteen ninety-eight visibly shows a strong cash position, a strong current ratio, a reduction in debt, and improved net worth. While we have some future challenges, the financial strength of the organization has never been better." Phil nodded his approval.

The financial strength of the organization was a critical stage-setter. He asked for comments from the Chairman of the Finance Committee. They had actually rehearsed his response. Phil performed flawlessly; but then again, he was a banker used to convincing audiences that things were in order.

Once the Board was convinced that the organization was in sound financial shape, Christopher went into the Strategic Objectives for 2000. He started with a common theme, growth. QualityCare was frequently asked to expand its service area, most often from physicians who wanted to get on the physician-owned HMO train. It was self-preservation. The QualityCare model was growing in popularity and the franchise opportunities were plenty.

So, responding to that, Christopher had devised a plan to expand the HMO's service area. "Phil, here is the answer to your initial question. Thank you for keeping your knickers on. I cannot imagine what would happen here if you didn't." There was a series of snickers from around the room. "We have built a better mousetrap and other physicians want us to help them do the same. What better way to reinvest in the community? While I use the term 'community' in its broadest sense, we have terrific and meaningful opportunities to do good things."

After about a half hour of financial talk, Mary Goodwin was still skeptical and asked, "Christopher, we're discussing expanding something that we've developed locally for more than a decade to physicians who have never run their own show before. What makes you think our skills are transferable? What makes you think they will preserve our primary mandate for 'patients first'?"

"I can tell you from previous experience that structuring the expansion and defining appropriate roles and responsibilities among the parties makes all the difference in the world. I am prepared to map out a plan that explicitly avoids that failed scenario."

Christopher then addressed Bill Bronner, a consumer representative and new member on the board. "Bill, I heard in your statement of purpose that you wanted to get a better handle on what would differentiate QualityCare from its competitors going forward."

"That's correct," he said. "I'm interested in how we'll continue to be a leader in customer satisfaction. I'm concerned that growth is detrimental to our strength in this area."

Christopher had the next PowerPoint slide brought up for the audience to see. "The market requires that we balance cost and quality. Stop and visualize the last personal computer you bought–how many of you have bought a PC in the last eighteen months or are looking for one today?" Everyone raised his or her hand except George Struthers. "George, you really need to get in the game. You still driving that 'sixty-eight Rambler?"

"You bet; it's a classic. As for computers, I will never trust those damn things." George was a retired autoworker. He hated change and championed tradition. It was in his union blood. The fact that he was also a former Marine just made him more determined to fight for the status quo.

"Okay, George notwithstanding, for the rest of you the value of that computer will go up if the quality goes up and the price goes down. The computer industry is a great example because the quality or functionality has improved. They are faster, lighter and obviously more durable if you don't drop them"–he gave his secretary a look; she'd destroyed two laptops that way–"moreover, the cost has come down. Now for your quiz: Does anyone believe that the value of computers is less today than two years ago?" There were no takers.

"So, Doctor, what the hell we gonna do, sell computers?" George griped.

"No. Our goal will be to differentiate QualityCare by focusing on the quality part of the value equation. Price is important, but quality is king. Insurance prices will continue to rise; we will all be in the same boat there, but we are an organization built by doctors and run by doctors. Who better than we to set the standards for care in the markets we serve?"

George wasn't done asking questions. "I still don't get how that's going to make us different," he complained, still not satisfied with the answers he was receiving.

Christopher ignored him. "Ladies and gentlemen, I remind you that the wise souls who started this organization gave it the name QualityCare for a reason. I say we make them proud. I say that we become the benchmark for measurable quality in our industry. I say we take this balance sheet for a spin and see what it can do. We will grow. What will fuel that growth is our dedication to optimizing quality. Doing what is clinically right for the patient. I tell you here and now that our competitors just don't get this equation. Would you like to not only grow but also be known as the quality leader?" He didn't wait for an answer. "Of course you would. We all want to be associated with a winner. Ladies and gentlemen, QualityCare is the market leader today and shall be for years to come."

He got a round of applause. Christopher concluded his remarks by giving the board a timeline for his plan. He was not seeking approval for expansion right then and there, that would take at least six months, but he was looking for their buy-in. He received it without exception. There were smiles all around, but the brightest may have been on the face of Roxanne Cromwell. To her, bigger was better. The hell with how the organization got there.

—Chapter 13—

The black-tie dinner following the Board meeting was elegant. The highlight was the after-dinner dancing. Julia was faced with another pleasant surprise. Andrew danced with her like never before.

"How on earth, or better yet, who on earth have you been dancing with?"

"Well, I'd have saved this special treat for our first dance together in August, but I have a huge problem."

"And that would be?"

"Now that I've taken some lessons on the side, I'm not talented enough to fake being a poor dancer, unless you're open to serious injury. I have long felt that a woman as special as you should not be seen on the dance floor with a complete klutz like me."

"My, my, you say and do the most adorable things, but don't let me catch you practicing with any of the other women here."

"It's a deal," he said crossing his heart and winking.

"Also, tell me that the woman you took the lessons from was as ugly as an alligator."

"Ease up on the alligators, I promise to leave that in my past from now on. As for the dance instructor, sorry, but I cannot lie. She was stunning. Her husband, however, was a massive hunk of a man; it made it difficult to flirt with her. It was also an odd class, two women for every man. You'd think people would go in couples."

"Likely story. I'm sure you loved it. Regardless, thank you for doing this for me." It was the simple and gracious things that Andrew did for her that she most appreciated.

At last, it was time to pick their celebrity/pro for the morning golf outing. Andrew's team was already made up of Julia and Martha Goodwin. He could chose a celebrity or professional golfer for their fourth player. Julia wanted Andrew to pick one of the three women from the Ladies Professional Golf Association. Not only did she think it would be fun to have a team dominated by women, she also thought that she might get some pointers on her own game along the way. Andrew, on the other hand, wanted to play with Steve Spurrier, the head coach of the Florida Gator football team.

Julia used the subtle pressure that often worked well on her fiancé. "Andrew, you're such a dear man. I'm very happy that you brought me with you. I would be even happier, however, if you'd do the right thing and pick a female professional golfer."

Martha, though she didn't care, got in on the action. "Come on, Andrew, do the chivalrous thing, do what your lady wants. Plus, if you pick a woman, it'll be a good test for your ego."

Outnumbered, he went with the flow. He decided on Annika Sorenstam. Besides being ranked second on the LPGA tour, she was by far the best looking, at least to Andrew. Chris Cromwell must have thought the same because he and Roxanne took Annika before Andrew got a chance. When Team Albright's pick came up, he went with Nancy Lopez, his second choice.

Monday morning dawned with thick dew and chirping birds. Julia took Andrew to the course early, because that was her habit. She was not an exceedingly competitive person until she got on the golf course. As she had in college, Julia still liked to sense the soul of the golf course; if she knew the monster she could slay it. The Cromwells arrived a little after nine.

Chris saw them and charged over with a purposeful gait. "We need to make this a much more interesting day. What say we wager some money on the outcome? Is two hundred fifty good for you, Dr. Albright?"

"I'm not sure that's such a good idea. We should be out here to enjoy ourselves and raise money for the charity."

"Poppycock, where is your competitive spirit? Besides, I never get tired of taking your money."

"Okay, Mr. Big Man on Campus, let's take your wallet for a spin," Julia said, jumping in before Andrew could respond. "I say we make it five hundred dollars. The loser also buys the winner dinner when we get back to Ann Arbor." It was a sucker bet; Andrew had gotten to be a pretty fine golfer since she'd started teaching him.

"Well Dr. Albright, we surely do know who has the balls in your family." He tossed a golf ball to Julia. "Pun intended." Roxanne jammed her elbow into Christopher's ribs–even she thought her husband had crossed the line.

The outing was a scramble format. Each player hit his or her ball; the team decided which was the best shot and then they all played from there. This made Martha's life easy; she never could have kept up with Julia or Nancy otherwise.

The first hole was a par five. Andrew's team reached the fringe of the green in two with a crushing drive by Nancy and a high, soft, five wood from Julia. Andrew chipped in for an eagle. After a round of high fives and hugs, he looked back into the fairway to make sure that Christopher was watching.

The front nine ended with the Albright team five under to the Cromwell team's four. Advantage Andrew.

Christopher decided to put some heat on his friend. "This is getting interesting. Raise the stakes to an even grand?"

It wasn't Andrew's style to bet that kind of money, but before he'd even thought about it he replied, "You're on, Mr. Big Man on Campus, and I hope you brought cash." He winked at Julia, who returned the gesture.

Annika and Nancy glanced at each other with raised eyebrows, a nod and a wink. Amateurs with spunk.

By the sixteenth hole, a short par four with water fronting the green, both teams were tied at ten under par. The game plan was to have Andrew hit a 210-yard drive, leaving the ball sixty-five yards short of the green and ten yards short of the water. Andrew commented that he had no clue how to hit the ball a specific distance and proved it by hitting it 240 yards directly into the pond.

Either Nancy or Julia had to go for the green. Nancy was playing the men's tees as a professional, but Julia was playing the women's tees, giving her a thirty-five-yard advantage. Nancy hit a perfect lay-up shot that would allow Julia to attempt driving the green. Before she hit, Christopher and his team came up to the tee.

Roxanne said, "Julia, it looks as if it's up to you. I'll bet you twenty bucks you can't land that white ball on that big comfy green."

"Not a problem," she responded.

Julia knew she had to tee it a little higher to get it to land softer, which was the key to keeping it on the green. She stepped up, took a practice swing, addressed the ball and hit it on the sweet spot. The ball was hit amazingly high for a fairway wood. The ball came down and even backed up two feet toward the pin.

After receiving congratulatory remarks from her teammates, Julia looked at Roxanne, who said nothing. "I'll take a Jackson, two Hamiltons, or twenty Washington's off your hands now. Your choice, it's all the same to me."

Roxanne searched her golf bag but came up empty-handed. "It looks like I'm short the cash right this minute." She stared at Chris, who shrugged his shoulders innocently.

"That's okay, you can owe me, dear," Julia chirped as they headed for the green.

Happily making up his pond shot, Andrew made the ten-foot putt and Team Albright was two up on Team Cromwell. Unfortunately, they let the eighteenth hole get away when both Nancy and Julia hit their balls in the water. It was the toughest hole on the golf course, and hubris caused both to try to hit shots farther than their skill allowed. Andrew saved par with a nice two-foot chip. The Cromwells needed an unlikely eagle on eighteen to tie Team Albright.

At the end of the day they fell two shots short.

Over drinks in the bar, no one could tell if Chris was kidding when he said, "This has been one expensive day, so far. You have my money and Roxy's ego in your pocket. So, I'm sure that you won't mind if I collect your room rent for tonight in advance." It was not the money that bothered him. He just hated losing. Roxanne hated it even more.

—Chapter 14—

The stories at dinner were the typical tall tales about the one that got away or the nasty wind that came out of nowhere to knock down the perfect shot. Andrew made it very clear to all who would listen that he had emptied Christopher's wallet. Julia was kinder to Roxanne and avoided making her eat crow. Maybe not schooled in politics, she sensed making fun of Roxanne in public would be a bad move, particularly for the new girl on the block.

As dinner was being served, Andrew clanked his glass to get everyone's attention. When he had it, he said, "Roxanne, it is with great pleasure that I donate today's winnings of one thousand dollars to your QualityCare charities. I'm sure that it will be better used there than what I had planned."

Roxanne was mildly surprised. "Well, Andrew, how gracious of you. Does anyone in the crowd want to match his generosity?" She knew how to take advantage of the moment; there were a number of takers who didn't want to look cheap.

The silent auction was always an enjoyable event. People were constantly getting up from the dinner table to check on who was bidding up the price of things. Julia had bid on and won a series of Irish church watercolors. She loved all things Celtic and these would be a good addition to Andrew's study. She was already planning to redecorate Andrew's house. Rather than being offended when she suggested it, he encouraged her to hire an interior designer to make the process go more smoothly.

Their spectacular weather repeated itself on Tuesday morning. Andrew and Julia left well before the sun came up to take a walk along the beach. They talked about the wedding and agreed they wanted something that was simple but elegant. They decided they would have a modest church service for fifty to seventy-five people, and then have a larger reception to celebrate with all their friends. They decided Julia would take the responsibility for the wedding and Andrew for their trip to Ireland and Scotland.

Andrew jumped right in. "I'm thinking that since we only have ten days, we could spend the first three in Ireland and the last seven in Scotland."

"What makes you think I'd want to spend the majority of my time in Scotland? Ireland is a much more scenic country than Scotland. Besides, it's warmer."

"Let's see: why would I want to spend more than the minimum amount of time in a country that's constantly fighting with itself? By all means, let's spend a week in Belfast."

She stopped walking before answering. "Scotty, you shouldn't risk being this cocky until *after* the wedding. Although small, there is *some* possibility that you could piss me off and find yourself standing at the altar all by yourself." She regretted the words as soon as they came out of her mouth.

"Ouch." He wondered where his teasing had gone wrong.

"I'm sorry," she said quickly. "I certainly didn't intend to bring you back to that dreadful place in your head. I've been so proud of you for putting that behind you. I know that it comes back every time Drew comes and leaves. Remember that God is smiling on us. We have each other and soon Drew will join us.

Should the heavens continue to smile on us, we will have a child of our own. Andrew, we are truly blessed, and I am among the most fortunate women alive."

"It's okay. I do on occasion have nightmares about you leaving, but I trust you, and I know that you're not going to do that to me. I sure do hate it when people leave me, physically or emotionally. I hated it with my parents, I hated it with Laura, and I hate it when my patients die, particularly the female patients. It all feels like abandonment."

"Why," she asked, "are the female patients you lose more difficult than the men?"

"I'm sure it goes back to feeling rejected by my mother. Until I met you, my life was a series of rejections by women. My mother was an emotional wasteland when it came to her children. My first girlfriend had her best friend break up with me–I guess it wasn't worth *her* time to tell me herself. Laura, well you already know she invalidated my manhood. When my female patients die, it's just another form of rejection. I know that it's not about me, but it does affect me. For some reason, my male patients don't create the same feelings. It hurts, but it's a different kind of hurt."

"Why didn't you tell me that before now?"

"I didn't have to tell you, you've played such a stabilizing force in my life. Although a bit of a cliché, you're the rock to which I tether my boat. The seas ebb in and out. The storms come and go. Sometimes they are severe, but as long as I'm connected to the rock, I know I'm safe. Julia, you are my safe place."

Back at the condo, Andrew checked his e-mail, hoping for, and finding, an update from Drew, who said he was keeping his promise to behave. He was focused on and nervous about the hearing, and he wanted to know what would happen if the judge did not let him come live in Michigan.

Andrew typed his response. "Little man, have faith. God is with us and this'll all work out right. Judge Parker has always said that she'd do what was right for you. Julia and I are looking forward to your coming to Michigan."

He responded to a few things from work and turned the computer over to Julia.

Julia had taken a shower and was ready for the day. She pulled up her e-mail account and found three messages. Two were from colleagues wondering if she was having fun, and one was from Andrew. While tempted to jump right to his message, she first answered her friends, telling them about having set a date. She copied the message to Carol, figuring that Andrew would forget. Then she went to the e-mail from Andrew. As soon as she opened it, she got a lump in her throat. He had found a way to pull at her heartstrings from 1,200 miles away. The e-mail read:

My Dearest Julia,

I am already taking you for granted, which is a horrible sin for which I need to seek your forgiveness. I need to thank you for creating an environment where I feel safe. This poem is but a piece of my heart and the gratitude that I have for you being in my life.

Safe Place

Our hearts need to find a safe place to be
Where we can come out and always be free.
It's the place to share our dreams and our tears,
It's also a spot we bare our schemes and fears.

Sometimes my safe place I can call all my own

For there are times when it's safe to be all alone.
There are others, however, when I need less space,
For there are times when I need you in my safe place.

Do you, my sweet love, need a safe place to go?
Are you in need of shelter when the cold wind blows?
Am I there in that safe place where you so want to run?
Where our souls and our spirit join together, as one?

We need a place where we share complete trust,
For feeling safe and secure is one of life's musts.
I would gladly give all that I have to be
Each other's safe place for all eternity.

Julia was in tears when she found Andrew in the bedroom. "Andrew, I will always be your rock and you shall always be mine. You can trust me to always be there for you. I will always love you and I will always protect you from that dark place that so many have created for you. I am your sunshine and you are my rain. Together we will help our seed grow."

She hugged him, and it was his turn to wipe the tears away.

—Chapter 15—

As the QualityCare Board got ready to reconvene, Christopher had a cup of coffee with his wife in the corner of the room. He was mentally taking the pulse of the group. If his long-range plans were going to work, he needed them to be confident about their future. He judged them ready. "Roxy, I do believe I have them right where I want them. This morning should be the start of a new era at QualityCare."

Roxanne nodded her head. "Yes. Just like we talked about. This is the opportunity and this is the time." She gave her husband a squeeze of encouragement.

He put down his cup and walked to the podium. He tapped on the mike to get their attention, then began. "Ladies and Gentlemen, I trust that everyone had a good time and spent lots of money at the auction last night?" There was a round of applause and a few brief snickers. "Good. As promised, we will be done here by noon. Everyone will then be free to do his or her own thing. As for Roxanne and I, we are dragging the Albrights back out to the golf course. The rumor you heard regarding our loss yesterday is real and today we'll be out for revenge. Anyone want to place a bet on the outcome?"

Phil teased the boss. "Christopher, you are a five-handicapper who lost a thousand dollars on the golf course. I believe that both of those facts are evidence that you're spending too much time on the golf course and not enough at the office. If QualityCare weren't doing so well, I'd say our CEO had a conflict with his priorities."

Christopher grinned and let the laugher die down. "Okay, I get the message. The comedy portion of our program is now complete. So, in that spirit, let's get back to business." Boos and hisses emanated from the crowd.

Christopher reiterated that growth was the theme for 2000, and quality of care would be the driving force to create that growth. He recognized that HMOs were coming under fire, which he used to drive home his next point. "HMOs might rank near the bottom of the trust scale, but people trust their physicians, and we are going to take advantage of that fact. We are going to press for patient's rights. We are going to focus on evidence-based medicine, doing the right thing at the right time. We are going to earn the trust and respect of the public."

He did not have to convince the Board. They knew a winner when they saw one and this was a winning formula.

He moved on to a different subject. "I want to give you one clear example of the respect that the insurance industry has for our model of health care. We have been asked to collaborate with an insurance company out of Great Britain called the British Insurance Group. Their CEO, Arthur Bishop, is interested in how we operate, as a potential model for their socialistic form of health care. The fact that he chose QualityCare is an honor and a privilege."

Arthur Bishop would be spending a lot of time at the Ann Arbor offices and Christopher had just laid the groundwork so people would not wonder why.

Andrew snapped to, suddenly seeing the connection that had started on the private plane ride from Orlando.

There was a round of questions and answers about the overall plan. Even Andrew saw no harm in growing. He did, however, have a gnawing feeling about Chris and Arthur's relationship. It wasn't so much what they did, but it had everything to do with not being forthright.

On his way out of the meeting he whispered to Julia, "We're going to have to watch this one closely. It looks innocent enough on the surface, but it doesn't feel right underneath all the platitudes. These two have been up to something for awhile. I wonder what all the secrecy is about? Maybe it's just greed that's the driving force here."

"You're just being paranoid, don't you think?"

Andrew didn't respond, but hoped Julia was right.

In spite of Chris's threat of revenge, he couldn't make good on it. Tuesday's golf outing took a different twist: It became a game of the ladies against the men. No money was involved. It was an excellent opportunity for Julia to get to know Roxanne better.

The ladies spent the front nine talking about the wedding. Roxanne being Roxanne, she insisted that the bride let her help with some of the arrangements. She knew how to get things done. Julia said they could make up some plans together when they got home. She was hoping that Roxanne would get distracted and forget about helping her, but she doubted it. Roxanne was too pretentious for Julia's taste. She made their wedding sound as if it should rival some royal couples's. For Roxanne, anything worth doing was worth making a big production.

On the back nine, Julia did not remember where, she asked Roxanne, "How did you come to meet Chris?"

Roxanne took her own route to an answer. "I always wanted to be a doctor. My father, grandfather, and great-grandfather were all physicians. *I* was going to be the first female doctor in the Stanton family. My grandfather and father were pioneers in the radiology business. They made a bloody fortune."

"But, you aren't a doctor, are you?" Julia couldn't envision Roxanne doing the hard work necessary to get through medical school.

"No. Oh, I got into medical school all right, but left after the first year. Allegations were made that I bought the answers to an anatomy final exam. There was no proof of that. People were just jealous of my family name. After all, Boston Med's Stanton Science Hall is named after my father."

"What'd you do next?"

"I cried and then sucked it up and moved on. I had enough background to easily complete the Physicians Assistant program at the University of Massachusetts. I went to work at the Boston Health Plan and that's where I met Chris."

"Where's your father now?"

"Not in Michigan, thank God. Dear father and I had a falling out three years ago. He thought I was using my trust fund money improperly. I was using it for political purposes that he apparently didn't approve of it. Well, daddy cut me off and I sued the son-of-a-bitch. I lost it all except for three hundred grand that was already in a Michigan bank account. That'll soon be gone, too." She took a vicious swing at her ball, perhaps using it as a surrogate for her father. "Damn the man. Who did he think he was to take my money away?"

"How sad you had to go through that. I'm sorry for you." Julia was anything but sorry, but she felt compelled to say something.

"Well, Christopher is just going to have to find a way to keep me living in the style to which I am accustomed. He's a good boy; he can do it," she said with a wry smile. "If he can't, then I'll have to rely on a hero who wears a black hat instead of a white one."

Julia, startled and curious by such a comment, started to ask Roxanne what she meant, but Roxanne was already several yards down the fairway.

The golf match ended with Julia firing a birdie on the last hole to tie up the match. Roxanne had played better than usual and Christopher was not on his game. He complained that he was emotionally flat after having played cheerleader to the Board for two days.

The flight home to Ann Arbor was quite nice since they were cruising in Arthur Bishop's private charter. It made it easier to face the dreary clouds of Michigan that awaited them. On the way home, Chris talked in more detail about his vision for QualityCare. He spent considerable time making sure that Andrew understood that to pitch quality of care as the differentiation factor, Partners Medical Group would have to be a central piece of the strategy.

Out of curiosity and concern Andrew asked his host, "Why the fast lane, Chris? What's the rush with all this growth stuff?"

"Because the market is ripe right now, Andrew, and we pick our fruit before it rots, do we not?"

"Humpf. That may be our problem: I don't think of PMG or QualityCare as fruit trees. Or anything else. PMG is a medical clinic and shouldn't be confused with a bounty-laden tree to be plucked."

Chris raised his eyebrows, but didn't bite. He changed the subject. "Andrew, on another matter. Bruce Meyers could be instrumental in helping us bring other physician groups into the fold. He is uniquely qualified and talks their language. It would make closing the deals so much easier. Can I buy twenty-five percent of his time from PMG starting in June?"

"I'll talk to the PMG Board, but I'm not sure that Bruce will want to go down that path. I guess we'll see."

Christopher saw no reason to tell Andrew that he had already talked Bruce into supporting his plan. He hadn't given the young doctor the whole picture, but he certainly led him to believe that he could personally benefit by supporting the growth plan.

Once they settled into the comfort of their own home, Andrew made both of them a drink and they compared notes about their trip to Florida.

Julia started. "Would you like to hear the life story of Roxanne Stanton Cromwell in five minutes or less?"

"Sure. I still don't know what Chris sees in her."

"Maybe it was her money."

"I know she was into some family money, but what're you referring to?" He didn't think any amount of money could make her baggage worth putting up with all the time.

"Did you know that Roxanne was a medical student at one time?"

Andrew stopped to think. "She was a graduate of UMass's Physician's Assistant program, I think. She went on to work in a local clinic in Boston. That's where she met Chris."

"Correct. But she was a freshman in medical school when she got the boot for buying the answers to some final exam. She told me there wasn't any proof; I suppose she thought I'd think that meant she was innocent. Ha."

"I've known her for ten years," he said, "and I have never heard that one before."

"How many intimate conversations have you had with her in ten years?"

"I'm not sure."

"Yes, you are. Trust me. I'm not the least bit jealous of that woman."

"Well, I guess I can admit that Mrs. Cromwell and I have had the grand total of one intimate conversation. She was falling down drunk at the time and wanted to know if I wanted to get in her panties. So, how about the rest of the story?"

"In a minute. Did you oblige her? She is a beautiful woman."

"Oh my God, she's a head case to rival all head cases. I've always pitied Chris."

"Not exactly a complete answer. Never mind. Her grandfather and father both made a mint in radiology, and got a science hall named after them."

"I knew that her family was heavily involved in many of the advances in the radiology field. You don't get the wing of a major medical school named after you without having done something genuinely special, or by writing a humongus check."

"Right again. Roxanne came into a whole lot of money when her grandfather died, but it was in a trust. She figured out how to get around that and started taking money out of it. She says she was using it for 'noble' fund-raising, if you can believe that. Her dad caught her and cut her off, but not before she'd stashed like three hundred grand of it. She even had the nerve to sue her own father to get back into the trust fund. She lost. Now the three hundred is running out and she told me that Chris was just going to have to find a way to keep her in the life to which she was accustomed. She even babbled something about guys in black and white hats. Well, there you have it, what does it mean?"

"I don't know, but with Roxanne anything is possible. On a personal level, I feel sorry for Chris, for sure. On a professional level, I just don't know." He did know though, that he was starting to have some doubts about his friend's plans for QualityCare. Did he want the company to grow for himself, or for the good of the patients, like he said?

—Chapter 16—

Life returned to some sense of normalcy over the next two weeks. Andrew met with Beverly McNeil once a week to discuss the upcoming custody hearing. There was not a great deal of preparation that needed to be done, but it made Andrew feel better to get together.

During their second visit, she said, "Andrew, we may have a problem."

"What on earth could be a problem at this point? You haven't discovered that Julia was a prostitute in Indiana, have you?" He was trying to be funny, but Beverly went right past it.

"We've had word that your ex-wife is fighting the jurisdiction of the Michigan courts and particularly Judge Parker. Her attorney is arguing that she's a legal resident of California and wants to have any and all hearings held there."

"You've got to be kidding me. She agreed long ago to allow the Michigan courts to have jurisdiction. Why on earth would she do this now?"

"Because she's scared she's going to lose out here, of course. We'll have a resolution to this on Monday. I don't think his tactics will work, but you never know."

Andrew went home and went into his quiet mode. He had faith in the legal system, but nothing but contempt for his ex-wife.

As usual, Julia was a comforting force. She kept telling Andrew to have faith. The ironic thing was that Andrew was telling Drew the same thing. He found it much easier to say than do.

Beverly came by the clinic on Monday morning. Just seeing her made Andrew fear the worse. If it had been good news she would have called.

She got straight to the point. "We're good to go. The courts have sided with our position. Laura has always agreed to let the Michigan courts have jurisdiction, so there's no precedence for change. Frankly, she received poor legal advice from her attorney. Now there's some chance that she won't show up, but I think it a small risk. I hate to say it, but right now it just sucks to be her because we are going to win this thing."

"Well, well. Aren't you the lawyer with the funny bone today."

"Levity comes with victory. Just you remember that, Dr. Albright."

"Is there anything else we need to do?"

"No, we're all set. You may want to talk to Drew to make sure he's as calm as possible. I'm confident he wants to be here in Michigan, but if he gets emotional, Laura's attorney will play that up in her favor. I lost the battle with our attempt for him to stay with you the night before the hearing. The judge didn't want us to create any undue influence. We can live with that decision. I'll use it to my advantage."

"I'm sure you will. You don't miss anything."

"There is one more thing. Judge Parker decided that she'd interview Drew in her chambers. Counsel is welcome to attend, but we won't be allowed to question him. It's only fair to young Drew to not be intimidated by us sharks."

Drew and Laura arrived on May 9th, just in time for Andrew to have a late lunch with his son. Their conversation was about everything else but the next day. Drew was nervous, but mostly all smiles, happy to be with his father. That night though, he faced a different set of circumstances. Lindsey kept after him, asking him why he wanted to live in Michigan. She reminded him that he would have to leave his school and his friends. He was just learning how to surf on the beaches of California. Where would he do that in Michigan? It was a long night for the boy.

Laura walked into the courtroom hand-in-hand with Lindsey at ten the next morning, with Drew walking several paces behind. Andrew's first thought was that Lindsey's trip to the sperm bank had obviously been successful–she had to be at least seven months pregnant.

Andrew moved to say hello to Laura. She ignored him.

Lindsey said just loud enough for Andrew to hear "Just tell frog face to go to hell."

"What she said," Laura whispered to Andrew as she took her seat.

Everyone stood when Judge Parker entered. She asked them to be seated and immediately launched into her review of the legal briefs and psychological profiles presented by an independent third party. She asked counsel from both sides if they had any comments they wanted to make before she talked with Drew in her chambers.

Laura had her California attorney, Robert Ramsey, with her. "Judge, are you absolutely sure that it is appropriate for you to have jurisdiction over this case?" he asked.

"Mr. Ramsey, is it?"

"Yes, your honor," he said smugly.

"Are you a member of the Michigan bar?"

"No, your Honor, but I understood that I could be heard in your courtroom today."

"Mr. Ramsey, is that your client's Michigan counsel sitting at your right?"

"Yes, he is. I believe you know Mark Patterson?"

"Mr. Ramsey, your rights to be heard in my courtroom have now been terminated. Had you asked me an intelligent question rather than insult this bench, I would have given you some leeway. Since you just stepped in a heap of Michigan dung, I do not want to hear anything further from you. Is that understood?"

"I object, your Honor."

She stared at him for a long moment and said, "So noted. Now, the next sentence out of your mouth will run you the risk of a contempt citation. Do you have a flight back to California this evening?"

"Yes, I do."

"Well, the only way you're going to be on that plane is if I hear nothing but your breathing. Ms. Donaldson, is there anything you wish to share with the court?"

"I just want to tell the court that every child needs his mother. I love my son and he is better off with me than with his father."

"Ms. Donaldson, I appreciate the love you have for your child, as I have children of my own. But I'm more interested in what impact the child that Ms. Resnick is carrying might have on this situation. Can you share that with the court?"

"Uh, Lindsey and I have certainly proven ourselves to be loving parents to Drew. We don't believe this is any different than if Ms. Osborn were to have a child with Drew's father." Score one for the California team. Beverly wanted to jump in and point out the difference, but she knew that Judge Parker already knew it.

"I have just one more question for each parent before Drew and I have a chat." She looked at Drew and smiled, hoping to put him at ease. "Dr. Albright, how did you spend your time with Drew yesterday?"

"We caught up on his progress at school, our upcoming wedding, and we talked about girls." He grinned at Drew, who was too mortified to return the favor.

"Girls?" the judge asked.

"Yes. It appears that Drew has a crush on a classmate of his."

Aghast, Drew shook his head wildly at his father.

"Well, that will happen to boys; it happened to my husband. I met him in the sixth grade." The courtroom broke out in laughter, which made Drew feel better, even though he didn't get the joke. "Ms. Donaldson, how did you spend your time?"

"Mostly with what we always do, except that we talked about being here in Michigan and why. I tried to calm my son, the same as any good mother." She saw no reason to include Lindsey's grilling.

"Drew, do you understand what we are going to do now?"

"I think so."

"Do you have any questions?"

"How long will it take?"

"Not long, and I promise that if you want to stop and take a break at any time, you can just tell me, okay?"

The judge, Drew and the three attorneys went into her chambers. After he was settled, Judge Parker asked if Drew wanted anything to drink. After the clerk got him some orange juice, she started. "Now, Drew, I want you to tell me all about yourself."

Drew expected this question and did a credible job considering how nervous he was. He told her about his life in California, his friends, and his school. He even talked about the crush he had on his classmate. Dad ratted on him, so he had nothing to lose. No, he hadn't told his mother about the girl. Judge Parker noted how lively he was when he talked about his dad, and how hostile he felt toward Lindsey. Of course, she already knew from his psychological profile that Drew, in his boyish mind, viewed Lindsey as a surrogate father for his real father. It was common to resent that relationship.

"Judge Parker, may I interrupt?" Mr. Ramsey decided that he had a question that couldn't wait.

"Not unless you want to become an honorary citizen of the State of Michigan for twenty-four hours."

"But, we are in chambers, Judge."

"Mr. Ramsey, do you see the court reporter to your right?"

"Of course," he said crossly.

"Well, that means that we're on the record in here. Were my instructions outside beyond your comprehension?"

"No, but–"

"But nothing." She held up a finger to her lips.

Next, Judge Parker asked Drew to describe the last twenty-four hours. His words were the kiss of death to the California contingent. Drew repeated Andrew's version of their visit and offered that he wasn't happy with his dad for sharing the crush he had at school. That was "private man-to-man stuff." When it came to his time with his mother and Lindsey, he talked expressly about Lindsey asking him several times why he wanted to live in Michigan. "She was just a big pain in the, uh, the neck."

Judge Parker sighed, disappointed with this typical type of manipulation that often occurred with children. The fact that Laura had allowed Lindsey's interference was confirmation of everything else she'd interpreted in the legal briefs.

"Okay. Now I'm going to ask you an unfair question. I want to start with making sure that your answer in no way is asking you which parent you love more. This question has nothing to do with them. Do you understand?"

"Uh-huh."

"If you were the judge here, what would you do with Drew Albright?"

"I-I don't know," he stuttered.

"Fair enough. What if this case involved a friend of yours and you were in my shoes. What would you do?"

"That's easy. I'd send the boy to live with his dad," he said with confidence.

"Is there a reason?"

"Every boy wants to be safe and my friend would feel safest with his daddy." If Andrew could have heard Drew's words he would have melted.

"Drew, we're done now. Do you have any questions for me?"

"What are you going to do?"

"I'll let you know after lunch, is that okay?"

"Cool, you bet," he said with a smile of relief on his face.

Judge Parker led her ducks back into her courtroom and announced that she would recess for ninety minutes.

As soon as she left the courtroom, Andrew was all over Beverly. "Tell me what happened."

Beverly gave him an almost word for word description of the discussion in the judge's chamber. She patted Drew on the head. "You were a little champion in there."

"What is she going to say at one?"

"You know I can't possibly know that, Andrew. It's always hard to tell in a case like this."

"Stop, stop, stop; I just want to know what you think. I promise not to file a malpractice case against you." He knew what it was like to avoid personal opinions with his patients, but this was different. At least he thought it was different.

"Personally, I hope his room is ready at your house."

Andrew and Julia hugged each other and then Beverly. They took a brief walk outside. The world looked bright even though it was a typical cloudy Michigan spring day. The April showers had brought May flowers, and Andrew walked hand in hand with Julia and compared the spring flowers to new beginnings in their lives.

Judge Parker returned promptly at one. She spent a few minutes going over some preliminary material to make sure it was in the court records. She then launched into her decision. The room was so quiet it made everyone self-conscious.

"I came to the court today with a good idea of what was right for Drew Albright. Sometimes, I hear things that either change my mind or at least create doubt. Neither of those events happened today. While I appreciate the rights of a mother to care for her child, my responsibility is to do what is in the best interest of the child. In cases like this, I try to determine the most stable environment for that child. In this case, it's clear the environment being created by Dr. Albright and Ms. Osborn is the most stable, pending their marriage. Thus I am awarding custody of Drew Albright to his father effective August twenty-third, nineteen ninety-nine."

Laura jumped up. "No, no! You can't take my baby!" She was about to say more when Mark Patterson took her by the arm and made her sit down.

"Dr. Albright, I'm allowing Drew to stay with his mother this summer for two reasons. The first is that she deserves some time to transition her role appropriately. The second is that I've always found it better not to let a child get caught up in two transitions at once. For Drew to adjust to your world at the same time you're preparing your wedding would be unfair to him."

Beverly stood and addressed the bench. "Your honor, Drew is an integral part of my client's wedding plans. He also believes that Drew would be better served by getting to know some kids his own age prior to school starting."

"I appreciate your input, but the fact is that Drew will be attending private school in the fall, according to your brief. As such, he is likely to have different friends in the neighborhood and school. I see no significant advantage on that argument. And I believe that it's right that Drew has some time with his mother before uprooting his world. I cannot discount the fact that this is a significant change for Ms. Donaldson, and I respect her need to create a healthy transition, which I fully expect her to do."

"Would it make any difference if my client and Ms. Osborn were to marry sooner?" She already knew the answer and didn't want to appear greedy, but Andrew wanted her to ask.

"No, it wouldn't. Mr. Patterson, any questions?"

"No, your Honor." He'd known his case was lost the minute Laura told him she was bringing her West Coast attorney with her. He wasn't going to alienate a judge he was likely to see in the courtroom again soon.

"Mr. Ramsey, do you have any questions?"

"Yes, your Honor."

"Frankly, Mr. Ramsey, I was being polite. Please go home." She paused and then concluded, "There being no further questions, this court is adjourned."

"The judge made a good call all the way around on this one," Beverly said, as soon as the judge was out of the room. "I know you wanted Drew to come as soon as school got out, but this will be better."

Jubilant, Andrew high-fived Beverly. Julia was in need of another mascara repair.

"Well, as disappointed as I am on that count, I think God smiled on us today. I've waited years for this day; I can certainly wait another ninety days. Thank you for helping me through this, and I don't mean just the legal end. Any attorney could have done the legal part; it's the emotional support that I most appreciate."

"I keep telling you that I'm not your average attorney. When will you believe me?"

They left the courtroom laughing.

—Chapter 17—

Andrew saw his son briefly before their plane departed. Drew was more nervous now than before the hearing. He didn't know how either his mother or Lindsey would act in the coming weeks. No child wants to disappoint a parent on purpose, but Drew felt like he had done exactly that. It made him sad.

Andrew spoke to Laura. "I'm sorry it came down to this day. I know how you must be feeling."

"Until you're a mother who's had her child taken away, you will never know how I feel," she snapped back at him. "I trust you did this because you feel it's best for Drew, but I'll never forgive you for it. I can't talk about it now, but I want you to know that I intend to win this battle in the long run. This isn't over." She shoved past him, glared at Julia and grabbed Drew's hand.

The plane left and Julia and Andrew celebrated by going to their favorite Italian Restaurant, Gratzi's. They didn't gloat. They talked about their future and whether Julia should return to Greenhills in the fall and figured yes. They had already decided that Drew would attend the fifth grade there; she might as well continue to teach until the time came for them to have a child of their own. They would revisit the issue then.

The day after the hearing, Julia got busy planning the wedding and working with her interior designer. She placed her condominium on the market for sale and planned to use the proceeds to finance her makeover project. They'd debated selling his place, too, but felt that Drew was too comfortable there to change.

She had to keep reminding herself that the wedding was supposed to be "simple." Up first were the invitations. In keeping with the theme, they would be simple; getting the guest list down to a manageable number would not. She moved on to picking a dress–ivory satin with a hint of lace; the flowers–lilies; and the music–a combination of traditional piano pieces with a live bagpipe player. She set out to nail down all the details by July 4th.

Andrew had some time to make up at the clinic. He had become distracted from his patient care duties. He enjoyed his administrative duties, but missed his patients and they him. He also had to prepare for the work that he would inherit from Bruce Meyers, who was going on loan to QualityCare in a few weeks.

He got home quite late one night to find Julia in bed reading. She was giddy with excitement about their wedding plans; she told him all about it, except the dress.

He shared his day. It started with hospital rounds at the crack of dawn and then he saw twelve patients before lunch. Instead of a leisurely break, he attended a business lunch, complete with stale sandwiches. He followed that with an hour of phone calls to patients and other physicians with eleven more office visits. Then he put in an hour of paperwork, leaving another hours' worth for another time.

His next comment surprised even him. "I was surprised at how hard it was to keep up the pace today. All the admin work has made me soft. In that capacity, I'm usually in control of my time. With patients, they're in control."

"How do your patients control how much time you spend

with them? Shouldn't the front office schedule them so the pace is manageable?"

"Actually, they do a good job of that. There are always exceptions, though. For example, I had two patients today who couldn't be neatly folded into the schedule."

"Why not?" Julia really didn't get it. It always felt easy when she went to the doctors.

"The sicker they are, the longer I have to take with them. Today, I had Jim Velucci in; he's been a patient of mine for some time. He's an autoworker at the Ford plant in Saline; he has chronic lung disease. He sees a pulmonary doctor at least once a month and me for all the byproduct issues that come up; he gets a lot of upper respiratory infections. I used to golf with Jim from time to time. I doubt that he could get around the course today. He loves his grandchildren, but seldom has the wind to play with them. It's sad to watch him go downhill."

"Can anyone do anything for him?"

"The one person who could have helped Jim the most was Jim. The guy smoked three packs of cigarettes a day–for the first twenty years they didn't even have filters. He never even tried to quit until he landed in the hospital. His heart is in reasonable shape, but his lungs are beyond shot."

"Tell me about the other patient, and please make it a happier story."

"Sorry. Her story is even worse than Jim's. Nancy Ours. She was diagnosed with ALS three weeks ago."

"Stop," Julia interjected. "What's ALS?"

"Have you ever heard of Lou Gehrig's Disease?"

"Yes, from the baseball guy. It's fatal, right?"

"Amyotrophic lateral sclerosis, ALS, is a neurodegenerative disease that attacks bundles of nerves in the brain and spinal cord. The sad part of this disease is the slowness of its progressive paralysis and atrophy of muscles. The good news is that the patient can go for more than a year before the symptoms become evident. The bad news is that you know it's coming. It starts in the hands as a rule, and then affects other parts of the body, including the ability to speak, chew, and in due course breathe. This is one of the hardest diseases for me to watch patients go through. Nancy will receive the best neurological care available here in Ann Arbor. My job is to coordinate her overall treatment plan. She'll see many physicians and take many different medications. Keeping all her care straight and making sure that all the doctors are talking to each other to optimize her care is a good thing for the patient. It's part of our care management program at QualityCare."

Andrew switched topics to a happier subject: what they might do in Scotland. Given a five-day limit in each country, he thought they should focus on Edinburgh and St. Andrews. After starting in Scotland, they would go to Ireland. Catching a flight home would be easier from Dublin than anywhere in Scotland. "I think that during our stay in Ireland, we should just rent a car and drive around and look for things to do. How about that?"

Turning her lips down in a pout, Julia replied, "You tried that once before. Don't do it again." She attacked him with some pillows. He defended himself poorly. What started out as physical playfulness soon turned to lovemaking.

After she had her way with him, she looked deep into his eyes and thanked him again for being in her life. "I cannot believe that you came into my life and swept me off my feet."

"It is you, sunshine, who has brought the light and warmth to this union. As they say, I once was lost but now I'm found. Thank you for finding me and thank you for loving me."

"You're very welcome." She fell asleep in his arms, feeling a level of peace and belonging she never thought possible.

—Chapter 18—

Memorial Day came and went in a blur. The couple had to arrange the first Saturday in June to stop and take stock of where they were. Julia decided to cook at home; she could describe her decorating plans and give him a walkabout so Andrew could get a better visual idea of what it would all look like when it was finished.

Andrew and his ex-wife had custom-built the eleven-year-old red-brick colonial. It had a center staircase and stained, six-panel doors. Andrew loved the dark wood floors. The formal living and dining room were in excellent condition for lack of use, but maybe they would entertain more after the wedding. The kitchen contained dark oak cabinets and laminate counters. Most of Andrew's time was spent in the family room, which was adjacent to the kitchen. It was a step-down room with a coiffure ceiling, stained moldings, and a natural stone fireplace that was both gas and wood burning.

He called to say that he'd be forty-five minutes late, hardly a rare event. It often took Andrew and his buddies an hour to settle all their wagers from the golf course. Julia took a bath, freshened up, and put on a yellow sundress with green piping.

Andrew was so delighted with how she looked, like a flower, that he practically stumbled attempting to give her a hug.

"Oh yuck, Andrew. March yourself upstairs and wash that cigar stench off your body. How do you expect people to take your medical advice seriously if you don't follow it yourself?"

"I smoke twelve cigars a year, if that. Besides, getting my friends to eat lots of red meat, drink heavily, and smoke cigars is good for my business."

She smiled, falsely. "The longevity of your friends does not concern me. I expect you to take care of me in my old age. Your behavior indicates that you really don't love me."

"Honey, the chances are that with my genes, I'll outlive you." He snuggled up next to her.

"Go away, you ashtray, I will not even kiss you until you meet my inspection requirements. Go."

"And you mine," he said, walking up the stairs.

After he'd dutifully scrubbed up, they shared a bottle of Pinot Grigio with his favorite meal, Shrimp Scampi. The dinner conversation centered on the need to slow down. They made a pact to not overplan the wedding or honeymoon trip. They wanted to enjoy this time, not be exhausted by it.

After dinner, Julia took Andrew into the living room. They normally didn't spend too much time in there, so Andrew knew something was up.

She held up the renderings her interior designer had drawn up. "We're going to take a trip. Do you want to take a trip?"

"Yes, we are taking a trip, but don't tell me you want to plan that, too?"

"Enough wisecracks, this is not audience participation night at the comedy club. We're gonna take a trip through the house and I'm going to paint you a picture of what it's going to look like when we get done with our project."

"Julia, I trust you with this project; you don't need my permission."

"This is your house–"

Andrew sat straight up and said, "Please, don't make me say this again. This is *our* house." It took her a few minutes, but Julia did get it through to him that this was still *Laura's* house, with Laura's look. "So, what you're telling me is that when the project is finished, *then* this will be *our* house?"

"Correct. How you got through medical school is an ongoing mystery to me. Now, here's the plan: You walk with me and I'll paint you a word picture. Please ask questions as we go. If you hate the idea, keep it to yourself or lie to me."

Julia began the tour. "We're going to go with more neutral colors to lighten up the interior. Too much dark wood. We'll be going with new wall-to-wall carpeting in here. The wood floors in the kitchen and living room will be sanded and finished with a lighter stain and high-gloss finish. I want you to see my beauty in these floors."

"That takes me back to grade school when we could look up the girls' skirts with their shiny patent leather shoes on."

"You are one sick puppy. When we entertain here remind me to insist that the women wear pants. Skirted women will not be admitted, but kilted men can stay. Now back to the picture. Stay focused, will you?"

"I'm having trouble getting your skirt out of my mind."

"Behave now and I'll make the effort worth your while later, but don't make me remind you again. In the kitchen, the cabinets are going to be painted white and glazed brown. We'll have new granite countertops and we're going for broke on the appliances by going with Viking Professional Appliances." She pulled out the kitchen drawings and he studied them with what she thought was the appropriate focus. "We'll paint the moldings and ceiling beams in the family room and we'll tie everything together with new custom window treatments. Look at these drawings, aren't they beautiful?"

"Absolutely." To Andrew they just looked like drapes.

She continued, "We'll paint the interior and hang some new wallpaper in the bathroom. The major change upstairs will be to replace your beat up, broken down, pathetic bedroom furniture. My cherry wood furniture will look awesome with a new bedroom carpet. We'll update Drew's room in Wolverine colors, maize and blue. Lastly, in the fall, we'll add some exterior trim paint and get to work on the landscaping."

After a long pause, she finally asked, "Well, what do you think?"

"You mean it's my turn to talk? I was still focusing on the painting. My first problem is that you invaded my territory."

"What territory?" she asked with some concern.

"Landscaping." He smiled down at her. "In all seriousness, you've done a terrific job. This is going to look incredible."

"Do you have any questions?"

"Two."

"They wouldn't have anything to do with time and or money, would they?"

"Yes, they would. How'd you guess?"

"Does it matter how much it costs? Remember, we agreed that this was my project and my budget."

"Julia, let me repeat myself: I trust you with this project."

"I don't mean to be defensive. In a nutshell, the overall cost is seventy-five thousand. I'm using cash from the proceeds of my condo sale to cover it. The timing part of the project is the good news: my interior designer will oversee the project while we're in Ireland."

Satisfied, Andrew lightened the mood. "You mean when we're in Scotland, don't you?"

"Why, yes dear, I guess I do."

"This is going to be special, but are you sure you want to spend that much money?"

"I do," she said with confidence.

"I like the sound of those two words. Just remember them when you're standing up in the front of the church with me."

"I will, you can count on it. Besides, I'll be homeless in a month. You're going to have to make an honest woman out of me. Do you want to do that?"

"I do," Andrew said while holding Julia's hand to his heart.

"Good answer. Now let's take you upstairs and reward you for your good behavior."

"At last, a job I can handle," he said as he led her up the stairs.

—Chapter 19—

The first week in June was busy for both Julia and Andrew. She was wrapping up the school year, as well as finalizing the wedding plans. Andrew was immersed in clinic business. He thought he might have used poor judgment, or at least poor timing, allowing Bruce Meyers to spend his time working for QualityCare. He was having trouble keeping up with the load.

Things were going well for Julia, and she wanted to share her final wedding plans with Andrew. She called him on a Thursday to see if they could have a late lunch. Greenhills was in its half-day session mode for the last week of school and she would be free by one.

Andrew's nurse told him that he had an urgent phone call. When he picked up the phone and discovered it was Julia, he was happy to hear her voice. "How's the nut farm?"

"The animals have gone home for the day, the zookeeper is taking care of the wild animals still left in their cages and I'm footloose and fancy-free. I want to take my future husband to a late lunch to paint a new picture. This time it's our wedding day. You up for that?"

"Sorry. The only way you're going to see me this afternoon is if you come to the clinic with a severe head wound. Even then, I'm likely to send you to the ER."

Disappointed at having her plan shot down, she asked, "What if I show up with a broken heart?"

"Then we'll shoot the bastard who caused the injury. I'm sorry, but it's crazy here today. Can I chat with you later?"

"How about–" She heard the click of the phone. She was annoyed that Andrew had cut her off–this was *their* wedding day she wanted to discuss, after all. Disappointed, she packed up her remaining work, and walked to her car. She had some errands to run, but all of a sudden she wasn't in the mood. She went home and pouted. She was talking to a girlfriend on the phone when she got a great idea. She made several phone calls and added two new errands to her list. At 5:45, she showed up at the clinic and was ushered into a waiting room. Andrew's nurse, Amy, told him he had one final patient to see.

"Can't one of the other physicians take care of this?" he grumbled.

Amy stuck with her instructions. "Nope, you're the only physician who can treat this patient's problem." Andrew's ego clicked into gear. He grabbed his stethoscope and took off as if he'd been called to war. He entered exam room three to find his bride to be.

"Ah. Ms. Osborn. I thought we'd talked about your condition over the phone earlier today. Has it worsened?"

"You know, if I have to make appointments to see you, we're in big trouble. So, I've taken care of the details and you're free until your precious committee meeting tonight. That means you have ninety minutes to spend with me."

"Okay, okay, okay. But a ninety-minute appointment is going to be very expensive for you or your insurance company."

"Scotty, you charge me a nickel for this time and you'll get bills from me that I know your insurance company won't cover." She led him outside to the park across the street from the clinic.

She had brought a picnic, which was a good thing since Andrew had skipped lunch. "I know your time is precious, so why don't you start by telling me about your day? What was the best thing, the worst thing and the most surprising thing?"

"Well, the best thing is this surprise." Excellent start, she thought. "There were actually two worst things. Two care management patients I was following up on for Dr. Meyers. They're both part of QualityCare's program to focus on chronically ill patients. One, Paula Callaway, is just twenty-three years old. She has AIDS. Contracted it overseas while serving in the Aid for Africa program. Her boyfriend came in with her today; it was an emotional meeting. The second was Sandra Horn, who has breast cancer. We treated her with a lumpectomy and radiation late last year with great success, but the tumor's back, and she has to have a mastectomy next week. The most surprising part of my day was Chris dropping in with Arthur Bishop. Do you remember him talking about the British Insurance Group in Florida?"

After thinking for a moment, Julia remembered. "Yes, he said something about helping BIG–a funny acronym for an insurance company I might add–learn more about our American healthcare system."

"You were listening, very impressive. I don't know why Arthur keeps showing up everywhere, but he'll be at our Executive Committee meeting tonight. Still feels too intimate to me for a cooperative learning project. I guess time will tell. Your turn, sunshine. Same three questions."

"The worst part of my day was our phone call. It shouldn't have been, and I reacted badly. I just get concerned that we'll fall into this pattern of busy lives not connecting. We can cover that later because the best part of my day is looking really good so far. I was fitted for my wedding dress today. Fit like a glove, which means that I'm going to have to watch what I eat for a few weeks.

Not much room for any new me." She didn't describe it for him, but it was an off-white, satin, sleeveless dress with a lace neckline. It would fall just below her knee and be accented by a headpiece made of mother-of-pearl and lace. She would wear her hair up and wear pearls on her neck and ears.

He teased her. "I can't wait for you to model it."

"Silly boy, I'm not doing that, you know the bad luck thing. You, my loving husband-to-be, will be wearing black pants and a white tux. We will have wild, green-and-yellow lilies on the altar and in the back of the church; they'll be taken to the reception as centerpieces for the head table. We have a soloist who will sing several songs. For you, and just for you, we will have a bagpipe player at the entrance to the church and reception. He will play a series of Scottish and Irish songs, including your favorite, 'Scotland the Brave.' Just before the wedding march the pianist will play my favorite, 'Cannon in D,' and you will cry. I will be wearing industrial-strength mascara, no runs, no drips, and no errors. As you know, we will be writing our own vows, so you better wow me, none of this weak poetry crap that you give me. Understand?"

"Completely, but when your industrial-strength mascara breaks down and there are black spots on your dress, don't blame me. In fact, maybe you should be safe and wear a black dress."

Julia retorted with pride, "Ten bucks says you'll be crying before I do. You remember that I'll be speaking my vows first? We already agreed to that."

"Make it twenty and you're on. I figure I'll show up in my kilt and you'll laugh so hard that you will be crying before you get anywhere near the altar."

"You wear a kilt and I'll cry at your funeral because you'll be dead. Care to describe our upcoming trip?"

"I wish I could, but I have a few things to do before the

meeting in twenty minutes. This was a delightful picnic. Could you do me one favor?"

"Sure," she said, gathering up the remnants of their outing.

"You know how much I like you in black. How about you wear black lingerie under that shear wedding dress? That way I'll get to see it long before the end of the evening."

She punched him as she walked off with the blanket and picnic basket.

She'd decided not to tell him what she'd cooked up for the reception; she'd gotten the idea from a friend's wedding. She had gathered 150 pictures of their time together, with a few of their own baby pictures thrown in for good measure. The pictorial review would be shown on video with music appropriate for the period of their relationship being shown. She had a voice-over message at the beginning that would start: "*These are the pictures of our memory past. Today we create a memory present. Tomorrow, we begin making a whole new set of memories. I can already tell our grandchildren that they were all memories of joy. Thank you, I am so glad that we finally got this over with.*"

—Chapter 20—

July Fourth fell on a Sunday and Andrew and Julia were both planning on going to California to see Drew. At the last minute, Julia asked if Andrew would be upset if she did not join him. She was getting ready for Home Design Concepts to start the house project and wanted to be there to pick out some window treatment material. Andrew knew how important this was to her and so encouraged her to do her thing. It also saved him from being asked his opinion; he was of no use on that front.

It was a restless flight. Andrew was looking for a way to communicate his love for and his faith in his son. As he sat skipping across the sky at 37,000 feet, it dawned on him that he had never written Drew a poem. He sat there for a few minutes and thought about what Drew reminded him of. The first thing that came to his mind was a tree. He was growing up both physically and emotionally. He got his computer out of his bag. Within thirty minutes he had written:

Dear Drew:

I am so proud of you. You ended the school year on a very positive note. More importantly, you kept your promise. It is fun watching you grow, and now I will be able to do that every day. This poem is for you. Read it often.

Growth

I am but a growing tree.
All I want is to be a better me.
Somewhere out there is a bright sun
And it shines on me; its work never done.

There are days full of clouds and rain.
I cannot understand why people complain,
For with every drop of rain that falls
I am a tree growing forever tall.

As a tree, I have a number of seasons.
I lose my leaves for obvious reasons.
And yet in spring I renew and grow.
Continual growth is my survival, I know.

Will I grow up to be big and tall?
Or will I remain forever small?
I am so lucky, for it is my choice.
I choose growth! I shout in my loudest voice.

My love always,
Dad

It was late evening when he arrived. Grabbing his rental car, Andrew headed for the Hilton in Huntington Beach. Given the late hour, Drew's mother would not bring him to the hotel until Saturday morning. When he checked into the hotel he found a pleasant surprise: a cookie bouquet with a card that read: "*To the two most important men in my life, sorry I couldn't be there. Enjoy the cookies and think of me, for I will be thinking of you." Love to you both, Julia*

Laura brought Drew to the hotel an hour late. Andrew hated this passive-aggressive behavior that had become even more routine since the custody hearing. While Drew settled in, Andrew walked his ex-wife to her car.

While she was getting in the car she commented, "Lindsey will be having her baby any day now. You might want to talk to Drew. He acts very hostile toward her and I can't reach him."

"I'll see what I can do. I also need to discuss our August plans for him. I want to make sure that we're all on the same page. You and I need to decide how we're gonna get all of his stuff to Michigan. We should arrange to have the majority of it shipped a week before so he has it when he gets there. Does that work for you?"

"I assume you're paying that expense?"

"Sure, no problem." He had that all-to-familiar feeling: This was going to get ugly.

Laura pressed her luck. "I'll be coming to see Drew once school starts. Are you paying my way out there?"

Trying not to laugh, Andrew said, "When pigs fly. I'm sure you can handle it."

"Actually, I lost my teaching position at Long Beach State and Lindsey is on maternity leave from Cypress College. Besides, I wouldn't have to incur this expense if you weren't taking my son away from me."

"How does it feel, Laura? Does the pain hurt like a hot poker lodged in your gut? I know that pain. I've lived that feeling." He felt bad saying it, but the anger and bitterness were still alive.

"You are a heartless bastard." Sadly, she meant it.

"I'm sorry you feel that way, but I can't undo what's happened. And, as I recall, this was about *you,* not me. I've changed in ways I couldn't begin to describe. I wish I'd been half the man with you that I am today. I doubt it would have made a difference, but I'd have been a better person—even if it would've been wasted on you," he said, as calmly as possible.

She slammed the car door and left in a huff, tires screeching. He hadn't intended to push her buttons, but every time he spent more than five minutes with her, he was reminded of the hole she'd left in his heart. That hole was patched very nicely by his love for Julia, but it still did not ease all the pain. As he returned to his room, he wondered why he was unable to let go of the anger.

Drew was munching on a cookie when Andrew returned. "Why isn't Julia here?"

"She had some things to do that are very important."

"More important than seeing me?" The question burned into Andrew's brain; he could sense the insecurity from both the question and its tone.

"She's at home getting ready for you to come. She's making it a much nicer place to live. She is even redoing your room in maize and blue paint."

"You mean like the University of Michigan?"

"Yes."

"Way cool. Can we call her to see how it's going?"

"Sure we can. What a great idea."

He dialed the phone for Drew. After four rings, the answering machine came on. "Um, Julia, this is Little Man Drew. I called to see how your project thing was coming. I can't wait to see it. Thanks for taking good care of daddy and me. The cookies are good. See ya soon." He hung up, satisfied.

The boys spent Saturday at Knotts Berry Farm. It was a favorite of Drew's and he enjoyed showing his dad around and being in charge for the day. At dinner, the boys covered many topics, including the wedding.

Puzzled, Drew asked, "Dad, will Julia be living with us?"

Andrew laughed and said, "We're getting married, you understand that, right?"

"Of course, but I know she has her own house, too."

"She sold that, so we're stuck with her. By the way, I have a very important question to ask you, man-to-man."

"Shoot."

"You and Julia are the most important people in my life. Being together is a dream come true for me. I want that dream to start right at the wedding. Do you know what a best man is, at a wedding?"

"Sort of. He's like the main man in the posse for the guy getting married."

"Interestingly put, but yes. He's often the groom's best friend. So, would you be my best man at our wedding?"

"You mean it, Dad? I'm your best friend?"

"I mean it with all my heart. It's an easy job, but the best part is that you'd get to stand on the altar with me, Julia, and her maid of honor."

Drew was bouncing up and down. "Wait 'til I tell my friends! I bet none of them has been best man before!"

"You're probably right. Before we head for the barn, little man, what do you want to do tomorrow?"

"Can you take me to church? Mom never takes me."

"Sure, and then we'll catch some breakfast at Dukes." Drew's favorite because it was right at the base of the Huntington Beach Pier where he was learning to surf. "After that?"

"How about we go hit some golf balls? I want to show you what I can do with a five iron. There is a place in Cypress that has junior clubs. I think it's the same place Tiger Woods learned how to play golf."

Andrew was surprised at the request. "Terrific. We are *all* over that."

They got back to the room and the message light was lit: Julia. "Little man, I am here in Michigan getting ready for you to come be with us. I'll always be here for you. I love you."

Sunday brought bright sunshine and cool ocean breezes. After church and breakfast, father and son headed to the Cypress Municipal Golf Course. Andrew picked up two sets of golf clubs and two buckets of balls. Andrew gave his son a few quick lessons on grip and then watched as Drew hit three seven irons in a row a hundred yards or more. He struggled with the five iron, not unusual for beginning golfers. Feeling cocky, Drew pulled the driver out of the bag, intent on crushing a few long ones. Andrew stood back. Drew's swing went a little wild and the ball nearly hit two people practicing to the right of them.

"Whoa. Stop. Let's get this out of the way up front. Golf is about control and mental focus," Andrew commented and Drew nodded. "Like everything else in life, golf requires one to prepare for success and accept constant failure. For now we'll just focus on control. Do the same thing and swing half as hard."

Drew did what he was instructed and was amazed at how far the ball soared. After he hit several 175-yard drives he got cocky and tried to kill a few more. The results were consistantly bad.

Andrew reiterated, "Remember, success is not guaranteed and failure is assured if you try too hard."

"Okay, Dad, I think I got the lesson."

Drew finished up his own bucket of balls and then polished off the rest of his dad's as well. He was getting tired, but that didn't matter to him; he got what he wanted, praise from his dad.

The rest of the day went by quickly, and it soon became time for Andrew to take Drew home. He was catching a 7:30 AM flight back to Michigan, so there wasn't enough time for Drew to spend the night. They were talking about how quickly six weeks would go by when they pulled in the driveway. There they paused; it was always so hard to know how to say good-bye.

Andrew gave his son the poem he had written. He knew that the meaning would be lost on him for the moment. Regardless, he hoped he would cherish it later in life. Regrettably, his mother threw it away before he ever got a chance to read it.

—Chapter 21—

The week before their honeymoon trip was the busiest of the summer. Julia finished the plans for the house project, closed on her condo, and moved her things into Andrew's garage. Andrew finished up all the loose ends at the clinic. He called Chris to make sure he had the needed materials for the August QualityCare Board meeting. The finances were heading south; it was going to be an interesting evening. Andrew had been given a heads-up that his renegotiated contract might come up, too.

The couple left Detroit Metro Airport on a muggy Saturday evening. Their flight would arrive in Shannon, Ireland, the following morning–Andrew having given in and reversed the itinerary. He had done so only after he had discovered that Julia's family lines could be traced to Ireland, through her birth mother, whose maiden name had been O'Brien.

The flight was peaceful but not restful. Neither of them had much luck sleeping on the overnight flight. Andrew worked on his wedding vows.

"You still righting those, Scotty? If you truly loved me, you would have finished those a month ago. Mine have been done like forever."

"Darling, I will never stop writing these vows. I will always need to recommit myself to my girl." This received no verbal response, just a smile and a squeeze of his hand. If her man wanted to write vows to her every day of her life that was fine by her.

Once safely landed at Shannon Airport, they had a short, eight-mile drive to Dromoland, a 16th-century baronial castle. The facility only had seventy-five rooms, but each was decorated in stunning period pieces. Their room was larger than what they'd expected and it overlooked a quaint 16th-century courtyard.

Although each wanted to get some sleep, they forced themselves to keep moving. They took a tour of the castle and the gardens. They learned all about its history and how this particular land was involved in the royal bloodlines that dated back to Brian Boru, Ireland's 10th-century high king. After a light lunch, they decided it was time for a nap—jet lag had caught up with them.

Dinner in the castle was a real treat: an 18th-century meal with the wait staff and cooks dressed in authentic clothes from that century. The food was also true to the time period, as was the entertainment. The music was made up of flutists, fiddlers, pipers and *sean nos* singers. It was unlike any Irish music that either had ever heard. The drink was wine or mead. Had it tasted like it did in the 18th century, no guest would have tried it, so this was the one departure from the authenticity of the evening.

Back in their room, Julia wondered out loud, "I wonder if they lived like that all the time? If I live like that for ten more days, I won't fit into my dress. We'll have to postpone the wedding."

Slipping his arms around her from behind and running his hands over her stomach and hips, he said, "How could my beautiful bride worry what other people think? For my money, you're perfect and always will be. It's your heart and mind that I am attracted to. The fact that I love your body is just pure bonus." While she hadn't been looking for a compliment, she was pleased to get it. "Besides, what happens to pregnant women? You think their bodies don't change?"

"Of course they do, silly. So you better enjoy this one while you can." She turned around and kissed him. "This is technically our honeymoon night, isn't it? Better yet, why ask the question? Come here and treat me like you will on our special night."

He did.

Monday was their first golf outing, at Tralee, a short drive from the castle. They drove along the Cliffs of Moher where they were rewarded with spectacular views of the sea pounding relentlessly below. It was just after dawn and the fog was still lingering, which made the sight even eerier.

The golf course was challenging, with plenty of visual distractions. The highlight was the Irish couple they played with. It was a day of history lessons. When Julia told the couple that she was of the O'Brien clan they were told that they must visit the Blasket Islands. This was not on their itinerary, but then again, there was no rule that said that they couldn't play it by ear. Neither Andrew nor Julia broke 85 on the golf course that day. It didn't matter to either.

Day three was equally busy. They started by catching a boat to Great Blasket Island. After lunch in a café, they returned to the mainland and went off to visit Cork and Blarney Castle. Exhausted, they headed to their new home for the next three days, the Killarney Park Hotel.

The most memorable day in Ireland was their last. They took a bus trip to the Old Head Kinsale Golf Course. The Kinsale countryside was mostly rural, but with some impressive coastal scenery. The bus made a side trip to Mizen peninsula, another spectacular cliff scene overlooking the Atlantic Ocean. They both played better golf that last day in Ireland although it was the sight and smell of the ocean that they remembered the most.

The return trip was all it was advertised to be–a pub-crawling sample of Ireland's nightlife. Their bus traversed County Cork and Kerry while stopping to sample the stout with the locals in at least six different pubs. By the second of the six planned stops, everyone on the bus was aware of their upcoming nuptials. They were celebrities everywhere they went. They participated in a sing-along in Cookstown and led the locals in American tunes in Monkstown. At the end of the evening, Andrew was glad he didn't have to drive or get up with the sun the next morning.

Morning came regardless of their desire to sleep. Julia gave Andrew a playful nudge. "Rise and shine, party boy. Today is the day we finally get to your beloved Scotland. Pity, don't you think?"

"At last, on to civilization," he mumbled.

"Yes, well, thank you for taking me to Ireland. Can we go home now? I have so much to do before the wedding."

"Surely you jest? We have yet to see God's country. You're welcome to go home, but I shall be stayin' a wee bit, lassie."

"I hope I can make you as happy as you've made me these last few days. But, so you don't get confused, Scotty my love, you may get to call the shots in Scotland, but I'm still going to kick your royal butt on St. Andrews Old Course. Imagine getting embarrassed in your own country."

Andrew admired her spirit, but he had a secret weapon that he planned to use to distract her: with a bet riding on the last golf day, he would employ psychological warfare.

—Chapter 22—

They both slept on the flight over the Irish Sea. Once they arrived at Edinburgh Airport, they arranged to have their bags transferred to the porter stand where they would catch a train at Waverley Station to Leuchars, eight miles outside St. Andrews.

"You know dear, if you were a real man you'd carry my bags for me."

"If I were man enough to carry your bags and mine, I'd be a circus freak. You've got Jimmy Hoffa stuffed in these bags somewhere, don't you?"

The Old Course Hotel was located on Old Station Road. The word "old" was everywhere pervasive at St. Andrews. The evening started out in the library, where Andrew and Julia sat in overstuffed chairs and sampled different types of scotch. The room was adorned with numerous oil paintings of the golf course and seaside. The antiques were plentiful, which just added to the charm. Given Scotland's geographic location, it stayed light well into the evening hours, so plenty of golfers were coming in off the links. Plenty of stories were being told. The most frequent story was of life in the deadly sand traps named Coffin, Grave, and Hell. No matter how bad the score was though, not one golfer complained of the difficulty of the golf course. The beauty and charm of the Old Course made it worth playing even in the worst of conditions.

Dinner was at the Road Hole Grill in the hotel, which overlooked the 17th fairway, just as their room did. The food did not disappoint either diner, and the ambiance was as opulent as the rest of the hotel. Julia kept commenting that brides shouldn't go on trips before their wedding or they should get their dresses fit one size larger. She felt better after they had taken a long stroll around town.

Friday morning's tee time at the New Course came with the dawn's first light. It was an odd name for a golf course that had opened in 1896, but relative to the Old Course where some form of golf has existed for 600 years, it *was* new. Easterly breezes off the North Sea leant considerable challenge to the game and made club selection particularly difficult. It also made it very cold. Julia's experience was evident that day; she had better command over the wind.

Andrew had to ask, "Have you made a woman's pact with Mother Nature? You appear to know precisely what move she's going to make next."

"We women do have to stick together." She laughed and winked, leaving Andrew to wonder whether he'd hit the mark or not. When they finished, she had beaten him by eight strokes. "I hope you put up more of a struggle on the Old Course on Sunday."

"I'm planning on it. I have a secret weapon that's sure to throw you for a loop."

"Give me a break, Andrew. I know more about your golf game than you do. There is no surprise, outside of a sniper, that could catch me off guard."

"We'll see now, won't we?"

She let it drop. Andrew's game was improving but she could bury him at will. She usually spared his ego, but Sunday was a different day.

They had dinner at the Rufflets Country House Restaurant. This was an experience every bit as good as the Road Hole Grill and much more reasonably priced. They shared the monkfish and kidney pie, but the highlight was dessert: hot, sticky toffee pudding with cream. Andrew ate all but one bite of the dessert; Julia was showing great restraint. She had a dress to get into.

Over coffee, she commented, "This has been such a good idea. I'm glad we made this trip. It beats sitting home and fretting."

"This trip is a great reminder of why we're getting married: The time we have together to grow and love each other is precious. It's times like these that keep me from taking it for granted."

"If I were in the wedding planning business, I might suggest this to all my clients. I'm glad you insisted that we do this before the wedding."

"I just got lucky. It was the circumstances surrounding Drew coming to Michigan that dictated this timing. I miss him and not having e-mail messages from him every couple of days leaves me wondering how he is."

"I miss him, too. I haven't seen him since May. I sure hope he accepts me as a mother-figure in his life. I know he has a mother and I will never replace her, but I so want to be a good maternal influence in his life."

"You already are, and when we have children of our own he'll be a big brother. We shouldn't wait too long though, or he'll be in college before our baby gets out of diapers."

Julia paused a moment, took Andrew's hand in hers and said, "I'm ready when you are, Scotty."

"Are you ready, Julia? Because I'm ready right now."

"Are you suggesting we move up our timetable for having children?"

"Why not? We're two adults deeply in love. We both want

children and now is a good time." Julia looked him a question. "Yes, I mean *right* now. What difference would waiting do? I say we go for it and let the good Lord decide on the timing."

She looked off in the distance, then turned back to him. "I've wanted to have a child for so very long. I can be patient, but I can also be easily convinced that now," she paused, "and I mean *right* now, would be a good time. What say you take me home and sweet talk me?"

"Not a problem."

They walked back to the hotel and spent the next three hours making love over and over. It was two parts passion and one part purpose that sustained them. When they finished, they took a soothing bath together and discussed names for the baby. Without voicing a preference they spent more time on names for a baby girl.

The remainder of the trip to St. Andrew's was anti-climatic. Services at Holy Trinity Church were memorable, as was the golf at the Old Course but neither could compete with the memories created the night before. Even Andrew's secret weapon to win their last golf match was useless. He waited until the sixth hole to start asking her about the redecorating project. He figured it would be a major mental distraction.

She shot him down. "Thank you for asking. I called this morning while you were in the shower. The project is on time and under budget. Isn't that great?"

"Swell."

Julia went on to kick his ass, just as she promised.

In the dusk of the evening, Julia and Andrew said good-bye to St. Andrews. They headed back to Edinburgh, where they stayed two nights at the Witchery Suites–which actually only had two rooms. They stayed in the Old Rectory Suite. The room was adorned with plenty of crystal, live plants, and a hand-carved

French bed. The ceiling was hand-painted and the furniture was Louis XIV antiques.

The Witchery by the Castle Restaurant was just as eclectic. Dark wood, dark drapes and eerie shadows cast by candlelight created an ominous atmosphere. Julia ate light and did not drink any alcohol. When quizzed by Andrew she simply said she'd had enough to eat and drink during their trip and now it was time to get into dress-fitting mode. She didn't want to spook him; she'd had a dream the night before that she was pregnant.

Their last day in Scotland was busy until mid-afternoon. They toured the Royal Mile and in particular spent significant time at the Edinburgh Castle. After a brief tour of the National Gallery of Scotland, they called it a day. They did nothing that evening but bask in the glow of a memorable trip before heading for London the next morning to catch their flight home.

It was a true sign of how exhausted they were that they both slept a good part of the eight-hour flight. They arrived home on a sweltering summer day, with plenty of pictures and a fair number of gifts and mementos.

And a child.

—Chapter 23—

The first thing that struck Andrew when he got home was that his house no longer looked like his house: It was brighter, lighter, and had the smell of fresh paint and carpet. The kitchen was something out of a magazine. He walked through each room, amazed at Julia's vision come true.

He picked her up and swung her around. "This is fabulous. I can't believe how astonishing this looks. Now I have a house that matches the beauty of my bride. You're the best."

Julia was all smiles. "You're welcome. I can call this *our* home, now. It's a good thing too, since I don't have any other home to go to."

They spent a little time rearranging Drew's bedroom so that his computer would fit in the farthest corner from the door. Andrew wanted him to have more privacy to e-mail his mother just as often as he wanted. Andrew's bitterness was easing, or at least it wasn't as noticeable. Winning could do that to a man. It was easy to bury pain when things were going well.

Andrew went back to getting caught up on his clinical work. It wasn't his patients who were driving him crazy, but the load that Bruce Meyers had shifted to him. Of the four patients Andrew inherited, three were doing well and one was not. Nancy Ours's ALS was in a dormant stage. It was early, but the illness was not progressing rapidly. Paula Callaway's case of AIDS was also under control. Jim Velucci's COPD was getting worse and he wasn't expected to live much longer. Sandra Horn's cancer was responding well to the chemotherapy.

The one patient he cared about most was undergoing a significant change. Julia was due to get her period around the fifteenth of August. She was late. She was hopeful, even though she had never been the most regular girl in the world. She would wait until she was positive before she said anything to Andrew. He had suffered so much loss in his world that she wanted to be absolutely sure.

In spite of the recent financial slump, the August QualityCare Board meeting was upbeat and positive. The meeting started with Christopher introducing QualityCare's new corporate counsel, Antoinette Vincenzo.

"“Ladies and gentlemen,” Christopher bellowed to get the group to simmer down, “I have very good news to start our meeting. The young lady at the end of the table is our new Corporate Counsel. Please say hello to Antoinette Vincenzo. Toni, as she is better known, comes to us from Washington D.C. where she spent the last seven years working for several of our congressmen and senators. She's an expert in health policy. Washington's loss is certainly our gain. This is a homecoming of sorts. Toni attended Pioneer High School right here in Ann Arbor. After graduating summa cum laude from Eastern Michigan University, which she attended on a swimming scholarship, she graduated from the University of Michigan Law School in nineteen ninety-two. Please, join me in welcoming her.”

Impeccably dressed in a blue pin-stripe suit with a white blouse and red scarf, Toni was diminutive in size, but carried herself with confidence, back straight, head high. Her brown eyes were warm and her smile bright, but there was no doubt that she was a serious professional woman.

The Board gave Toni a round of applause and then Chris introduced each member to her. Toni gave them some added background on her life in the nation's capital, but left out her reason for coming home: Her plan and career were well on track when she met a man and got engaged. That fell apart when she got pregnant and refused the abortion her fiancé insisted on. He took off and Toni, alone, couldn't handle the Washington grinder as well as raise her daughter, Maria.

Christopher brought the Board back into focus. "I did not know we'd hired a celebrity. I'm sure Ms. Vincenzo will be happy to tell you more stories about Congress after the meeting. For now, I have some important business to get through."

Phil Kunkle seized the moment. "Christopher, I'm sorry, but her stories are much better than yours. Why make her regret that she came to work for you?" The rest of the Board laughed.

The Board received the financial report, which did not look as bad as had once been projected: After a brief blip in the financials, things were looking better and year-end projections were slightly under budget. The growth plan Christopher had outlined in the spring was brought back to the Board for final approval, much earlier than anticipated, but then it had to be to meet Arthur Bishop's agressive time frame. Lansing and Jackson were their first target cities for growth and Christopher emphasized that aligning with just the right physicians was the key component for success. Bruce Meyers had spent a significant amount of his rented time meeting with physician groups in each of those markets.

Bruce was asked to give an accounting of his activities. "Members of the Board, part of the materials you received for this meeting includes my report outlining the specific steps our team has taken to complete the due diligence for our expansion plan. I won't go into all the details here tonight, but I will be happy to answer any questions. You'll also find the names of the physicians we've contacted in Lansing and Jackson in Section Four of the report. They are prepared to come meet with the Board, should you request it."

After twenty minutes of walking through the materials and a few clarification questions, the Board was left feeling a new confidence with the risk their CEO was asking them to take.

Christopher pushed for a decision. "Time is of the essence here, ladies and gentlemen. The window is open for expansion next year, but we mustn't delay."

After some questions and debate, the Board voted unanimously to approve the growth plan. Christopher was on track.

On Tuesday, August 24th, Julia's home pregnancy test turned positive. She went to see her gynecologist and tested positive in his office, as well. Now confirmed, she could tell Andrew they were going to have a baby.

Drew would be arriving that evening, a day late. It was going to be a hectic evening, so Julia decided a celebration dinner on the following night would be the best time to surprise both the men with her news. She was a little nervous though about how Drew was going to react when he discovered that he was going to have company in the house.

Drew's first reaction when he walked in the house was similar to his dad's. "What on earth did you do to this place, Dad?"

"Do you like it, little man?"

"It looks so much brighter."

Julia was pleased with the impact her project had on both Albright men.

Andrew smiled and said, "This was all Julia; didn't she do a great job?"

"This is way cool. Can we go see my room?"

Julia led the way, lost in thought about making a nursery out of the adjoining alcove to their bedroom.

Drew admired the new maize and blue wallpaper and window treatments, then he stopped dead in his tracks, smiled at his dad, and asked, "Is that what I think it is?" In the corner of the room was a golf bag with a red bow on the outside.

"Why don't you go find out?"

In two heartbeats, Drew was in the bag checking out the clubs. "Can I take these out back right now and swing 'em?"

"Of course you can, but no hitting golf balls. We'll go test these tomorrow after I get home from the . . ." Drew was not around to hear the rest, he was flying down the stairs, golf bag in tow, ". . . clinic." He turned to Julia. "Well, I guess that worked. Glad I picked those up."

"You're his hero; he wants to do whatever you do."

"Sunshine, you'll see more of the golf course with him than I will. It won't take too many lesson from you before he's whipping me."

"We're going to have a blast after school."

"I sure hope so. I want him to be happy and adjust to this change."

"He will. I'm sure of it."

Later, Drew played with his putter in his bedroom. Andrew picked up a book to read, and Julia wrote in her journal: *It's so hard keeping my secret–we'll have one more guest at the wedding, the baby. I can't wait to see his face. And just think: When people ask me when I conceived, I can honestly tell them it was on our honeymoon.*

By Wednesday, time was running out and things had to be done before the wedding on Saturday. Julia had to go by St. Patrick's to drop off some sheet music for the soloist, pick up groceries for her celebration dinner and stop by the bookstore to pick up a book on infant gestation. She would wrap it up for Andrew and Drew to use as her opening.

The last thing Drew wanted to do was run errands so she called the golf pro at Stonebridge and asked if one of his staff was available to give Drew a golf lesson. She thought he would have fun.

Hearing the news, he hugged her. “You’re the best,” he said.

“That’s funny, your dad said the same thing to me yesterday.” She winked at him and slipped into Irish-speak. “Aye, and isn’t it that we’ll be havin’ the fun together? I’m so glad you’re here.”

“Me too. And I’m happy you’re gonna marry my dad. He looks happy.”

“He loves us both very much. Little man, I love you too.” She ran her hand through his short blond hair and they headed out the door.

He jumped out the door at the golf course. Right before he slammed it shut, he yelled, “I love you, too!”

She headed toward her first stop, St. Pat’s, but got caught up in a terrible traffic jam. Rather than risk the highway construction, she headed up Whitmore Lake Road. She called Andrew from her car to make sure he would be home for her celebration dinner.

With a smile that he could not see she said, “I’ve got a really terrific surprise for you guys this evening.”

“I’m sure I’ll love it. See you tonight. I love you,” he said, distracted as usual by work.

Slightly north of Joy Road a black SUV came speeding toward her, out of the blue, out of control, careening across the lanes. Julia had a split second to make a decision. She jerked the wheel to the right. The SUV hit her broadside, continued its forward progress, finally coming to a stop with both cars in the ditch beside the road, steaming, hot metal clicking. Julia's airbag popped out, she slammed against it, and was crushed between the crumpled door, her seatbelt, and the bag.

"Please God, no," she said as she passed into unconsciousness.

—Chapter 24—

Two cars behind Julia ran off the road to avoid the collision in front of them. Within seconds, EMS was called. There was no movement inside Julia's car. An autopsy later revealed that the woman in the SUV had suffered a heart attack and was already dead when the paramedics arrived. They removed Julia carefully from the wreckage. Her blood pressure was dropping and the paramedics were concerned with her internal bleeding. She arrived at University Hospital in less than fifteen minutes. She was in the emergency room for less than half an hour, just long enough to get stabilized, before she was sent to surgery.

At 11:12, Dr. McBride, chief of the ER, called Andrew. As soon as he heard who was on the phone, his heart thudded against his chest, stopped, started again. This couldn't be a social call.

Yelling over the normal commotion in the ER, Dr. McBride said, "Andrew, I hate having to tell you, but your fiancée's been in a car accident. Hit head-on by a woman in an SUV on Whitmore Lake Road."

"Oh my God. How is she, Bill? Can you tell me how she is?"

"She's in surgery. We're looking for a small puncture wound in her aorta. The paramedics were on the scene within five minutes, and she's already been transfused with three units of blood."

"Was anyone else in the car?"

"No, she came in alone. I'll be in surgery checking on her. Meet me there."

Andrew was out the door before he hung up. He tried to call Drew from the car: no answer at home. Why would Julia leave him at home on his first day in Michigan? He called his receptionist to help find his missing son. He arrived at the hospital in twenty minutes, screeched into a Reserved parking spot–not his. He bolted up the hall to surgery, and found his colleague waiting.

"Any news, Bill?"

Dr. Murakami, the vascular surgeon, made eye contact with Andrew and nodded to his scrub nurse to bring Andrew into the scrub room. Andrew grabbed a gown and mask. "I'm sorry to see you here under these conditions, Andrew. She is stable for now. She lost a lot of blood. The force of the collision broke her ribs, causing a small puncture in her aorta. The bone fragment actually saved her from bleeding out. She also ruptured her spleen. The paramedics did an excellent job; had they not, she would not have made it here alive."

"How long will she be in surgery?" He saved his neurological questions for later, when they were all in the Intensive Care Unit.

"We are done repairing the damage we could find. We are checking everything else one more time and then we'll close up." Murakami, the best surgeon on staff, turned around and headed back to his patient.

Andrew collapsed into a chair–it had just hit him that Julia was in deep trouble. The blood and oxygen loss gave her a high probability of impaired brain function, but it was too soon to tell.

Dr. McBride cut into the Andrew's terrified silence. "I know this is a difficult time and I'm sorry. I'm also sorry about the baby."

It didn't register. "Was there a baby in the other car?" Andrew stood slowly. "Bill?"

"We're talking about Julia's baby. We discovered her pregnancy during some blood tests in the ER."

"Oh my God, Julia was pregnant?" Andrew's legs wobbled; Dr. McBride helped him sit down.

"You mean you didn't know?"

"No." Tears poured down his face. He put his head in his hands. Through the tears, he said, "Julia told me she had a surprise to tell me tonight."

"We called her OB doctor from the ER; he told us he'd confirmed it for her yesterday."

It was a long night.

He called Carol first; she came immediately, stopping first at Andrew's to pick up Drew, who had caught a ride home when Julia failed to pick him up at the golf course.

Standing bedside in the recovery room, Andrew had plenty of well-wishing colleagues who stopped by to offer support. A cursory nod was his only reply. He was too busy watching the monitors, waiting for her vital signs to improve.

Carol arrived with Drew and the three of them stood vigil for three days. Julia came out of surgery well, but her internal injuries and other bodily trauma were too much to overcome. She never came out of her coma. Her brain functions ceased on Friday.

Andrew held her hand constantly while talking to her, refusing to face reality, refusing to let her go. "Julia, sweet Julia, today is our wedding day. Please don't leave me on our wedding day. I know you can do this. Wake up, please. Wake up and let's go to our wedding. Everyone's waiting. We can't make them wait, sweetheart, we can't . . ."

Julia had a living will, explicitly defining what her wishes were in this kind of circumstance. But Andrew wanted a miracle. He went to church on Sunday, even though it was hard on him to be there. If God had not allowed this to happen, he would have been married in this very same church less than twenty-four hours earlier. Their flowers still adorned the church. Conflicted out of all reason, he asked a benevolent God for a miracle, at the same time cursing Him for allowing the accident to happen.

Carol approached him after the service. She took him by the hand and forced him to look her in her eyes.. "Andrew, you need to step back and look at what you're doing."

"I can't let her go. Not now, not ever."

"What would you do if she were a patient of yours?"

"Sis, she is *not* my patient. That's an irrelevant question."

"I know you're hurting. I know Drew is hurting. But we're dishonoring Julia by not allowing her to go to her heavenly kingdom."

"No. God does not get her yet. He cannot have her. He doesn't deserve her. She is too good for Him. She was an earthly angel. This is where she belongs."

"Oh Andrew, you cannot believe what you just said. If you truly believed she was in God's hands, what would you do for the woman who gave you her heart and soul?"

After another round of tears, Andrew whispered, "I would let her be at peace."

"Of course you would, which would be the right thing to do. Let's go see her. Please, look in your head and do what it tells you, not what your heart tells you. And remember: Whatever you do, you do it for Julia, not yourself."

They left St. Patrick's, Andrew taking an arrangement of lilies with him. He wanted Julia to have them in her room. Normally, they would not have been allowed in intensive care, but the ICU staff accorded him the special privilege.

He set the flowers down next to her bed. "Julia darling, these are your flowers. Open your eyes and see their loveliness. Smell the lilies, my Irish girl. They are so full of life. Julia, I love you, please come back to me."

He sat and held her hand.

He thought about what Carol had said.

Hours later he went home to be with Drew.

On Wednesday, he spoke with several physician colleagues–had it not been for their respect for Andrew, they would have taken Julia off the respirator days before. They gave Andrew some space and he took it.

His last words to her on this earth came slowly, through a tidal wave of emotion. "Julia, my sunshine, thank you for coming into my life. I will see you in my dreams. Please talk to me often. I love you and I will join you soon."

—Chapter 25—

September was an act of survival. Andrew struggled to make the funeral arrangements. He went through the motions of laying her to rest in the cemetery at St. Pat's. Drew started school. Andrew stayed home.

His colleagues tried to get him to a grief counselor, but Andrew wanted to mourn in his own way.

His work did not matter; the last thing he wanted to do was see his patients.

Late in September, Laura and Lindsey decided to move back to Michigan. Laura had lost her job and wanted to be closer to Drew. Lindsey had delivered her baby girl, Olivia, and wanted to be closer to her family in Ohio. Now was a good time, so in October the three of them moved to Ypsilanti. Laura had gotten a new job at Eastern Michigan University. Lindsey planned on staying at home until the following fall, after which she hoped to get a position at either EMU or Washtenaw Community College. Secretly, though not without the occasional twinge of guilt, Laura thought that with Julia gone, she could win her son back.

The maturity with which Drew had handled Julia's death was well beyond his years; many commented on it. Maybe he was compensating for his father not dealing with it well. Andrew grew to depend on his son, looked forward to the end of each school day, fixed him dinners, helped him with his homework at night, but couldn't bring himself to play golf with him yet.

Drew dropped the next bomb into Andrew's life. "Dad, mom is going to move back to Michigan."

With an unintended vicious stare, Andrew asked his son brusquely, "Where did you hear that?" The last thing he wanted to do was to share his son with that damned woman. Every bad thing that had ever happened in his life had been at the hands of evil women: an overbearing mother; Laura had run off with a woman; an evil woman had had a heart attack and killed his Julia. Now, the evil ghost was returning to take away his son, again.

"She just told me on the phone. Isn't that great news?" he answered, totally unaware of Andrew's simmering rage.

"When?" Andrew stopped. It wasn't fair to put Drew in the middle. He would call Laura later that night. "Is this what you'd like her to do, Drew?"

"Well, it means I don't have to go so far to see her."

In his selfishness, Andrew wanted to make his son understand his feelings, to be on his side only, to hate the woman as much as he did, but he knew that'd never happen. And it wouldn't make him happy anyway.

Lindsey answered when the phone rang that evening. "Hello, Lindsey here."

"Lindsey, this is Andrew Albright, is Laura home?"

"She's outside cooking steaks on the grill, Dr. Albright." She never called him Andrew.

"Can you get her? This is important."

"Sure, I will. I bet I know what this concerns." She actually laughed out loud.

"Please, just get her," he said, annoyed at her hubris.

"Andrew, how are you?" Laura said. "I suspect you're calling about my conversation with Drew this morning?" She didn't laugh, but she had a smile on her face that could be heard two thousand miles away.

"Why the hell are you coming here? Why didn't you call me?"

"I don't owe you a phone call. Put simply, this is a good time for Lindsey, Olivia, and me to move to Michigan. And besides, who're you to question either my actions or motives?"

"This is lousy timing; it'll just confuse things for Drew."

"Andrew, I'm sorry for your loss. I was happy for you and Julia," she lied, "but now you're just going to have to deal with another reality."

"When will you be moving?"

"The house here in Huntington Beach sold in forty-eight hours. An all-cash deal. We close on October fifteenth, and leave on the sixteenth. I've got a teaching position at EMU and Lindsey will stay home with Olivia for a year. We'll be looking for a house in Ypsilanti. I already have a real estate agent sending me information."

"This is a stupid idea. You're acting selfish." Andrew said, gripping the phone so hard his hand turned blue.

"Well then, it's a good thing you're not in control of my life. This is best for everyone, including you. Deal with it." Even that little bit of revenge tasted sweet.

Andrew hung up the phone. He went into the den, poured himself a drink and cursed all of womankind. He called Beverly and much to his dismay she said there was nothing illegal or sinister about what Laura Donaldson was doing. She, too, suggested Andrew find a healthy way to deal with it.

By October Andrew had to go back to work, even though his

heart wasn't in it. Laura arrived and made his world a very difficult place: Drew was gone much more frequently.

November and December were no better. As the weather turned bitter cold, so did Andrew. He still had primary custody of their son, but Laura, and Beverly McNeil, informed him that early in the new year she was going to challenge that and ask for joint custody again. Given how far Andrew had drifted, she wanted to seek sole custody, but Drew would be the one penalized if she did that–and it was Andrew she wanted to punish.

After Julia died, Carol boxed up her things. She didn't want to throw them away and she didn't want Andrew to have to deal with it either, so she put them out of sight in the basement. She labeled the boxes. When the time was right, she would go through them with her brother.

By New Year's Eve, the darkness in Andrew's life was stifling. He had turned down every invitation to join the last New Year's Eve party of the millennium. He went to the cemetery during the day to leave her flowers. He hardly noticed the twenty degrees and eight inches of snow on the ground– he wanted her to have something with life close to her. At nine that night, while the world partied, he went to the basement. He opened a box that wafted out with her perfume. He could smell her. She was right there with him. He could see her when he closed his eyes.

He opened a box of her clothes and pulled out the black dress she had worn on their first date. Then he did what he swore he would never do: He took the box with the wedding stuff upstairs. He let it sit on the floor in the family room for an hour while he wrote.

Dearest Julia,

The Bear

It is the dead of winter,

With just nowhere to go.
My heart is as cold as ice.
Is there shelter around? No.

I hibernate the season away,
Hidden deep in the ground,
Nature's way of surviving.
I simply cannot be found.

If only it were springtime
Awaiting a warmer day.
Alas, I am not the bear
So I wait for you . . . I stay.

Andrew placed the poem on the counter, intending to leave it for Julia in the morning, then opened the box marked "Wedding." The first thing he pulled out of a garment bag was Julia's wedding dress, with her pearls and earrings pinned to the collar. How stunning she would have looked in it. He held the dress close. He wanted to be next to her. His tears fell on the satin and lace.

He spoke out loud. "Why, Julia? Why did you leave me? Why did that woman have that heart attack? Why was she even driving? Why did the angels come for you?"

The next thing he came across was an envelope marked austerely, ***VOWS.*** He choked back his tears and opened the envelope. He looked at the words, but did not read them. He could not read them. Finally, he opened the parchment paper, and on it he read:

My dearest Andrew, my dearest husband:

The night you proposed to me, you sent me directions for the night.

You told me to bring my heart and my head and I did, just as I do today.

But, today I bring something else. Today I bring my soul, for you have touched me there in ways that I thought only God could do. You had my heart from the start. Today I offer you my soul. You are that part of me now. It is the mantle on which I place my trust in you. I ask that you place your trust in me, as well. I will be your light, and you will be my wind. Together we shall bask in the holy grace of God, forever.

Andrew lost all sense of control, making no attempt to stop the river of emotions pouring over him, washing through him, drowning him. The last thing he took from the box was the video Julia had made. He put it in the VCR. It started with baby pictures and had photos of their brief life together. The background music leaped and danced in trills and slides and giggles. At the end of the tape she'd included one last photograph: Julia in her wedding dress, her sweet voice in the background. She finished by saying, "I am now Mrs. Andrew Albright. I didn't think that I would ever be this happy or lucky. I want you all to know that I love Andrew Albright and together we shall truly bask in the holy grace of God."

Andrew cried until he fell asleep, crushing Julia's wedding dress against his chest.

—Chapter 26—

Andrew felt surrounded by darkness. Laura successfully petitioned the court for joint custody of their son on Valentine's day, and when Drew was with his mother, there was no light at all in Andrew's life. Andrew would typically spend the time beside Julia's grave while Drew was gone. Even an intervention from Carol failed; as much as his sister tried, she couldn't bring him out of his despair. His work deteriorated. Chris and Roxanne tried to involve him in their social life, but there was growing tension on the Board, which made it difficult for the two men to split their relationship.

The problem that surprised people the most was Andrew's attitude toward his patients, particularly his female patients. The PMG staff had great empathy for Dr. Albright, but his attitude was growing tiresome.

On one occasion in late March he left an exam room in a rage. His nurse confronted him as soon as they got out of earshot of everyone around. "Doctor, that patient didn't deserve to be treated with such disrespect. What the hell were you thinking?"

"Stay out of it, Amy. She got just what she deserved. She's making her whole family miserable. She's selfish and doesn't think about anybody but herself. The whole world is not here to take care of her."

Amy pulled him into an empty office. "It's not the whole world that concerns me," she said. "The only person and the only place that concerns me is the here and now. It's our job to take care of her. Specifically, Doctor, it's *your* job. Are we clear?"

Andrew spit out, "Let someone else take care of that parasite. In fact, let God have her. She and those around her would all rest in peace."

"Andrew, stop! You *can't* mean that. I know you don't mean that. Tell me you don't mean it."

"The hell I don't. She and all the rest of 'em like her need to go away. They need to make peace with God and die."

"Take a minute, Doctor. Sit down, cool off, and rethink what you're saying. I've known you for too long to listen to this crap. I won't let you disrespect this clinic, our work and your reputation."

Andrew hissed, "You can go straight to hell."

His next patient went unseen.

The Annual Meeting of the QualityCare Board came in April, 2000, as usual, but without the trip to Florida. Many thought it was due to financial difficulties.

They held the meeting on the campus of the University of Michigan at the Women's League Ballroom. The opening night agenda included dinner, live entertainment and dancing. Andrew was in no mood to dance. He ate dinner with Chris, Roxanne, Toni Vincenzo, and Arthur Bishop.

When he had a moment, Andrew asked Chris, "I'm surprised to see Arthur Bishop here. What's up with that?"

"I will explain that tomorrow morning, but if you stick around after dinner, we can talk." Chris wanted Andrew's support, but he avoided seeking it due to the tension between them. It would require too much political capital and there was precious little of that to go around.

Andrew hadn't seen much of Roxanne since Julia's death, though she had been concerned about him. After a couple of drinks, she tried to check up on her distant friend. "Andrew, you doing okay? I know it must be hard to adjust to a world without Julia."

"You have no idea," he snapped. "I'll be fine. I'm thankful for good friends and a forgiving God." He grabbed up his own drink and turned away from her.

After a lengthy pause, Roxanne tried again. "It's so cute that Arthur thinks Cromwell is such a good British name. He likes Christopher."

"Why is he here? Every time I look around that guy is here."

"Why, Andrew, he's here to save the day. Didn't y'all see that white horse he rode up on?" she said, in her best southern accent.

"Save who from what?"

Roxanne leaned in close and whispered, "He's going to clean up the mess you helped create when you re-negotiated that QualityCare contract."

"Jesus, that was over a year ago. What is there to clean up?"

"That's for Chris to discuss tomorrow. Where have you been? Your cave that deep?" Roxanne winked, shrugged a shoulder and left him.

Andrew decided that it was time to go, but he didn't want to leave without talking to Christopher. He located him across the room and shouldered his way through the crowd, ignoring several people who started to say something to him, intent on confronting his friend the CEO.

"Christopher, I need to get home to Drew." A lie; Drew was with his mother, but it was effective for his purpose. "Can we chat before I leave? Walk me to my car?"

"Sure, give me one minute and I will meet you by the stairs."

It wasn't one minute; it was more like five. Chris must have known that Andrew was pissed at him for the delay. "Sorry I kept you waiting," he said, "but I had to put a leash on Roxanne. She has had one too many drinks."

"Speaking of Roxanne, I just talked with her. She tells me that Arthur Bishop is a man on a white horse. Now I know someone is going to step in some horseshit, so why don't you square with me about what's going on."

Christopher was politically savvy: He had already lobbied for and lined up the Board member votes he thought he'd need to push through his plan in the morning and Andrew's wasn't one of them; Roxanne had convinced him to leave his friend out of the loop.

"Well, we have a very important decision to make tomorrow." Christopher stopped walking and stood close enough to Andrew to violate his personal space. He looked down into his eyes.

Andrew backed away. "Wait a minute, I didn't see anything earth-shattering in the Board package. Did I miss something?"

"No. It wasn't there to miss." Christopher didn't want his plan leaked to anyone but the six Board members he could count on to vote with him. "We've already covered the subject: our expansion plans, to which we have already committed the organization. Arthur is going to help us achieve that goal."

"How the hell is a man from Great Britain going to help us grow?"

Chris patted Andrew on the shoulder, "I'm afraid that will have to wait until tomorrow."

"No, damn it, I want to hear it now."

Christopher threw a red-hot spear. "Andrew, if your head wasn't so far up your ass, you would know what was going on.

This is business and I need my business partners to come dressed, on time, and ready to play. You, my friend, have sat on the bench for eight months. I have tried to help you get on with your life, but you choose not to. It's a choice. You want to play in the game or stay on the bench?"

"I don't know what the hell your game is."

"This game is called Success, just like always. The same game we have always played."

Although he said it, even he didn't believe it. He was so far into his own game now that he was stuck. Pulling out would certainly destroy his credibility with Arthur and ruin any chance of getting Roxanne out of Ann Arbor—which she heartily wanted to do. He needed Andrew, but to some degree he was trying to protect him, too. At least that's what Christopher told himself.

Andrew went home mad, confused, and hurt.

Christopher just went home mad. When he got there, he pumped his wife for information. "Roxy, why the hell were you talking to Andrew about Arthur?"

"Come on, he's going to find out tomorrow. It would be nice if he got on board. Pun intended."

"You are the one who suggested we leave him in the dark."

"You know he's not cut from the same cloth as you. He doesn't have your killer instinct. He'd be quite happy staying right here in second-class Ann Arbor. I'm happy that I married a man who has bigger plans. I bet you he won't vote with you. You mark my words."

Monday morning came and with it an April snowstorm, which made the meeting get off to a late start. Christopher made some introductory remarks and launched without delay into his presentation, which was no ordinary Power Point presentation; this was a high-caliber graphic-arts display. The first thing the

Board saw was a message that flashed on the screen over and over. Pictures of groups of happy, smiling people, and happy, smiling staff, popped on and off the screen. Graphics faded in and out:

We Are The Solution

We Are The Answer

We Shall Make A Difference

QualityCare:

Making It Happen;
Making A Difference

Christopher spent the next ten minutes explaining what making a difference meant to himself and QualityCare. He and Arthur Bishop had laid the plans well for this meeting: they'd commissioned a survey of key points for the Board and leaders in the community to consider. Now he was just basically telling them what they wanted to hear.

He concluded, "Ladies and gentlemen, people want to work for a winner. People want to be on the winning team. People want that team to make a difference. It's time for our team to make a difference."

He took a break, per the pre-scripted plan, giving the Board an opportunity to digest this portion of the meal.

The meeting continued with Christopher reintroducing Arthur Bishop. Chris asked him to speak to the Board, a surprise to most of the people there. Arthur told a couple of cute and powerful stories. He was funny and he was charming, and he had that British accent. Somehow that gave him credibility he had not yet earned. He finally came to the point of his presence. "I'm going to ask you some questions, and I'll assume your answers are in the affirmative unless you tell me otherwise by raising your hand."

Christopher gauged the members's reactions. So far so good. Chris hooked them; it was Arthur's job to reel them in.

Arthur started by asking, "Do you believe in the sanctity of medicine as an honorable profession?" After a brief pause and a look around the room he continued. "Do you believe that QualityCare is worthy of its name?" He paused even longer, waiting for some brave soul to argue. "Do you believe that you make a difference in how health care is provided in your community?" Now came the tug on the pole. "By a show of hands, how many of you have loved ones who live outside of Ann Arbor?" One hundred percent of the hands went up. "How many of you wish that your loved ones could get the same level of care that *you* give to our community?" Again, one hundred percent of the hands went up. Andrew took note of the words *our community.*

They were taking the bait, just as pre-scripted.

"If you could, would you step up and make a difference to make that a reality?" Nods all around. Arthur smiled. "Fine. You have a blank sheet of paper in front of you. Please take ten minutes to list at least five things that you personally can do to make a difference. Also, describe five things that you think QualityCare can do to make a difference."

They all thought, scribbled, sighed, took a break. The members drank some coffee or tea, ran to the restrooms, stared into space.

Once re-gathered, Arthur recorded the answers on a flip chart. The reason for asking people their personal preferences was to match each individual's personal vision with an organizational vision. When that occurred it was much easier to get people to go along with the business vision. Today, the results were close to what had been anticipated: The top three conclusions indicated that QualityCare should: 1) Continue to set a benchmark example (keep doing it well), 2) Create a broader vision (success breeds success), and 3) Take the show on the road (grow).

Lunch was just another pause in the action to create the right pace–a pace too fast would blow the plan. When the Board had settled back in, Christopher took the growth plan that the Board had already approved and expanded on it.

"Ladies and gentleman, our managed care industry is extremely complex. To optimize and achieve the behavior change results we desire, we need to invest in QualityCare's infrastructure."

Andrew interrupted out of a sense of duty. "Christopher, I know what *we* usually mean by being in the 'behavior modification business.' What do you mean by it?"

"Payers and patients both want healthcare providers to produce better health care outcomes. They want them to do so without the waste of resources that are so prevalent in our business." Chris had used Andrew's soapbox argument against him, just as he and Arthur had expected to do. "This investment is the key to our future success. It is the key to making a difference. There are several options that will allow us to capitalize on both the market opportunity and our strategic plan."

He discussed each option, but spent the majority of his time discussing a change in corporate structure. He outlined a plan to convert from non-profit status to for-profit status and then how they would go public. Chris knew from his planning sessions with Arthur that this was the place to stop and take questions. In fact, he had planted some questions amongst a few of his strongest supporters. He knew he would get the obvious questions concerning control, costs, and taxes, and there were plenty. Phil Kunkle asked several questions about the tax implications of converting to a for-profit corporation. Philip worked for a publicly held corporation; he knew the answers, but thought the Board should know as well.

Christopher had also asked Toni Vincenzo to give an overview of the legal and tax issues involved. She presented a very polished overview of what would happen, spending considerable time covering the Michigan Insurance Department's role in the conversion. She explained in detail how the economic value of the current corporation would be placed in a charitable trust to take care of the poor. The public offering would then re-capitalize the company. Whereas the community owned the not-for-profit QualityCare, the shareholders would own the reconstituted company.

It all made sense, but it left open a question Christopher and Arthur had long anticipated. They expected either Andrew or one of the other physician-Board-members to ask it and were surprised when it was Martha Goodwin who spoke up. "Dr. Cromwell, we built QualityCare on the backs of the physicians of this community. If we go in this direction, those physicians will lose control over everything they fought for when they started this company."

"Ah, well, that's why Mr. Bishop is here. As I told you long ago, the British Insurance Group has been looking for a way to invest in the American healthcare system. It is not just the return on investment that turns them on–it's the long-term ability to export our methodologies–the way we treat illnesses–for patient care to England."

Arthur got up and explained the second half of the plan. His company was prepared to purchase 53% of the new for-profit QualityCare so that the physicians could remain in control after the company completed its conversion. He would then stack the new Board with local physicians–at least that's what he said he'd do. He presented a set of pro forma financial statements. QualityCare would have the capital to grow, invest in information systems, and become more efficient administratively. The money saved in operations alone would allow the HMO to pump eleven million more dollars a year into patient care.

The argument was compelling and appealing, but there were a few detractors. They'd known there would be, but Chris and Arthur expected to be able to count on the votes they'd lined up before the meeting, sway several of the others to their side, and be able to ignore the detractors.

They took their last break of the day. Chris quietly tapped each "sealed" voter on the shoulder and confirmed his or her vote, but they were still one short. The holdout was Bruce Meyers, Andrew's partner at the clinic. Arthur bought Dr. Meyers' vote, on the spot, with an offer too attractive to turn down.

The Board reconvened. Arthur was excused and the debate began. Martha and Andrew, along with two consumer Board members, argued that this was not what they'd all started years ago and pleaded with the Board to reject Christopher's plan. They would have had a more successful argument if they'd had any idea how large Christopher's cut of the new deal was going to be.

Christopher only needed seven positive votes. His vote would break any tie, regardless of his conflict of interest.

After an exhaustive debate, Philip Kunkle made the motion. "I wish to move that we give the Executive Committee of the Board the authority to pursue the conversion and public offering of a great institution, QualityCare. This will, of course, require final approval by this Board, but this motion will allow the appropriate investigative work to begin."

The vote was nine in favor and five against. Andrew threw

up his hands in disgust and left. Christopher stayed around and accepted congratulatory remarks from several Board members.

As soon as Christopher got in his car, he made two phone calls, the first to Roxanne. "Sweetheart, we did it."

"I knew you would; the champagne is on ice, waiting to celebrate. Hurry home, dear."

He hung up, dialed another number. "We hit a home run. Everything you said was right on the money. I wish you could have seen the vote; it was even better than we expected. You are a master."

"You did this one very well. You're a terrific pupil. I congratulate you."

"Arthur, we make a great team. This is going to be a lot of fun. It will be hard work, but it will be fun."

"Yes indeed. But don't forget that it's also going to be very lucrative. We just need to keep the organization on the financial upside; no one wants to invest in a financial dog. We have a few months of hard work in front of us. *You* need to make sure the financial picture improves. Goodnight, Christopher."

Christopher was concerned with the last statement. It ate at him that QualityCare's financials weren't as rosy as he'd painted them over the past several months. He would have to fix that immediately if he was going to stay in Arthur Bishop's good graces.

—Chapter 27—

Andrew wandered around his redecorated home, touching this, straightening that. He thought about the Board meeting, annoyed and disappointed that Christopher had won. He fixed a drink, finished it, and fixed another. His arms ached. He wanted so badly to hold Julia one more time, though it wasn't just Julia he missed, but the feeling of stability and that elusive security she'd represented.

He needed to talk to someone, so he called the first person on his go-to list, Carol.

"Sissy, how are you?" He didn't call her often because he hated answering that same question. "I thought maybe you needed some brotherly love, eh?"

"Little brother, with a sense of humor, have you been drinking?" Andrew had never been a big drinker, but the bottle had been his solitary friend of late. Insecurity, loneliness and booze: a bad combination, even for the strongest of men, and Andrew had never been that. "Let's start with my asking you how *you're* feeling?"

"Low. I am the proverbial rudderless ship drifting aimlessly at sea."

"Okay. Describe that for me, Andy," Carol said, searching for clues.

"I was this buttoned-up individual for so long. After I got married and Laura and I had Drew, I just added buttons. I used to blame myself when Laura left me."

"And now?"

"I wasn't done, Sis. Please let me finish or I'll never get this out."

"I'm sorry, please continue."

"Like I said, I always thought it was me until Julia came into my life. She made me *me*. She found a way to dig into my soul to find me. Now I am *him* again and I want to be *me* again. Does that make sense?"

"Sounds perfectly normal to me. Andy, I hate to throw this at you, but maybe you're ready to hear it: You are not very good alone. You need a partner to be secure. You may not see it now, but some lucky woman out there will step on the path to your heart again. You just have to keep the boulders out of her way."

"I want to feel that way again, but I just don't know how. Damn, I just want to feel the right way for the right reasons. I have a feeling that needing a security blanket isn't the right reason."

"Well, Andy, the fact that you've got your sense of humor back and can see the sun over the horizon is an indication that the world isn't as dark and bleak as you've been thinking. Congratulations, you're done mourning Julia."

"I still talk to her everyday," he said, almost embarrassed.

"Our mother was a real piece of work, but I loved her. I miss her and I visit her in my memory everyday. I still talk to her. There's nothing wrong with keeping the memory of loved ones alive. It's only when that process gets in the way of living in the present that creates the ultimate problem."

"You're right. Unfortunately, I've been a real ass and I'm afraid I've burned some bridges."

"Your friends and family know who you are and we accept you as is. Watching you be in pain has been very hard, but I'm sure you can get on with what's important to you now. Are you ready for me to find you a new woman?"

Laughing, he replied, "Only if you're ready for me to find you a new husband to replace that knife-happy doctor you married."

"I'll check with him to see if he's done with me. In the meantime, keep smiling. I love you."

"I can see why the Hoosiers in Indiana elected you to office. I love you too, Sissy. Thanks for believing in me."

"You're welcome, just keep believing in yourself." She was not convinced that he could or would.

Andrew signed up for the Memorial Day Father and Son Golf Tournament at the Oak Pointe Country Club, in Brighton. The day would be a challenge given Oak Pointe's sand traps and water hazards and that Andrew's golf game had deteriorated badly in recent months. The reward was being with his son; they hadn't had many good times together since Laura had returned to Michigan. Drew played well and the Albrights finished with a sixty-five, good enough for third place. It was the first trophy Drew put on his dresser, but not the last.

"That was quite a display you put on today. I was very proud of you. Your practice is paying off," Andrew said on the way home.

"Well, it all has to do with the mental part of the game."

That sounded like something Julia would've said. "Did Julia tell you that?"

"It was one of the last things she ever said to me. I figure she's watching me from heaven and I wanted her to know I heard what she said." It made Drew sad to talk this way and he normally avoided conversations about Julia.

"Do you miss her?"

"Sure, she was great. I don't think mom or Lindsey liked her much, but I'm not real sure."

"Why do you say that?"

"They just never had anything good to say and Lindsey was always calling her a spoiled brat or something like that."

"Little man, she was a princess. I sure hope you find your princess someday." Andrew took Drew's hand in his.

"Dad, I don't even like girls."

"Whatever happened to the crush you had on that girl in California?"

"She dumped me before I moved back. I'm done with girls." Spoken like a true Albright man.

"I doubt that. Some girl will sweep you off your feet someday, mark my words."

They stopped for ice cream and discussed Drew's summer plans. He told his dad that Laura wanted to take him with her to California for a month in July. Typical Laura, no phone calls; it was easier to let Drew drop the message. Andrew wished to himself that his ex-wife would just disappear. In the end he said fine, so he could get another witner vacation in Florida with Drew.

He continued to struggle on the work front. He was starting to come around, but he was still bitter and Lindsey and Laura weren't helping his opinion about women. Christopher avoided Andrew as much as he could. He sent Toni Vincenzo to talk to him about the BIG plan, as it was now called, as part of Toni's job as corporate counsel to educate the Board members about the for-profit changeover process.

She scheduled a lunch meeting with Andrew on Tuesday, June first. As instructed, she passed on the news to Andrew that the conversion process was going very well. The Insurance Commissioner was prepared to approve the process pending an audit of the financials. The fact that the state would pocket $240 million for their indigent care fund didn't hurt. She then covered a topic that would soon become both public and a problem: an internal audit had shown that QualityCare had lost over two million dollars in the first quarter. The Finance Committee would meet in three weeks to discuss it. She detailed the remainder of the process over coffee. She found Andrew to be a good listener who asked intelligent questions.

Impressed by her knowledge and delivery, Andrew could sense that she was struggling with some aspects of the deal. He wondered why she had come to QualityCare. He finally asked her point blank, "Why did you come to work for Christopher Cromwell?"

"Well, I didn't come to work for Christopher per se. I came home from Washington to be near my family."

"Why'd you give up your career as a political lobbyist?"

"My daughter Maria was born in early nineteen ninety-seven. I couldn't raise her well and compete in the cut-throat world of Washington politics at the same time."

"So where's her father?"

"Gone. The scum left me when I wouldn't have an abortion. However, I refuse to dwell on him. He's turned all men into serpents that I now must tolerate in this life." Trying to be cute, but too serious for it, she failed.

"I can respect that, but at least he didn't leave you for another man." Toni looked puzzled. "That'd be a two-beer conversation for another day."

In his car, he laughed to himself about the picture of a woman-hater and a man-hater being friends. Then he called and asked Christopher if he could stop for a visit that night. They set it up for 7:30. Andrew finished up his clinical work and had dinner with Drew before going over to the Cromwells'. Chris hadn't made it home yet when he arrived. Roxanne answered the door and hugged Andrew more affectionately than he thought necessary.

"I'm sorry, Andrew, but Christopher got caught on a conference call with the attorneys in New York. Apparently they ran into a problem today. He should be here soon. Drink?"

"No thanks. I'll take a diet pop though, if you have one." He didn't feel comfortable being alone with Roxanne when she was drinking. The fact that she was wearing a very revealing dress didn't help. Their friendship, what little of it there was, hadn't recovered since he'd won the contract battle. Or maybe it started when Julia died. He didn't know or care.

"You mind if I have one?" she asked.

"Your house. Go ahead."

She returned with his diet cola and her vodka on the rocks. She made small talk for awhile until the subject of the public offering came up. "Andrew, are you going to screw with this deal? Why you'd want to ruin a good thing is beyond me."

"First, I'm not confident that this *is* a good thing. Did Christopher say what was up with the public offering that was creating such a problem?"

"Something to do with the due diligence process uncovering some financial irregularities in the books."

"Money. Financial irregularities. Audits. I get the feeling we're more concerned with money than with QualityCare's original reason for being: taking good care of our patients. Roxanne, my biggest concern is that we do this thing for the appropriate reasons. It *may* be the right thing, but I'm still concerned with the reasons."

"Andrew, my dear, trust me, the reasons are so right." She got up and fixed herself another drink. When she returned she sat on the couch right next to Andrew. "Let's talk about you. Are you lonely?"

"Not really. I stay busy with Drew and work." Uncomfortable at being so close to her, he shifted his weight away and hoped Christopher would arrive soon.

"Well, isn't it time for you to get back in the saddle again?" She stood up and sat in his lap. She kissed him while she was running her hands through his hair.

Andrew was caught completely off guard. It took him a few seconds to realize he was kissing the woman who was married to his friend. He stood up abruptly, tumbling Roxanne to the floor. She grabbed everything she could to break her fall. She grabbed his hair with one hand and his shirt with the other. She landed on the floor with a handful of both.

Andrew looked at her with contempt. "What the hell are you doing?"

"Oh Andrew, come on. Don't you find me attractive? I just want to help you move on with your life. I'm not looking to have children with you, but a roll in the hay might do us both some good." She raised her eyebrows, ran her hand up the inside of his leg, pouted a bit. Her act was pretty convincing.

"Not now, not ever. Christopher is my friend and you're his wife. Besides, I honestly don't find you all that attractive." She was model-attractive, but too shallow to be anything more than a trophy as far as he was concerned. "I need to leave. Please tell Chris that something came up at the clinic."

Mission accomplished. Idly wiping her hands on a Kleenex and just as unconsciously sticking the hairy tissue in her pocket, Roxanne called Christopher. "You can come home now."

Christopher arrived to find Roxanne sitting on the couch with a drink in her hand. "So what'd you find out?" he asked immediately.

"Andrew Albright is going to be a definite problem in completing this deal. I had to come on to him to get him to leave, but he's a big boy and I'm sure he'll get over it."

She wasn't totally honest on either front, but her husband didn't need to know that, now did he?

—Chapter 28—

Nancy Ours, Andrew's ALS patient, slept in the first floor bedroom of her house. Things had not gone well for her recent disease progression; she was rapidly losing use of her motor skills. Nancy's husband and three children were at Houghton Lake up north. It was a family tradition to open their summer cottage the first weekend in June, but Nancy hadn't felt up to going and her physician, Dr. Andrew Albright, had suggested she stay home and rest. She regularly received home health visits every other day; QualityCare paid for these as a necessary part of her treatment plan, but they had agreed to check on her daily while her family was gone.

The intruder knew her story well. He was paid to know. He opened the side door at 1:30 AM with a borrowed key. The intruder was a slight man, covered from head to toe in black clothes. He slipped down the hall and stood by the side of her bed.

Nancy came awake, startled, but not yet afraid. The medication she was taking made her groggy. She mumbled, "Who is it? Who are you?"

The man in black wasted no time. "Do not struggle with me. Tonight you are going to join God in heaven."

Starting to lose control of herself, Nancy pleaded, "Please don't hurt me, please."

The man in black stayed with his script, ignoring her pleas. "You're going to follow my directions precisely as I give them to you, or I'm going to kill your oldest son and then your husband, but I'll leave your two girls alive to remember the three of you.

"I have a tape recorder in my hands. I'm going to turn it on and hand it to you. You're going to thank your family for their support and tell them that it's time for you to go. You don't want to burden them any longer. Depart from that and I'll have to go to plan B. You don't want me to have to go to plan B, do you, Nancy?"

Nancy was crying too hard to say anything. That wasn't a problem for the moment because the killer had several things he needed to do. He took off his backpack and removed a bottle of vodka that had been laced with sleeping pills and narcotics. He told Nancy to take two swallows; it would help her "relax"–not to mention paralyze her lungs, but that would take at least an hour. The killer was in no hurry. Nancy complied, but it took her three attempts to get the drink down. She was sitting in a puddle of tainted booze. She tried to get out of bed, but her muscles failed her.

Twenty minutes later, with the tears drying on her face, Nancy mumbled into the recorder. "My dear family, I love you." She choked back a new set of tears and the man in black snatched the recorder out of her hands.

"You need to calm down and get this right!" It was no use; she was going to cry her way through the recording. But what could he do? He had to stick to the plan. If it went perfectly, his employer would double his fee.

He turned on the recorder, and she started again. "My dear family, I love you and I love what you have done for me. I no longer wish to be a burden to you. It is time for me to be with God in heaven. I shall await your journey there, too. I will see you all in heaven. Please be kind and loving to each other. Do not hate those who hate you and always forgive–"

He cut her off. He would edit the last comment with the eraser button.

He forced her to drink several more ounces of the vodka. Nancy fought to live but couldn't keep her eyes open, couldn't breathe and finally couldn't even pray.

It took another twenty minutes before the drug cocktail paralyzed her breathing completely. The man in black pulled a stethoscope out of his backpack and checked for a heartbeat. None. Nancy Ours was dead. For a man who had never done this before, he remained rock steady. He packed up all the goods he had brought and before he left, took a picture for his boss. He also left a small token of his appreciation next to Nancy's bed.

It didn't take long to discover Nancy Ours' death. The home health nurse called the police immediately. They arrived within a few minutes, along with the coroner for Washtenaw County, and Chuck Schmeidekamp, the county's police investigator. His colleagues knew him as Schmidy. He was an average man who did above-average detective work.

Schmidy asked the home health nurse, "Did you touch anything?"

"I checked her pulse to see if she was alive. I saw that her color was awful, but thought maybe she was having difficulty breathing again."

"What was Mrs. Ours's medical condition?"

"She had a debilitating disease known as ALS."

"You mean Lou Gehrig's disease? I've heard of that. In fact, there was a sergeant in the Ann Arbor police department who died from ALS. Sad to watch him wither away. Where's her family?"

"Up at Houghton Lake, opening up their cottage."

Schmidy listened to Nancy's voice and words on the tape recorder, sighed heavily, shook his head and said, "This is sad, and now I'm gonna have to call her husband and tell him his wife committed suicide. I hate this part of the job. I'll be thinking of that poor family driving all the way back from Houghton with this on their minds."

While the death looked like suicide, Schmidy told the forensic squad to treat the bedroom as a crime scene anyway, bagging the woman's medicines, the tape recorder, the still sopping bed sheet, and other items near the bed.

Andrew received a call at 11:00 Wednesday morning informing him that Nancy Ours had committed suicide. He asked if there was anything he could do for the family. He had Nancy on his mind as he headed for lunch with Arthur Bishop. He didn't want to go, but Arthur was leaving for London that night and if Andrew was going to learn any of the things Christopher wasn't telling him, he had to meet Bishop now. They were to meet at the Lord Fox Restaurant where Arthur's driver would take him to the Willow Run Airport to catch his private plane home.

After they had eaten their salads, Andrew asked, "Arthur, I simply don't get why you want to invade Ann Arbor."

"This really doesn't have much to do with Ann Arbor. This is about taking what you and your colleagues have built and franchising it in other communities. QCare will bring them a better medical model and they will bring us, we hope, a good return on our investment. Please, make no mistake about this venture: It is strictly business. Sometimes doctors see medicine as a noble profession that need not succumb to the pressures and opportunities of normal market dynamics, but it just isn't so and I bring that reality to the table. Your customers want me to bring that reality to the table."

"Okay, I can accept that part of the plan for the moment. But why QualityCare?"

"Because it's the right size to invest in. Frankly, the British Insurance Group doesn't have the capital to fight with the big insurance boys. We looked everywhere in the United States before we decided on QCare."

"How long has this been in the works? And what is Chris's role?"

"We've been discussing this for a well over a year. We are a publicly traded company on the London Stock Exchange; we desire to add the New York Stock Exchange to our portfolio of financial markets. The capital is better here in the states. This is a winning scenario for everyone. As for Chris' role, you should talk to him on that subject." He grabbed up his drink, swallowed, set it down.

"What's the timing on this thing and how will our current financial slide affect it?"

Arthur slid a slice of beef into his mouth, chewed. "Good question. We have to close this business deal by September if we're going to do it at all. My Board will want to go in another direction if we cannot get this done in a timely manner. We've jumped our biggest hurdle: The State of Michigan's approval. The current financial slide is a bit troubling; a positive turnaround is critical before we can go public. Every insurance company in the world is hurting. If QCare can turn the ship around while others continue to slide, it will pump up the initial stock-offering price. The higher the price, the more capital we can raise to stabilize the balance sheet."

It was starting to make sense to Andrew, and he didn't like it any better now than before. This sounded too much like a get-rich-quick scheme. The question was who would benefit? The legal documents would openly identify the benefactors. Andrew made a mental note to get a draft copy from Toni Vincenzo. He was allowed; he was a Board member, and he was president of PMG. "This just feels a little greedy to me."

"Stop being naive, Doctor. This is the way business works. You know it's not too late to get on board the train. I am prepared to make you a very handsome offer to back our venture." He paused a moment, took a sip of coffee and eyed Andrew over the edge of the cup. "We will need a new CEO after I retire and Chris moves up the ladder. In the interim, the stock options will be most valuable."

Incensed that Bishop thought he could be bought, Andrew wadded up his napkin, threw it on the plate and stood up. He gave Arthur what he considered some advice. "You're working with an organization named QualityCare. Every time you refer to it as QCare, you dishonor the founders. Get it?"

A nod in understanding–that Andrew wasn't going to get on board the train, though Arthur figured Andrew could take any meaning he wanted–was the only response Arthur offered as Andrew left the restaurant in a huff.

That evening, the man in black made a phone call, looking for his bonus money. "The job is done and done right. Can you go ahead and deposit my bonus in the account just like the first deposit?"

"Of course, but don't be getting greedy or go throwing money around. We're not done yet. Phase Two is coming real soon. I'll contact you in the usual way," his boss whispered.

"Are you alone?"

"No, so don't call me here again. Ever. Stick with the plan."

"You bet." The man in black hung up the phone and headed out to go shopping. He had money to burn and more to earn.

The following day, Nancy Ours's autopsy showed what the

police had expected. A combination of alcohol and prescription medication had killed her. Her death was ruled a suicide.

Andrew called Toni to get some answers. She told him that the draft documents being filed with the Securities and Exchange Commission were not yet public.

"So when will the QualityCare Board have a opportunity to approve the final transactions?"

"I don't know, but I could ask Christopher if I can make the draft documents available to the Board."

"No thanks, I'll talk to him myself."

He headed straight to the QualityCare offices to see Christopher, calling first to let his secretary know he was on his way. She told him that Dr. Cromwell was tied up. He came in and waited anyway. The longer he waited the more upset he got, not because of the wait itself, but because it gave him more time to let his anxiety about the deal build up.

Chris eventually came out to greet him. "Andrew, how nice of you to stop in. Is this a social call or is it business?" He led Andrew back to his office.

"According to Arthur Bishop everything is business, so let's stick to that, for the moment. I want to review the Security and Exchange Commission filings," he said, taking a seat squarely in front of Chris's desk.

"Why?"

Hardball-time. "As President of Partners Medical Group, I have concerns regarding this deal and I'm not sure I can support it. I was hoping to read the documents to find something that I could support."

Chris planted his hands solidly on the top of his desk and leaned forward. "The Board is going to sign off on this, Andrew. I don't need your support. I want it, but I don't need it, you egotistical jackass."

Andrew stood up, jammed his hands in his pockets, took one out, and pointed a finger at Christopher. "You can do whatever the hell you want with the structure of this organization, but you remember this fact: You do not have a valuable product without our clinic. You can't make a successful public offering without PMG as part of the package. If we–no, if *I*–were to terminate our contract with the required twelve months' notice, it would kill everything." He turned around and walked out the door.

He ran into Toni in the lobby. "I can't believe you support this sham offering."

"Wait just a minute, Andrew. You don't understand."

"Then explain it to me."

"How about dinner this Saturday? We can discuss the reality of public offerings until you're sick of the topic."

"Is this business?" He wasn't sure if he wanted it to be strictly business or not.

"Strictly."

"Good, then you buy. I assume, as a 'Vincenzo,' you know some good Italian restaurants?"

"I think we'll try something else, maybe a Greek place downtown?"

"You're buying, so you pick. I'll be by to collect you at six-thirty. Address, please?"

"You're a smart boy, look it up," she said, smiling and walking away.

Banter. The kind he had relished with Julia. It hit him hard just how much he missed it.

—Chapter 29—

Saturday came and Andrew got a case of the sweats thinking about dinner with Toni. He didn't know why; they had established it was supposed to be strictly business. Maybe it was the "supposed" that had him up tight. What if it wasn't?

Toni introduced Andrew to her parents, Celeste and Salvatore. Mom and Dad lived one block over and Toni's maternal grandparents lived less than a mile away. Family pictures on the walls clearly indicated that the Vincenzo family was close besides simply being neighbors.

The smell of pasta made its way from the kitchen. Mama Celeste was heating up some rigatoni with ragu sauce that she had made at home that morning and brought over for dinner.

Andrew thought the Vincenzo kitchen was far more inviting than fighting the traffic downtown. He would have been just as happy to stay and eat with Toni's family. They would've loved to have him, but Toni was ready for a night out. She picked Maria up, said, "Oh boy, for a three-year-old, you sure are heavy," hugged her, and tapped her on the head three times. She told her parents she would be home early.

Dinner was peaceful, no debates. Andrew got a fresh perspective of both Toni and the public offering. "Andrew, this public offering could be a bad thing. Seen it happen plenty of times. But, I think this one feels good. Arthur is willing to allow the docs to keep control. What more could you ask for? Besides, this may be the only way to capitalize our growth."

"Yeah, but at what expense? Growth is not always a good thing."

"Correct, but stop and consider who truly controls the ethics and purpose of the new organization."

"That would be the shareholders right?"

"Theoretically yes, but shareholders rarely have anything to do with the day-to-day operations of any publicly held company. You know, and apparently have already reminded Dr. Cromwell that without the docs the HMO has no product to sell. It's a win-win situation. The community wins, the doctors stay in control, and Arthur gets his financial jumping-off point to franchise QualityCare."

"It still doesn't feel right," Andrew said with a grave look of concern on his face.

"It'll be fine. If it weren't, I'd quit." She placed her hand on his forearm for reassurance. He felt the electricity.

They gradually got away from business talk and wandered into personal stories. Toni apparently wanted to change the world. She wanted to be a force in reforming American healthcare politics; she thought she might even run for public office one day to do it–she didn't think her having a daughter without a husband would ruin her chances in this day and age. But damn the Serpent; he should've married her.

"Okay, I spilled my guts, now it's your turn," she said. "I've bought you dinner and the obligatory two beers. So, let's hear your story." She'd heard the rumors and wondered how close to the truth they were.

"No, this was supposed to be business, not the Andrew Albright Confession Session. And you didn't tell me the Serpent was your fiancé," he said, neatly sidestepping his own story.

"Oops, sorry, I left that part out. The bum was supposed to marry me in a big Italian wedding. We'd already spent a small fortune when he bolted. Papa was one angry man. Still is."

Andrew made a mental note to never cross Papa. "How long before your wedding did he dump you?" She looked surprised at his inelegance. "Sorry, bad choice of words. When did Serpent Boy slither back into the pond?"

"I found out I was pregnant seven weeks before the wedding. He was gone two weeks later. But I'm not telling you another thing until you give up some dirt about yourself."

He told her first about Laura and then about Julia. Toni was empathetic enough to recognize that to lose a soulmate and a child at the same time must have been devastating. They both had good reasons to be bitter. All of the sudden, this was a support group of sorts. It was easy. Neither had any desire to pursue the other in a romantic way.

At least that's what they said out loud.

Sandra Horn and her husband, Peter, were staying downtown to celebrate their anniversary at a concert at the Joe Lewis Arena. It was a perfect early summer evening, breezy and humidity-free, to walk along the Detroit River back to their hotel in the Renaissance Center. Given Peter Horn's duties as a lawyer in the District Attorney's office, they didn't get to go out often. But Sandra had long accepted his hours and the payoff: he was well respected and well paid. He was a fine litigator; his conviction rate was one of the highest in Oakland County. She enjoyed being his wife.

The man in black followed them for quite some time. He was in no hurry. He wanted an audience, but it needed to be small.

When the time, light, and audience were right, the man in

black stepped out from the shadows and yelled, "This is for Michael! You screwed him and now it's payback time!"

He shot Peter with three quick shots at close range, two to the chest and one to the head. Then he shot Sandra. Same pattern, two and one. Both were dead before they collapsed to the pavement. The witnesses ran for cover.

The man in black just ran.

During their post-dinner stroll through Greektown, Andrew said, "I'm afraid our personal story-telling got in the way of the 'strictly business' rule we set up, didn't it?"

"Well, yeah, and I hold you wholly to blame. Can I offer you some unsolicited advice?"

"Sure."

"I'm a lawyer, so I know: Lawyers can be your best friend or your worst nightmare. It all depends on how you treat them."

Andrew wondered which of the two Toni might be as this QualityCare thing played out.

When Andrew read the Sandra and Peter Horn story in the Sunday paper he felt snake-bit. This was the first time he'd ever had two patients die at the same time of non-medical causes. He got up, looked out the window, and locked the door. He told himself it was a coincidence and he was just being paranoid.

—Chapter 30—

Christopher knew Andrew was right about PMG: no PMG, no BIG deal. And Roxanne was sure Andrew wouldn't go along, no matter what Chris offered him. It worried him deeply. He conferred with Arthur on several occasions, who told him the best thing he could do was to make Andrew a player in the game: make it difficult for him to play the trump card. Christopher doubted he had any inducement big enough to make Andrew change his mind.

It was a phone call the morning of the Finance Committee meeting that brought Christopher awake, literally. The ringing of the phone was a sledgehammer against his subconscious. He had come to hate these early morning phone calls, particularly the ones that served as his alarm clock.

"Chris Cromwell."

"Well, don't sound so excited to hear from me."

"Shit Arthur, I'm seeing way too many sunrises working with you." He didn't have the courage to call Arthur what he was, a relentless corporate hardass.

"Dr. Cromwell, I told you long ago that this was hard work. You gave me the clear impression that you had the stomach for this."

"And I do." Christopher paused and failed to find the right words. "It's the looks I get that I don't like."

"What the hell are you talking about?"

"My friends and colleagues treat me like I'm a Roman soldier on the way to pillage their hamlet."

"C'mon Chris, I shouldn't have to give you pep talks. You've built a first-class operation. Wall Street is going to put up the money to take your better mousetrap to more people. Very noble indeed. Don't you agree?"

"Yes."

"Then what the hell is the problem?"

"It's the money. I feel like I'm stealing from the cookie jar in my mother's kitchen."

"There's nothing unethical about making money. I'll not tolerate ethical indiscretions. We are in this for the long run. You with me? If not, tell me now."

"Yes sir, I am with you."

"Nuff said, ol' boy. And stop whining about working early. I've taken plenty of your calls at midnight. Now, the reason I called was to make sure you call me as soon as you can after the meeting. I'm a little put off by all these audit findings."

"Yes sir, I will."

Quality Care's monthly Finance Committee meeting was tense, embarrassed by the audit report that showed their profits had been overstated. The cause was understated Incurred But Not Reported (IBNR) Claims.

Allen Kaminsky, the QualityCare Chief Financial Officer, explained the issue to the committee. "Picture yourself going to see your doctor. The minute you leave your physician's office the liability for that claim exists. Since the claim has neither been generated nor sent to us, we really do not know it exists. On average, it takes a physician's office four days to create a bill and fourteen days for us to get it into our claims system and write a check to the doctor. Estimating the amount of claims that have occurred for which we have not yet cleared checks is IBNR. The two things we monitor are the time it takes providers to bill us, and the status of our most chronically ill members. The longer the billing cycle, and the sicker our patients, the higher the IBNR factor will be at any given point in time."

Christopher, as CEO, and Philip Kunkle, Chair of the Finance Committee, took turns talking about what had happened and what the organization could do to correct it, Christopher constantly hearing Arthur's voice in his ear, instructing him to make sure that the IBNR improved before the public offering.

After the meeting, Christopher went home and shared his doubts with Roxanne. "I'm afraid we might have to pull the plug on the public offering."

"Are you out of your mind? You're so close! Why on earth would you want to do such a stupid thing?"

"Because we can't sweeten the PMG deal, we're way behind in our financial projections, and Andrew is likely to hold us hostage no matter whether we fix the financial numbers or not."

He didn't bother to tell her again that buying Dr. Albright's loyalty was out of the question; she knew it as well as he did.

But Roxanne was nowhere near ready to accept defeat. "How many times have we talked about this, Chris? Stop being so weak and stay focused on the end prize. Arthur's offering you the chance of a lifetime. Besides the stock options, he's already told you he's retiring in three years. This is *his* swan song and *your* coming-out party. So suck it up and stop whining."

"Roxy, these things are not the most important things out there—"

Practically screeching, she cut him off. "You want to work at this dinky little HMO the rest of your career? You want to live in this Podunk town the rest of your life? This is not London." Rather than wait for an answer, she filled in the blanks for him. "Of course you don't. There are much brighter days for us if you just stay focused, for god's sake."

"You're right. You're right, of course." Christopher *was* an ambitious man; Roxanne was simply the fuel that helped propel him forward. She had been since the day they'd met.

The following evening was Phase Three for the man in black. The schedule had been moved up. The target this time was twenty-three-year-old Paula Callaway, Andrew's AIDS victim.

Andrew dropped off some medication samples for his patient, Paula Callaway, early in the evening. He signed out the medicine from the clinic pharmacy and gave it to her on his way home from work. It was not a common practice, just an act of kindness.

"Thank you for doing this for me, Dr. Albright. Reggie is out of town and I wasn't up to going out."

"You're welcome. I hope you feel better. Please call me if you need me. You know the drill."

"Won't you come in and visit for a moment?" Paula was lonely and wanted company and thirty minutes of Andrew's time would be perfect.

"I'm sorry, Paula, but I have to get home. My son is waiting for me." It was the truth, otherwise Andrew would have been happy to stay.

"Oh. Well, thank you again."

"You're welcome and keep smiling."

The man in black made his way into Paula's house at three in the morning, after making sure her alarm wasn't set. Like with the Nancy Ours termination, he'd copied the key from the home health agency. He'd waited in the shadows for twenty minutes, partly to be safe but mostly to savor the moment. He was a Physician's Assistant by day; this, however, was more fun and certainly more lucrative.

The man in black headed to the part of the house where he knew Paula would be sleeping. He had waited until the wee hours of the night because Paula often had difficulty falling asleep; the virus had impaired her lungs and her breathing. He entered her bedroom and quietly moved her wheelchair out of the way.

He was surprised to see her awake and wildly hitting the buttons on the phone, but he terminated the call before she could get an answer. Flustered by the surprise, he said, "Be calm or this is really going to hurt."

Paula screamed, started to fight him, swinging her arms in wide arcs, and tried to struggle out of the bed. He fought to get his sedative-soaked rag up to her face. At first it just made her gag, but then she slumped.

He hooked a small canister of poisoned gas to her oxygen canister. Getting Paula to keep the mask on her face proved more difficult than he'd thought it would be, but he didn't panic and she didn't struggle long: Within seconds she went limp, within a minute she was in a coma, within several she was dead.

The killer crossed the room to Paula's computer and typed in a message:

I pray that you will forgive me for what I am about to do. Reggie, I love you with all my heart. For a long time I have wanted you to move on with your life, and now you can. Mom and Dad, I pray that you will also accept my decision. I will suffer no more, and I thank you for your love and support. Pauline

The man in black packed up his belongings and left two small presents, one on the bed and the other on the coffee table in the living room. He left the house, pleased with himself. It had been an efficient visit. He had just earned a quarter of his annual salary in two hours.

He slithered away into the night.

—Chapter 31—

Paula's boyfriend, Reggie Ryan, arrived at her house before the home health nurse the next morning. He was almost hysterical when he called 911, but he didn't tell the operator that Paula had committed suicide, he told her his girlfriend had been murdered.

The ambulance and police showed up together, read the message on her computer, got Reggie calmed down, and asked him why he'd called her death a murder and not a suicide.

"I haven't touched anything, and look where the wheelchair is. Paula had just had outpatient surgery on her foot. Between that and her lung ailment she went everywhere in that wheelchair. She couldn't walk two feet. She wouldn't have been able to get from the chair to the bed."

"Maybe she accidentally pushed it away after getting into bed?"

"How would she get to the bathroom in the middle of the night? She wanted the chair close, especially at night. It was her lifeline. Who would do such a bad thing to Paula? She was so kind to everyone."

"Is there anything else that looks funny to you here?"

"Well, Paula would never have signed her name Pauline, she hated it. This was a personal note to her family. She would have signed it like always, 'Paula' or 'Smallfry.'"

The police called Detective Schmeidekamp, who dropped what he was doing and sped over to the Callaway house. He debriefed with the Ann Arbor Police at the scene and talked to Reggie for as long as the young man held up emotionally. After he was satisfied, he supervised his crime scene unit while they bagged, vacuumed and fingerprinted.

Paula's autopsy took place the next morning. The cause of death: a lethal dose of poisonous gas. There was also poisonous residue in Paula's tear ducts, which had crystallized after her blood stopped circulating. Had she lived longer it would have dissolved. There were also very small bruises on the inside of Paula's left arm. The ME surmised that the killer–there was no indication of more than one perp–had held her by the arm while he placed the mask over her face, though the ME admitted it wouldn't take much of a bump to leave a bruise on Paula Callaway. She was severely anemic. But what would she bump on the inside of her arm? The ME ruled the death a homicide.

Exactly how the man in black had been instructed to make it look.

Given the fact that three women were dead within days of each other, and that they'd all had the same doctor, they revisited the Ours family and took another look at the Sandra Horn shooting. Originally, the police thought her killing was motivated by Mr. Horn's role in the District Attorney's office. Now they thought maybe Sandra Horn was murdered and her husband was an extra hit.

The amount of resources organized to solve the serial killing spree was unprecedented for Ann Arbor. The FBI labs were asked to help evaluate the forensic evidence collected at each site: unidentified hair near the body in Nancy Ours's bedroom and bullet casings surrounding the Horns's bodies. They hit the jackpot at Paula Callaway's when the hair strands found there matched those found at Nancy Ours's home. They also found a glass in the living room that had prints on it that did not match Paula's or Reggie's.

The fact that all the women had debilitating diseases caused much speculation by journalists and investigators.

On Friday, Schmidy decided it was time to drop in on Andrew Albright, the physician of record for all three victims.

After interrupting Andrew in the middle of an exam, Schmidy started with the obvious. "Dr. Albright, can you imagine why Mrs. Ours or Ms. Callaway would want to commit suicide?"

"No. Each had a very debilitating disease, both were suffering physical and emotional pain, but they were also fighters. Neither would have given up, in my opinion. I honestly don't consider either of them to be capable of suicide."

"Then you must believe they were murdered, is that correct?"

"I guess so. They would've had to be, wouldn't they? They're dead, and not from natural causes."

"Doctor, do you support physician-assisted suicide?"

"No, I do not. It violates the first law of the Hippocratic oath: First, do no harm."

"Do you know of anyone who would want the women dead?"

"None."

"Maybe Sandra Horn, Doctor?"

"How does she fit in?"

"She's another dead patient of yours, is how. The funny thing is that the murder was made to look like it was directed at her husband, but we think not."

"I really don't know," was all Andrew could say.

Schmidy put away his tiny notebook. "Dr. Albright, we appreciate your insights into this matter. I'm sure that we'll be talking more."

Uptight from the detective's visit, Andrew wanted somebody

to talk to, to bounce his thoughts off of. He thought about calling Toni, but went instead to see Julia. He wanted to feel her presence. He stayed by her grave for about forty-five minutes but left feeling just as antsy as when he'd arrived. So, after he got home, he called Toni.

She answered the phone brusquely. "Toni here."

"Hi. This is Andrew Albright. Have I called at a bad time?"

"I'm giving Maria a bath. What's up?"

"I just wanted to talk to someone about these killings going on in town. I apologize if this is a bad time."

"I tell you what, why don't you come over? After I get Maria in bed, we can chat. I'd like to talk to you, too."

Andrew made his way over to her house at the Polo Fields. He sat in her driveway for a moment collecting his thoughts. He wondered why he was *really* there. Yeah, he needed to unload, but why Toni?

Toni answered the doorbell. "Hey Andy, come on in. I was reading Maria a story in the family room. Make yourself comfortable."

Andy? he thought. He rolled it around in his mind for a minute or two and decided maybe it was okay coming from her. He wondered for a minute why he'd always hated it, then mentally shrugged: probably because his mother had called him Andy; most of his hang-ups started with her.

She continued reading the Dr. Suess book and Maria pointed and giggled at her mother, who used different voices for various characters. She looked different in her role as a mother than she did as the corporate attorney for an insurance company: looser, softer. She finished the story, looked at Maria and tapped her on the head three times. "Go on now, jump in bed and I'll be up to tuck you in." She turned to Andrew and asked, "Can I get you anything to drink?"

"I'd love a glass of red wine, if you've got it."

"In an Italian house? Are you kidding?" Returning with two glasses of wine, she toasted them both with "Here's to better days." They took a sip of wine and Toni headed for Maria's bedroom.

While waiting, he perused the family pictures that were everywhere, envious that he didn't have such a family background, and then wondered if he would ever overcome the bitterness he nurtured against his parents.

A picture of Toni and Maria in front of their house caught his eye in particular. Mom was holding her daughter, who was hugging her mother and beaming brightly. On the bottom was a hand-written caption: *Tap, Tap, Tap.*

Toni came back ten minutes later. "I'm glad you called. It's been a rough day." Andrew had the picture in his hands. Toni smiled. "That's one of my favorites," she said.

"It's a lovely picture. What's the tap-tap-tap mean?"

"Oh just something Maria and I have between us. 'Tap, tap, tap' means 'I love you.' It started in the pediatrician's office. Maria used to be afraid of getting her shots. I told her to feel how much I loved her instead and just before she'd get her shot I'd tap her on the hand three times. She'd be thinking about that and forget about the shot. We still do it."

"That's nice," he said, feeling a stab of longing for what he'd missed as a child. "What'd you mean with your toast about 'better days'?"

"Oh, my day. A homicide detective came by; he wanted to talk to Chris and me."

Andrew was almost afraid to ask. "What did he want? Why'd he come to you?"

"Because those three dead women were all QualityCare members."

Andrew, unaccountably on the defensive, said, "Well, there's some real news, but what's the significance of that? Twenty-five percent of Ann Arborites are members of your HMO."

"They're looking for patterns, of course. This just might be one."

"I don't see the pattern," Andrew stated, annoyed. At what, he wasn't sure.

"Each of the women was very ill, Andy, and they were all patients of yours. Surely you can see that the police wouldn't just accept that as a coincidence?"

"Actually, I hadn't thought of it that way. What would anyone have to gain by killing those women?"

"That's what the detectives wanted to know. One of them asked for their claim files and we told him we could only turn them over to him if he got a subpoena." He looked her a question. "That's standard operating procedure for us. But the worst part was that they were asking questions about you."

"What? What kind of questions? What did you say?"

"I didn't say anything because I don't have any information. Chris supplied most of the information." Toni felt a brief twinge of guilt in her stomach; she didn't want to be disloyal to either her boss or her friend.

"Okay, so what did Chris tell them?"

"He discussed your role at PMG and QualityCare. I don't know what else. I was dismissed."

"Dismissed?" He looked at her like a puppy in need.

"I just represent QualityCare, Andy. I was there to answer questions about that subject only. Once I was done with that, I was excused. Not that there isn't a whole lot of interest at the office, what with these patients being QualityCare members, which is bad enough, but when the detectives showed up to question Dr. Cromwell, the staff about went nuts wanting to know what was going on."

"About like what happened at the clinic when that detective came to see me. But I can't imagine that anybody in the healthcare profession would go around murdering people. Why would anybody want to kill people who're dying anyway?"

"A mercy killer, maybe?"

"Some mercy," he sniffed, "killing Paula with poison gas. And Nancy Ours by paralyzing her lungs. And shooting Sandra Horn to death."

"Money, maybe?"

"Money? How would a murderer get any money out of it?"

"I don't know. The mystery books I read always say 'follow the money,' so I just brought it up." She grinned.

Annoyed that she didn't seem to be taking the topic as seriously as he thought she should, which Julia certainly would've, always having known exactly how he felt, Andrew rose and put his empty wineglass on the coffee table. "Well, I need to go home and get some things done. Thanks for the drink."

He gave her a perfunctory hug as he left. She watched him leave from her front door, one eyebrow raised, a finger tapping against her lips. "I think maybe a little work in the humor department might be needed here," she murmured.

—Chapter 32—

Things were tense at QualityCare and even more so at the clinic. Schmidy and the detectives hovered around, interviewing doctors, nurses, and even patients. Everyone was on edge. The clinic's Board met and discussed what they could do, if anything. Since none of the murders had occurred on clinic property they decided they shouldn't do anything but cooperate fully with the investigation.

Schmidy was convinced that the murders were linked to QualityCare. They had a suspect in mind but wanted to process all of the physical evidence first. If Schmidy was right, this was going to be one high-profile case, so he wanted to do it by the book.

Toni called Andrew at the end of the week and suggested she get her parents to watch Maria while they went out for dinner and drinks. Andrew wasn't in the mood, being too caught up in his own emotions and anger at the police for disrupting his clinic and the murderer for killing his patients. He didn't know who to lash out at, or who to unload on. If Julia had been alive, he'd have had a sounding board, but with her gone, he was just stewing in his own bad thoughts.

"Thanks, but no. I'm way behind here at the clinic what with all these detectives messing up the schedule. I think I ought to stay here and get caught up with some paperwork," he fibbed.

"Oh come on. I need to get out for awhile, even if you don't. How about it, huh? For me?"

A small smile crept across his face. "Okay, fine. For you."

"You all right, Andy? You haven't said five words since we left my house," Toni asked as they sat down to dinner. She hated silence; Italians, as a rule, just didn't deal well with it.

"Sorry, I'm just preoccupied, I guess." He really hadn't noticed; he had plenty of noise going on inside his head to make up for it.

Maybe it was the Chianti that loosened him up, but she finally got him talking: about the murders, about Drew and the evil couple, about his regular clinic duties, and about college. On and on, one subject leading to the next. Or, maybe it was Toni. She seemed to know what to say and how to get him to respond. She even got him laughing a time or two. There wasn't any passion to speak of, but there was a comfort level; the relationship was comfortable. Andrew didn't think any woman would ever replace the passion Julia had brought to his life, but the more time he spent with Toni the more time he realized he wanted to spend with her.

He had a sudden idea. He put some money on the table, grabbed Toni by the hand and led her to his car.

"Where are we going?"

"It's a surprise."

"Oh good, a surprise. Any hints?"

"Just one: To understand me, you need to go sightseeing."

Understand him? Why am I supposed to understand him? It took about twenty minutes to travel far enough north to get where he was going. Toni saw the church.

"We're kinda late for Mass, aren't we? I like this church, though. I used to come here when I was a little girl growing up in Whitmore Lake."

Andrew was amused. "Why is it I haven't discovered that you're a Catholic, yet?"

"Good Lord, Andy, I'm an Italian girl who refused to have an abortion. You didn't put two and two together? How'd you ever get to be a doctor?"

It sounded so familiar. It was as if Julia was sitting right next to him. He looked at her in amazement. "Julia asked me that exact question. How ironic that you'd ask it at this moment."

They got out of the car. Toni thought they were going into the church, so she was surprised when they crossed the road and headed for the cemetery. She followed him reluctantly; graveyards weren't exactly high on her list of surprises, especially at night.

She saw it immediately, and stepped back awkwardly. Andrew knelt at Julia's grave and said a brief prayer. It was a warm summer evening. Although it was a moonless night, radiant stars were shining. Andrew didn't speak or look up for about five minutes, not intentionally rude, just lost in thought. He was thinking over and over about the poem he had written Julia the night before, the one now in his briefcase in the car, meant to be a private reading, the one that would allow him to let her go.

"Andrew, just what the hell are you doing?"

Yanked out of his thoughts, he looked up at Toni. She stood over him, leaning against a tree, arms crossed, a frown etched so deeply in her forehead he thought maybe she'd been cut.

"What? Oh, I'm sorry. I was just thinking. Talking to Julia."

"You do that often?"

"Uh, yeah, three or four times a week, I guess."

"And you brought me here why?"

He looked around the dark cemetery, just now realizing how odd his constant visits might seem to Toni. "Well, uh, I guess . . . Well, I thought since we were getting to be friends, this might help you understand me."

"Under*stand* you?" She tossed her head to the side, then looked down at the ground. She moved away from the tree and slowly walked around him. "Let me get this straight: We were having a pleasant dinner, getting to know each other and all that, and you suddenly decide I need to *understand* you, so you drive me out to watch you kneel at your dead girlfriend's grave?"

"Toni, I'm sorry. I just thought–"

"Thinking might have been the one thing you weren't doing. Testing me, is what you were doing. If I held your hand and helped you cry or say goodbye or something, I'd pass your test, wouldn't I?"

"What are you talking about? I'm not giving you any test."

The wind had picked up, flicking her hair across her face. She sighed. "I'm sure you don't think you were." She shook her head and sighed again. "The sad part is, I was really getting to like you. But this . . . this . . . this is too weird and certainly more than I care to deal with. Take me home."

"I apologize. I thought this would be okay with you. You know what it's like to be left. How hard it is to let go."

"You thought wrong. And by the way, saying you're sorry doesn't always work. It doesn't just automatically absolve you for completely screwing up."

They drove home in deafening silence. When they arrived, he started to get out of the car to walk her to the door.

"It's okay, Andrew, I'll find my way to the door," she said. He started to call out to her, but she was gone.

He slammed the gearshift into reverse, backed out of her driveway recklessly, punched the accelerator and shot down the street. Who the heck did she think she was anyway? Who asked her to judge his behavior? What kind of woman was she anyway, just jumping down his throat like that? Julia would never even have *thought* to say something like that to him. For crying out loud, didn't she realize he'd taken her to see the love of his life? That it was important for her to know Julia so she could know him? Know him so she could–

He hit the brakes. Pulled off the road and into a parking spot. Put the car in gear. Sat there.

Could do what?

Hold his hand and let him cry? Cry *with* him, even? Help him stay in his misery?

The sad part is, I was really getting to like you, she said. He wrapped his arms around the steering wheel and lay his head down. He *had* been giving her a test: Show Me You're Just Like Julia. The pathetic part was that he couldn't remember if he and Julia had ever liked each other. They'd had a great love affair and everything was just rosy between them as long as Julia did and said exactly what he'd wanted her to do and say–and vice versa. They'd both wanted to feel safe, to hold off the world and its insecurities and risks by wrapping their arms around each other.

Which was fine as long as they were both alive. The saddest part was that he had just realized that being like Julia was not what he wanted. He wanted to have the right feelings for the right reasons just like he had told Carol.

He lifted his head off his hands, put the car in gear, made a U-turn and headed back to Toni's.

She opened the door to him, an eyebrow cocked, one hand on her hip.

"Before you say anything, yes, you were right. I was testing you. I didn't know I was testing you, so I hope that counts. Does that count?"

She nodded, then smiled. "Yeah, that counts. You're still a jerk, but come on in."

"No, I don't want to come in, it's late, but I do want to know if you think there's any hope we can be friends. Have I blown it?"

"No, you haven't blown it." She grinned. "It was a close call, though."

"Just friends?"

"I think maybe we'd better stick to just friends right now, don't you? I'm not ready to stop being angry at men, and you apparently are nowhere near ready to take another risk on love, are you?"

A fleeting wave of sadness swept through him, Julia's face momentarily perched at the peak, and then it passed. He nodded solemnly. "Just friends, for now. That's plenty."

Andrew slept well for the first time in months, both that night and the next. On Sunday morning, a bright, sunny day, he left for church without feeling like he was moving in a rain cloud, feeling more optimistic than he had in a long time. He parked his car, jumped out, pocketed his keys and then looked up at a man approaching him.

Chuck Schmeidekamp. Schmidy.

"Dr. Albright, can I have a moment of your time?"

"Of course, Detective. What can I do for you?"

"I have a warrant for your arrest."

"What the hell are you talking about?"

"You are under arrest for the murder of Paula Callaway."

Schmidy read him his rights and placed him in the police car.

And the rain cloud was suddenly back.

—Chapter 33—

Schmidy hadn't wanted to arrest Andrew Albright in the parking lot of the church, but he'd had no choice. Word had leaked that an arrest was imminent. They had been processing evidence for several weeks and the District Attorney was ready to move. The Managed Murders case had been assigned to Rebecca Bridgeman, a young, ambitious prosecutor with eyes for a seat on the judicial bench. She'd made her bones in the DA's office by taking on men-on-women assault-and-battery cases, two of which had resulted in the death of the female victims. Rebecca had successfully convicted both batterers of murder. Dr. Andrew Albright was a high-profile male and three women were dead. Rebecca saw the case as getting her one step closer to the ultimate goal, a judgeship.

Andrew was taken to the West End Police Station, where he was processed in the usual way. He refused to answer any questions until his attorney was present. It took the better part of the afternoon to locate Beverly McNeil, who was out with the girls that Sunday afternoon. As soon as she got the phone call from her husband, she excused herself and rushed to the police station, signed herself in as Andrew's attorney of record, and headed to the interview room to meet her client. "Andrew, are you okay?" she asked immediately. She knew the answer was no but she wanted to ask anyway. She was looking to gauge his mood. It was not good.

"Hardly. I don't understand what's happening to me. Why would someone want to do this to me?" His mind was going faster than he could talk; he was thinking out loud. "What made me a target for this? What kind of pervert would do this to me? I didn't kill anybody. I don't hate women. I would never–"

Beverly put her hand on Andrew's arm and stopped him. "Stop right there. Let's not discuss any of this here. You don't need to answer any questions right now." She had looked briefly at the arrest warrant and it would be awhile before she could get through the whole document and evaluate the evidence the state had against him.

"How long am I going to be in here?" His first thoughts were of Drew and how he would react.

"It'll likely be Tuesday before you're arraigned and have a bail hearing. I need to review the evidence the state's got, but bail shouldn't be a problem; you're an upstanding member of the community and you have lots of ties here, so the judge probably won't think you're a flight risk."

Andrew paced the small interview room while Beverly talked. He scratched his head, crossed his arms, sat down, stood up, and then sat down again. When Beverly finished, he asked, "Beverly, will you do me a favor?" He was trying so hard to keep the river of emotion behind the dam.

"Of course I will, what is it?"

"Will you call Drew for me? He's in California with his mother. I don't want him to hear this from anyone else. I wish I could tell him myself, but they won't let me."

"Yes, of course." She wrote down Laura's number. "Andrew, I need you to know that I'm not the right person in our firm to handle this case. We have other, more experienced defense attorneys for cases like this. I'd like you to think about hiring one of them."

"No, I want you. You know me; I know you. You'll be the best for me. Besides, I trust and feel secure with you."

"Trust is not what you need right now. A knowledgeable, experienced criminal attorney is your best bet. Well, we can cover that later on. I'll let you know tomorrow what we're up against."

Beverly left, burdened with the fear that she wasn't professionally capable of representing Andrew in a murder trial. She had heard that Rebecca Bridgeman was going to be chief prosecutor for the case; she and Ms. Bridgeman had had some prior battles, which Beverly had lost. Rebecca was smart, sharp, innovative, ambitious and resourceful. Quite an opponent for an attorney with mostly civil law experience.

His jailers took Andrew back to his holding cell and he was left with his own worst enemy: his thoughts. He couldn't stop playing the tapes in his brain about how this could have happened. What evidence could the state possibly have that would implicate him?

Ann Arbor is a small community. The local radio station announced his arrest and the police reporters were all over the story before Andrew was even booked; the news spread from mouth to ear, leaping like flames into homes, offices and apartments. All but two of the people who knew him had the same reaction: shock and disbelief.

Toni was shocked, but she wasn't absolutely sure he couldn't be a killer; she didn't know him that well yet. Was this just part of the upsetting pattern that she would forever face regarding men? She had to wonder.

Neither the man in black nor his boss was surprised or shocked. There hadn't been any guarantees that their plan would come together, but so far, so good. The man in black demanded more money. He got it, but blackmail only worked for as long as he stayed alive; the time might come when he became a victim of his own game. He had videotaped his actions and recorded the boss's voice, and made sure his boss knew that should any harm come to him, the tape would be made public. While not a professional hit man, he was acting the part well.

Beverly went over the evidence on Monday morning: there were hairs that matched Andrew Albright's DNA at both Nancy Ours and Paula Callaway's homes. They had a shoe print outside Paula's side entry door that was same size and make as a pair in Andrew's locker at work. There was also a drinking glass inside Paula's house that had her client's fingerprints on it. The sign-out log at the clinic clearly showed that Andrew Albright had intended to visit Paula Callaway on the day she was murdered. The telephone company listed a call from Paula's home to Andrew's unlisted home number at approximately the same time as her death. The police also had an interview tape with Amy Thomas, who'd told them that Andrew had yelled at her that some "patients should just die."

Whoever was behind this had done an excellent job of planting the evidence, and apparently Andrew had played right into their hands by shooting his mouth off.

She got to the police station at 10:45 Monday morning. She found her client to be anything but himself. It was clear he hadn't slept. She knew it would be hard. Physicians were so used to being in control. Her client was a caged animal that had absolutely no control right now.

"Well, the good news is that I think the case the prosecution's built is one we can attack. Let me lay it out for you. They can place you in both Nancy Ours and Paula Callaway's bedrooms."

Andrew gasped. "What? The detective never mentioned Nancy. I'm being charged with killing both of them?"

"They don't have to list all the charges, just make sure you were read your Miranda rights, so there's no issue there. They'll focus on Paula Callaway's murder because that's where they have the most solid evidence."

"How do they place me at the crime scene? I was never there."

"The pharmacy log book at the clinic shows that you delivered narcotic medication to her house on the day Paula Callaway was murdered. Is that true?"

"Of course it is. She was very grateful." Andrew's mood lightened. "Is that all they've got?"

"No. They've got strands of hair that match yours inside the house."

"But I never went in the house."

"They've also got a glass with your fingerprints on it. Found on the coffee table in the living room."

"That just can't be! I never went in the house!" Andrew, shocked, trembled with fear. He went back to pacing to try to stay composed.

"And one more thing: they don't have the exact time of death, but Paula called your house at three-twelve a.m. The prosecution's theory is that she knew she was going to die and instead of calling nine-one-one, she dialed the phone number of her killer to send the cops a message."

I was her doctor; she could've been calling me to help her."

"Right. I agree. It's one of the facts we can argue. There are hair samples at the Nancy Ours's crime scene as well, and shoe prints outside Paula's house that match a pair of shoes in your locker at the clinic."

"Anybody could've had the same kind of shoes; they're Nike's, for crying out loud. Hell, her son might have the same shoe size I do. Damn it, I would *never* kill my patients, ask anyone."

"Unfortunately, they did. Your nurse at the clinic said you said you thought 'these sick patients should die.'"

Andrew paused his pacing, stared at Beverly in shock and collapsed into a chair. "Oh my God, I remember saying that to Amy, but it was just a bad day. I was angry and frustrated. What with Laura leaving me and taking Drew and Julia getting killed by that woman driver, I was . . . I was just frustrated."

"And they'll use it to paint you as a bitter man. They'll have established motive and opportunity. It isn't looking good, but I think we've got some holes in their theory we can deepen, and they don't have anything but circumstantial evidence. Nobody actually saw you at Paula's. They're simply assuming you went there because the logbook says you were going to. But I can pound on that: why would you write down you were going to see her and then kill her? It'd be like pointing your finger at yourself. Let me get on to the bail issue and get you out of here. We can go over our defense when you're home."

Before she left, Andrew asked, "Did you talk to Drew?"

"Sorry, but no, I didn't. Your ex-wife wouldn't let me speak to him. She'd already heard the news." She watched Andrew's eyes flare open with rage. She wasn't sure if she should tell him the rest, but decided that Andrew might as well here it now so he could process it. "She also told me that under the circumstances she wouldn't be returning from California any time soon. She feels Drew is better served by not being in the middle of this issue."

Andrew flew off the handle, cursing and fussing about how wrong this was and how she had no right to keep Drew away from him. He even accused Laura of being in on the conspiracy.

Beverly made a mental note of that: Laura might have had a motive and she did leave town right after the murders. If nothing else, it went to establishing reasonable doubt.

—Chapter 34—

The Managed Murders Case was assigned to Judge William Bennett. This was neither good nor bad; he was tough, but fair, in the collective legal community's opinion. Their first appearance Tuesday morning before the judge went well. The DA's office had no opposition to allowing Dr. Albright bail. Beverly drove Andrew back to St. Patrick's, where his car had been since Sunday. On the way there, he borrowed Beverly's cell phone and called Drew in California.

Laura answered the phone. "Andrew, how surprised I am to hear from you." There wasn't even a hint of surprise that Andrew could have been charged with murdering his patients. "Before we go any further, I want you to know I won't be bringing Drew back to Michigan next week as planned. It obviously wouldn't be good for him. I told Ms. McNeil that, but I wanted you to hear me say it." She clearly wanted him to suffer.

His immediate response was to seek pity. "Laura, can't we talk about this? I could use a little support right now."

"Well Chief, you get none from me. I'm not your security blanket." She remembered precisely what would hurt him the most.

"Could you just twist the knife a little more? I've never chastised you or embarrassed you in public when you decided to alter your life. In fact, damn it, I supported your following your heart."

"Well Sport, I didn't alter my life by committing murder, now did I?"

"You think I'm guilty? You *can't* believe that I actually killed those women."

"Doesn't matter what I think, my son is not living with you under these circumstances." She couldn't have asked for a better way to keep Drew to herself.

"I haven't got enough energy to argue with you. Let me talk to Drew." He could hear him in the background playing some kind of video game.

"My son is out with some friends."

"Laura, I can hear him playing on the computer."

"You're mistaken, that's just Lindsey entertaining Olivia," she lied. "The baby likes the colors from the computer games. It stimulates her visual acuity."

Andrew hung up the phone and turned to Beverly. Without saying a word, she knew what he was thinking.

"I'll check on this first thing tomorrow. We'll see if we can get Laura's attention through the court," she said, dropping her client off in the church parking lot.

"It is time for some butt-kicking with that woman. She's played me long enough. No mercy." Andrew closed the door as he received a thumbs-up from his lawyer. He walked to his car, placed the paper he had bought on the way out of the jail on the front seat, opened his briefcase and took out the poem he had written Julia days before. "Let's get this over with indeed," he told himself as he headed for a final visit.

Andrew sat in the cemetery for a long time on that picturesque summer day, long enough to accomplish his task. When he returned to the car and finally saw the headlines in the paper accusing him of killing his own patients, he was afraid to go home and yet more afraid to be alone. Finally, pure exhaustion set in and he headed home. On the way, he called the clinic. He was instructed to stop by at his earliest convenience. He turned the car around and headed there immediately, calling Toni at the QualityCare offices on his way.

After a long delay, Toni came on the phone. "I can't believe this, Andy. What's happening is appalling. What are you going to do?"

Almost begging, he said, "I just need to talk to someone. I need a friend. Can I stop by this evening?"

Toni offered an alternative. "Why don't I meet you after work?" It would be difficult to have him come over; her parents had suggested she avoid having Andrew around Maria, and they were as likely to be at her house as at their own. No, no, they weren't passing judgment, but consorting with Andrew Albright was maybe not such a good idea right at the moment.

Andrew offered an alternative. "How about I bring some sandwiches to Gallup Park? We can sit next to the river and talk about what the hell is happening. Can we do that?"

"Sure, I'll be there at six-thirty sharp." Toni really did not know what she was going to say to him. This was having a negative effect on QualityCare and she had a job to do. The staff and employees felt just about the same way Toni's parents did. Chris Cromwell almost laughed; this was certainly a good way to get Andrew off his back. It was bad for Andrew, of course, but you use whatever weapon your enemy allows you in a battle.

The impact at QualityCare paled in comparison to Partners Medical Group. When he arrived at the clinic the Executive Committee was waiting. It took them all of five minutes to suspend him, with pay at least, pending the outcome of the trial. They would not allow him to see patients. He offered to do administrative work, but was told that PMG would not be well served under the circumstances.

Andrew went home, sat and stared at the wall. What was going to happen next? He was so down he called Toni to cancel their dinner meeting. She didn't answer her phone and Andrew didn't want to talk to her secretary. Maybe it would do him good to see her.

Before leaving, he called Carol. She hadn't even said hello before he blurted out "I'm in trouble."

"I know. I heard. I don't believe you killed those women, of course. Why do the cops think it's you?"

"Beverly says they've got my hair and my fingerprints at the crime scenes, and Amy, you remember Amy? Well my trusted nurse told the detectives about that time I flipped out and said I wanted some of my patients to die."

"Holy Jesus; did you really say that?"

"Yeah. I was just mad at everybody then; here these women were alive who were gonna die anyway, and my Julia was dead and shouldn't have been. I'm sorry I said it; God knows I didn't mean it. I guess I'm paying for that blunder now rather than in hell later. It feels like I played right into the hands of whoever is behind this."

"Andy, if there's ever been a time for you to believe in God, it's now. Use your faith. And believe in yourself too; you didn't do this, after all."

"Faith is a rare commodity right now in my life."

"Why don't you come stay with us in Ft. Wayne for a few days? It might be good to get away; I've got some pretty good clout with the reporters around here; I could at least make them leave you alone."

"I would love to, Sis, but I can't leave the state. In fact, if I'm going to be out of Washtenaw County overnight, I have to let the authorities know."

Carol was trying not to cry. "You're on my mind and in my

prayers. I love you and I have faith in you. This'll all work out right, I just know it."

"Thank you, Carol. I love you too."

He avoided the reporters already camped out on his lawn, stopped by Zingerman's Deli and picked up some sandwiches before driving out Geddes Road to Gallup Park. It was a favorite spot for him. He loved the soft flow of the Huron River and enjoyed watching life go by: the joggers, Rollerbladers, and mothers with babies in strollers. It was always full of life. It was peaceful. He wondered why he'd never brought Julia there. It didn't matter now.

Toni was late, not unusual with her job. She saw no reason to tell him she'd delayed leaving because she couldn't make up her mind whether she should meet him. She'd finally come down firmly on his side: the man simply wasn't capable of murder. She may not have known him long, but she trusted her own feelings. It was time to give trust its due. She'd smiled ruefully. Right, like she'd done so well with the serpent.

She gave him a quick hug and they picked a shady spot near one of the bridges to have their picnic. It was a bit warm, but a fresh breeze blew cooler air off the river.

"So what happened? All I really know is what the radio and newspapers say."

He gave her a synopsis of his arrest and release, then added, "My attorney thinks we've got a chance, at least. But my ex is going to keep Drew away from me and PMC put me on suspension."

At a loss for what to offer him as support beyond a few empty platitudes, she decided to change the subject and tell him what she could about QualityCare's public offering. "It's close to being complete. The QualityCare Board will consider a final vote in three weeks. Depending on the publicity surrounding your case–uh, you know, how involved they might get with it–they might have to delay it, though. The financial projections have improved, which is my good news. Rumor has it that the Wall Street analysts are excited about having us in the equity markets."

"And how is Christopher?" he asked. What he really wanted to know was why his friend hadn't called him to offer support.

"Dr. Cromwell is fine. He's busy with bankers and lawyers in New York and London. He did ask me to pass a message on to you in my capacity as the corporate attorney."

"What is it? No, let me guess: I've been suspended from the Board pending the outcome of the trial."

"Yes. It makes me sad, but I want you to know that I was the one who recommended it. I had to." She felt like a traitor and wished that were the only bad news she had to give him.

"I understand. I'm not happy, but I understand." He did understand it, but it still hurt.

"Unfortunately, it gets worse." He looked at her with sad eyes. *Please do not abandon me* ran through his thoughts. Every woman important in his life had abandoned him.

"I can't see you socially right now. The criminal investigation involves QualityCare and I can't give any appearance of impropriety," she said.

"I can't believe that you too are abandoning me, just like everyone else I have ever cared for," he whimpered, without thinking.

"Give me a break here, Andy, I'm not abandoning you. I can't go out with you, is all. We can still talk on the phone, and maybe we could arrange to meet at church or something. We agreed we could be friends; we are friends."

Andrew stood and headed for his car. "We'll see, won't we?" he tossed over his shoulder, refusing to come out of his sulk. "I gotta go." He did not wait for a response, which was good, since none was forthcoming.

He went home and got wasted. He wanted to bury the pain. The more he drank, however, the more pain he felt. Every drink opened the emotional floodgates that much further. His life was caving in all around him.

Toni went home, hugged her daughter, read her a story, tapped her on the head three times and put her to bed. She went to bed wondering if having Andrew in her life would be worth putting up with his moods. "Yeah, well," she said out loud, "I suppose he's entitled to them. I don't know how I'd react if I had a murder charge hanging over my head, a girlfriend in the grave and a son I couldn't talk to."

—Chapter 35—

July ebbed into August. The District Attorney and her investigators crafted their trial strategy. Beverly and Andrew crafted theirs as well, focusing primarily on her proving that anybody could have left the evidence that pointed at Andrew. It was a defense attorney's standard fallback strategy: Blame it on someone, anyone with a potential motive and means to carry out the crime. The SODDIT Defense: Some Other Dude Did It. Reasonable doubt and sloppy police work was a defensive attorney's best friend. Beverly would have to rely on the former.

Andrew finally got an e-mail from Drew. His mother had forbidden him to send e-mails from home, so he sent it from a friend's house.

Dear Dad, I'm not sure whats going on. I'm scared. Mom wont let me call you and I dont know why. Maybe you could come here and take me home? She says you're in trubble. What could be so bad? I miss you. I want to play golf with you. Mom says we wont go back home until school starts. I hope you do what you tell me to do and smile. I hope to see you soon. I love you Drew

Beverly had a talk with Judge Parker, who had some major

concerns about Andrew's ability to care for his son while preparing for a murder trial, but she did agree that legally Laura Donaldson couldn't change the custody arrangement. Laura was pronounced in contempt of court, but since she wouldn't respond to any inquiries from Beverly or her own attorney, Mark Patterson, and Judge Parker didn't want to go to the expense of sending a marshal to California, Laura was still holding Drew hostage. As far as Laura was concerned, her ex-husband was guilty and would fall like a wooden toy soldier under the District Attorney's guns, and she was going to get full custody soon anyway, so why worry about Judge Parker and her contempt of court citation? Laura even had the nerve to call the DA to see if there was anything she could do to help her case. After a relatively short conversation, the DA decided she could well become a star witness for the prosecution.

Laura told her Michigan attorney to inform Beverly McNeil that she and Lindsey and Drew would be returning to Michigan before the start of Andrew's trial.

Andrew had called Toni the morning after their shortened visit in the park and apologized for acting like such a fool. She'd accepted it, but reminded him what she'd said about being a jerk and saying "sorry." After that they'd kept in touch on the phone, and the more she listened to him, the more certain she was that he'd been set up.

At the same time, she was also becoming more and more uncomfortable with the financial underpinnings of QualityCare's public offering: There was too much money on the table for too few executives. There was no doubt that Chris, Arthur, Dr. Meyers, and others would benefit by holding stock in the new company. In fact, even Andrew would benefit. She had seen the documentation in which he'd been offered a significant financial position in the organization if he agreed to keep PMG in the fold. Clearly this was a bribe. What she needed to know was if he had accepted the deal. If he hadn't, could there be a link between that and the murders?

The legal and loyalty chasm between her job and her friendship with Andy worried her considerably, but on the first Saturday in August, she crossed the line. She went into the office long before the sun came up. She wanted to review the files regarding how the organization had overcome its dip in the financial bottom line. The secretary kept the spare keys to the CFO's file cabinet in her desk; Toni simply took them. She used the light from the parking lot security lamps to open and read a file called "Financial Turnaround Plan, 2000."

Astonished, she realized she was reading a plan that had never been discussed with the Board or anyone else. It had to do with manipulating the IBNR to create a false turnaround. A bullet point caught her eye: • *We need to more aggressively manage our catastrophically ill patients.*

Did murdering sick patients constitute aggressive management? It certainly seemed possible to her. She needed to talk with Andy's attorney, Beverly McNeil. Toni was holding a possible motive for the murders in her hands. She stopped briefly to ask herself if she was truly being objective.

The first she knew she was no longer alone was when she heard a key hit the lock in the office door next to the CFO's, Chris Cromwell's office. She quickly hid beneath the desk, sticking the file under her sweatshirt. When he went to make coffee she tried to sneak out, but hadn't made it out of the office before he returned to his own. She couldn't leave without being seen, so she waited, her heart pounding so hard she was sure Chris could hear it through the wall. Getting caught in an office not her own with a purloined file hidden under her shirt would hardly be a good career move, and given her new information, it might just get her killed.

She was positive Chris had spotted her. She was getting ready to come out in the open when his phone rang. She said a prayer of thanks and wondered who would call at that time of the morning.

She heard Chris answer. "Chris Cromwell here. Ah, Arthur. I have been waiting for your call. Any chance we could have these chats at a more decent hour?" He paused, obviously listening before responding. "I realize it's after ten a.m. in London and you have a golf match to get to, but it's only five-twenty in the bloody morning here." Toni heard another pause and another response. "Yes, I have done everything we discussed. The financials are fine and ready to be inspected. Yes, our IBNR has improved." After a long minute, Christopher laughed and said, "That will happen when you lose some of your sickest members. I'm pretty sure that Andrew Albright did not commit these crimes, but for the time being, we are better served with this hanging over his head." Pause. "Well, I know he can't vote against us or pull PMG out of the network as things stand now."

Christopher swiveled around in his executive chair and propped his feet up on his credenza, his back now to the door of his office. For Toni it was now or never. She wanted to hear the rest of the conversation, but getting out now was more important.

She had forgotten that she'd left her car in the parking lot right under Dr. Cromwell's office window. She still couldn't risk being seen, so she walked a half a mile to a small bagel shop and stopped for some coffee. She would wait an hour and go back. It was a long hour, but it gave her time to review the file and collect her thoughts. Finishing it, she was even more convinced that there was a link between the public offering and the murder of innocent, but expensive, QualityCare members.

"'Managed Murders,' indeed," she said to herself.

The sun had risen but it was the type of overcast day that made one want it to rain just to get it over with. She was halfway back to her car when the raindrops started, turning into a light but steady rain. She looked from a distance for Chris' car, but it was gone. She waited another five minutes to make sure no one else was around. When she got to her car she saw a piece of folded paper on the windshield. Her heart quickened when she opened the note and saw Christopher Cromwell's signature. The rain had made most of the note unreadable; she could only make out the last three lines.

. . . It would be easiest for us to discuss the above at my house tonight. Please join me at 7:30. Unless I hear otherwise, I will expect you then.

Toni spent the rest of the day in a panic. Had he seen her? Had somebody else seen her and told him? She decided that Andrew wasn't the only one in a world of trouble. Shoving her worry aside, she called Beverly McNeil, who told her to come to the office at 12:30.

At a little past noon, Toni left for downtown Ann Arbor and the law offices of Harris, Steele & Washington. She picked at the Chinese food that'd been delivered while they discussed the art that adorned Beverly's office. Finally too antsy for small talk, she said, "I need to get right to the point. I perhaps shouldn't be here right now, so please take that into consideration." Beverly nodded her head and Toni continued. "I wanted to talk to you about Andrew Albright's case. There is credible evidence that indicates someone inside QualityCare had plenty of motives to want those women killed. Someone other than Andrew Albright."

"That's some pretty serious stuff. You sure you want to divulge this to me, of all people?" It was Toni's turn to nod. "Without violating your employer's rights to privacy, what can you tell me?"

"That's the problem. As you know, there isn't much I can say, or divulge to you here. Can you tell me who you plan to call as defense witnesses?"

"No, you know I'm not at liberty to talk about the details of the case with you."

The lady lawyers were at a stalemate. Each wanted to share with the other what she knew, but they couldn't do it legally.

Beverly, instead, went fishing. "I'm thinking I should cast a much wider net for collecting defense material. I've been concentrating on the chain of evidence the DA's office has. I'm playing defense, but maybe it's time to go on the offense?" She looked quizzically at Toni, who gave a barely perceptible nod. "I believe now that the murders were a business transaction. I should maybe determine what gain and for whom?" Again, a quick nod.

It was enough. They were skating on ethical ice, but hadn't broken through.

Toni went home and called Andrew. She wanted to know the level of his financial involvement in the public offering, but didn't know how to innocently ask him.

Andrew answered the phone in a playful mood. "Toni, how you be?"

"Fine. I just called to see how you were doing." She hated to lie, but it was easier than the truth at the moment. She still hadn't come up with a reasonable reason for asking him whether he'd taken QualityCare's bribe or not.

"I'm doing well in spite of the fact that my attorney tells me that my defense case is weak at best. I've been placed at the scene with no alibi. I just got off the phone with her; she says I'm in bigger trouble today than yesterday. I'm not sure who she saw this morning, but it's caused a major setback in our case. I'm beyond upset."

"What? That isn't what happened. I was the one in her office earlier."

"So you're the new star witness for the prosecutor, eh?" he teased.

Now she knew she was being played. "Hardly. I was there trying in my own feeble way to save your ass. You're still a jerk, but worth saving, I think."

"Well, then tell me how we achieve that worthy goal?" He knew she wouldn't tell him, but it was worth a try.

"Well, I could tell you in detail, but then I'd have to testify against you in court to save my own ass. Let's keep your questions within the field I can play in."

"Then I'll avoid drilling you with questions. I merely ask that you treat me the same way. That just kind of limits us to a field the size of that jail cell I spent forty-eight hours in."

She decided to just go for it. "Andy, I need to ask you a question so I can sleep tonight." She paused just long enough to let him say something negative. Hearing nothing, she continued, "Did you accept any financial incentive from QualityCare–either now or promised for the future–for supporting their public offering?"

"Not exactly an in-the-field question, now is it? Another verbal contract violated?"

"Stop playing, I need to know. Please."

"Why?"

"Chalk it up to intellectual curiosity."

"Of course I didn't. Not that Arthur wasn't prepared to offer some pretty big inducements to get me to support the program. There's an obscene amount of money in those stock options. It wasn't so much that I saw it as a bribe as much as I thought it was a conflict of interest. Besides, I had my loyalty to PMG to consider. I couldn't sell out my partners for my own gain and look in the mirror every morning. I was pretty disappointed that my partner, Bruce Meyers, fell for the bait. He'll become the

Chief Medical Officer of the new company after the offering. Anyway, I told both Chris and Arthur that I'd recommend that PMG pull out of the QualityCare network if this business decision placed us in a position that would compromise our clinical integrity. The public offering can't go too far without PMG."

"Okay. Thanks for telling me about it. Gotta run. I have my own meeting with the boss in a little while."

"Odd time to be meeting, don't you think?"

"You wouldn't believe how busy it is what with this offering and all. I'll talk to you later." She'd gotten a second motive and an explanation for the note in the file about not worrying about "BM." Bruce Meyers had been bought. She said goodbye and while neither of them said so, they missed seeing each other.

Two hours later, she pulled into Chris and Roxanne's driveway. She wasn't sure how many of her thoughts she would admit to her boss, but it was unlikely he would like any of them.

Chris opened the door and smiled. He could be charming when he wanted. He took her out back to the deck and offered her a drink. She decided a beer would be good; it might relax her. Roxanne was the one who returned with the beer and a glass. She also brought out a tray of light snacks.

"Toni, how lovely to see you. It has been too long. Chris apologizes, but he had to take a phone call. He's always on the phone these days."

The Cromwells had gotten very good at the T.O.–turnover–game. Roxanne played nice to see if Toni would say anything to her that she might not say to Chris. Then Chris would come in and close whatever deal she'd softened up the bait for.

It had worked on Andrew and others.

Toni kept up her end of the small talk. She'd always found it easy to get Roxanne to talk about Roxanne; the woman was amazingly narcissistic. Roxanne talked about a recent stay in

London and how much she enjoyed its "high tea society" as well as Great Britain's old culture. She said she was looking forward to living there one day soon. She even made a big deal about the London glassware in her hand that Arthur had given them as a present during his first trip to Michigan.

Chris came out on the deck. The earlier rains had stopped, but it was still soggy outside. Toni didn't know if it was the saturated air or her nerves making the sweat drip off of her. The three made more small talk about trivial things: the weather, vacations, and summer-end activities.

Toni decided she'd follow Beverly's lead and go on the offensive. "Chris, I know you didn't leave a note on my car to have me stop by and chat about your trip to Europe and the weather. The rain destroyed most of what you wrote, so I'm not sure why I'm here. Why don't you just get to what's on your mind?"

Taken slightly off guard, Christopher hesitated. "I can do that. My note told you that I knew you were in the office early this morning. I told you I expect and demand your loyalty. The reason that I asked you here is to find out if I have it."

"Do you have my loyalty?" She had prepared responses to many questions that might come up, but this hadn't been one of them.

"That's the question on the table. A simple yes will do," he said, obviously trying to be cute yet intimidating.

"You've always had my respect and loyalty, Chris, and you'll keep them until they're no longer deserved. Do you deserve them?" she asked bluntly, not willing to be either cute or intimidated.

"Well, I certainly don't think I've done anything *not* to deserve them, if that's an answer."

"Sort of, I suppose. See, the thing is, I'm worried about this shareholder deal. I think there's a potential correlation between the financial deals on the table and the deaths of those women.

I believe that there is plenty of motive to go around and I may even know who's involved." Law School 101. Place an accusation on the table and see if the other party gets defensive.

Roxanne had heard enough and excused herself. She knew that the social side of the evening was over.

Christopher went cold. "If you are suggesting that anyone associated with this project is involved in these murders, you are completely wrong. I have a hard time believing that my friend Andrew Albright did this, but the evidence seems to clearly point in that direction. I trust justice will prevail, but only time will tell."

"Chris," she said, rising to leave, "I've grown more and more convinced that there was a calculated plot to frame Dr. Albright for those murders. I believe that Andy,"–Chris raised his eyebrows at the familiarity the nickname implied–"didn't do this, somebody else did, and I hope you aren't, and weren't, a part of it."

He made a mental note that it would be important to prove her assertion false. He looked away before answering. "Toni," he said, "your loyalty is very important right now. We go live on Wall Street in two weeks. The Board will finalize its position this coming week. You can't go soft on me now. The business community would see straight through you. Everyone would feel your doubts, even if you thought you were keeping them hidden."

Toni had heard enough.

As she reached the front door, she suddenly turned around and faced him. "You know what? I just made up my mind. I don't want to be a part of this hypocrisy. It smells like spring flowers on the surface, but underneath is nothing but putrid, spoiled crap."

She left. She didn't need a response from him to know what to do next. She knew in her heart that she had a bright future. She smiled at herself in the rearview mirror and tapped her head three times.

—Chapter 36—

Early Monday morning, Toni called Christopher's office to see if she could make an appointment with him for later in the day. She was told he was available right then and there. She had no time to collect her thoughts, which was a good thing. This was now going to come from the heart. Christopher was sure that he was in for another lecture on business ethics. He was in no mood for it.

Chris met her in his anteroom. "Come right in, but tread lightly."

She calmly shut the door. "I doubt you'll find what I have to say 'light.' I'm sticking to what I said last night. I'm going to resign my position as corporate counsel here at QualityCare effective September fifteenth. That should give you time to start looking for my replacement."

"Can you tell me where you're going?" He didn't care as long as it didn't impede his public offering.

"No, though not because it's a secret. Frankly, I have no job lined up." It petrified her to be jobless.

"So why are you really leaving?"

"Oh my God, Christopher, rewind the tapes from Saturday and ask me that again. In the corporate world, most people don't leave their job; they leave their boss. You've always treated me fairly, and I'm happy I got a chance to work here, but it's time for me to leave."

"So, why leave? Your timing couldn't be worse for me or the organization."

"Why leave? Try: 'because I don't trust you,' and that's very bad for both of us. You don't want me around dealing with the press and Wall Street under these circumstances, trust me on that."

"I'm distressed that you've lost faith in me. I fear that you see an unsavory intent in my heart. I can assure you that just isn't so," he said in his sincerest tone of voice.

She wasn't persuaded. "That's for the courts to figure out. I won't stand idle while you let a good man take the fall for your greed. Maybe you should be investigated. Regardless, I don't want to work here any longer."

"I guess I'll just have to accept that," he said with a sigh, wondering how to break the news to Arthur. Being a suspect in a murder case would hardly be good and the timing could not be worse.

He dismissed her. She started to say something else, shrugged, shook her head and left. At 5:30 that evening Christopher and the VP for Human Resources showed up in her office.

Chris stood in the doorway. "Under the circumstances," he said, "we believe it ill-advised for you to continue to work until your resignation date. You are to leave immediately. We will pay you through the end of September. Security will remove your things."

There were no more words. Christopher wasn't about to let Toni gather evidence to confirm her suspicions from his very own office. She couldn't even take her own books, files, résumés, or other personal items; they would be boxed up for her and sent to her home.

As soon as she got home, she called Andrew to let him know what happened. Andrew felt pangs of guilt. He cautiously asked if he was the cause of her leaving.

She put that notion to rest. "No. Given what I know now, I don't understand why on earth these financial deals haven't been challenged already. The good news is that I no longer have a reason to keep my distance from you. Maybe we can get together later this week?"

"I don't know Toni, my attorney claims you're Public Enemy Number One. Do you think it would be wise for me to be seen with you?"

"Ha. I may be the best friend you have right now. Thursday good? We can get together and commiserate while the QualityCare Board makes Chris, Arthur and Bruce Meyers rich."

Andrew bridled, thinking about Dr. Meyers's selling out, but shoved it away in the corner of his mind. "It's a date, or at least a get together."

"We can call it a date; even friends and good Italian Catholic girls date."

"Fine then, it's a date."

Andrew wasn't sure he was ready for a "date" with Toni, but he did want her friendship in the worst way. She, Beverly, and Carol seemed to be his only lifelines to the world these days. If he lost hold of any of them, he was afraid he'd drift off the planet entirely.

Toni had a difficult time explaining to Papa why she was out of a job, but part of being in a close Italian family required that one shares everything and Toni did. He was a traditional Italian man. He had spent thirty years working for one law enforcement agency or another. His latest stint was with the Michigan State Police. He was very protective of his daughter. This latest change of events was disturbing to him, and he went into paternal protection mode.

"Toni, you don't know what you're dealing with here. Someone is either killing, or paying someone to kill, people who get in their way. You have just quit an organization that could be very dangerous. Now you want to go out with the doctor who's at the center of the storm. Why not just take some time and we can take Maria away for a few weeks?"

"Papa, I love it when you try to protect me, but your first mistake was to raise such an independent daughter. You and Mama may live a block away and I appreciate how much you look after Maria, but I'm my own person, as scary as that may be at times. I admit, a part of me wants to run away and hide, but that's not who I am. I have to do what I believe is right. Do you remember when I told you I was going to Washington?"

"Of course, and I tried to talk you into doing something that would be less demanding to keep you here."

Toni continued. "I told you then and I tell you now, I want to make a difference on this earth. A brilliant and innocent man is accused of doing bad things. Am I to sit by and watch from the sidelines?" Not waiting for an answer she said, "I think not. Making a difference in this world is not always convenient and it is not always risk free."

"Please remember Maria, and be careful with what you do. There are plenty of people who can help. Should I call a few of my law enforcement buddies?"

"Papa, you know me. When I need your help I'll ask for it." She hugged him and he kissed her on the cheek.

Toni headed for bed and Papa for the phone. She wasn't asking for help, but he was going to make sure she got it anyway. He stayed to make a few calls before heading home to Mama; he saw no reason to upset her with any of this.

Thursday night came and Andrew met Toni at the Gandy Dancer. He remembered it as the place he and Julia had had their first date, and thought it ironic that he and Toni had so many reasons to avoid intimacy, which made it the primary reason they felt so comfortable together, where he and Julia had *only* been looking for intimacy.

Toni had suggested they meet at the restaurant at 7:30; she didn't want to provoke her father by having Andrew pick her up at the house. She was late getting to dinner and had to park a quarter of a mile up Depot Road. As she walked to the restaurant, she had a feeling that someone was watching her. It was still light outside and she put it out of her mind. She chalked it up to Papa making her paranoid.

Andrew was already seated and having a glass of wine when Toni arrived. "Ah, you look lovely," he said, with a smile and a hug.

She was wearing a black cocktail dress that made her face light up with the combination of her brunette hair and olive complexion. It was almost identical to the dress Julia had worn on their first date. He pulled her chair out and gave her a quick kiss on the cheek as she sat down.

"Thank you. I apologize for being late, but I have two good reasons."

"And they would be?"

She took the two packages out of a bag. "You told me that your ex was bringing Drew home. I figured the two of you had some catching up to do before he goes back to school, so I got you something that might help."

He opened the bags. Golf balls. "Hey, that was nice of you. My golf game is in such shambles, though, that these balls aren't likely to last long, but they'll make nice sacrifices to the golf gods."

She looked at him with puzzlement. He explained that losing golf balls was part of the game. If a golfer expected the golf gods to smile on him occasionally, you had to make sacrifices to them.

"Gee, I had no idea that golf was such a religious event."

"You have no idea." They both laughed. "And reason number two? Maybe because you were getting your hair done?"

She was delighted he noticed. "As a matter of fact, it was having my nails done that made me late." Again, they laughed. Deep down he was happy she'd made the effort to impress him and she was happy he'd not only noticed it, but also appeared appreciative. Neither of them talked about work during dinner other than to compare notes on how it felt to be unemployed.

Across town, Chris Cromwell and Arthur Bishop were having a tough night. QualityCare's Board loudly decried Toni Vincenzo's decision to resign. They also commented back and forth as to whether they thought Andrew Albright was guilty or innocent, but mostly they worried about his connection with the organization and how his trial would reflect on them. And they were particularly concerned with PMG's stability; Bruce Meyers assured the Board that the clinic was a stable supporter of their business venture.

The last bone of contention before the Board made its final vote was the financial incentives for the executives that were to be included in the offering. Chris was to get 250,000 stock options priced at sixteen dollars each. Arthur Bishop was to get 450,000 and Bruce Meyers was granted 100,000 at the same price. Stock options were typically used to create incentives for employees to stay with the company. It was also a tidy mechanism used to reward management for keeping the stock price increasing, which is what the shareholders wanted. Each recipient could exercise these options over a three-year period. For every dollar that the stock went up in price, Chris would have a paper profit of a cool quarter of a million dollars.

The Board asked that Christopher, Bruce and Arthur step outside. Mary Goodwin led the debate with Philip Kunkle playing counterpoint by justifying the virtues of good incentives. They argued the ethics of the stock options and after an hour concluded that they would support the final proposal, but only if the options were taken off the table until the organization could develop a more equitable plan for all its employees. The Board knew it was now or never for them–once the offering happened they would no longer exist. A new Board of Directors elected by the shareholders would take their place–a Board dominated by Arthur Bishop pawns.

The three men returned. None was happy with the outcome, but they were also realistic. It would be relatively easy to develop and incorporate a stock option plan with the new QualityCare Board. They were surprised to learn that the vote hadn't been unanimous: three holdouts thought that health care didn't belong in the hands of Wall Street. Andrew would have clearly been number four.

Andrew and Toni finished up dinner. Then they stopped in the bar for an after-dinner drink. Neither wanted to hurry home; neither had much to hurry home to. Maria would have been in bed for hours, and Andrew's home was lonely and dark. They dawdled over their drinks but finally had to call it a night.

"Where's your valet ticket?" Andrew asked her. "I'll have them get both cars at the same time."

"I didn't use the valet; I parked just up the street. I love to walk and I hate the valet. It makes us lazy."

Andrew pretended he was insulted. "So that would make me lazy, then?"

"No, just settled in your habits," she said, letting him off the hook. She hugged him and turned to leave. He grabbed her hand. She thought he was going to kiss her.

Instead, he said, "I can at least drive you to your car. I won't take no for an answer. There's no reason for you to walk alone at this time of night."

She didn't argue, secretly wondering if she wanted a goodnight kiss. They got in Andrew's car and he pulled up just on the other side of Depot Road from her car. She hesitated briefly before getting out. She didn't know if she was disappointed that he hadn't kissed her or not. Before closing the door, she touched her fingers to her lips and then to his. "Thanks for a nice evening. I hope there are more of these in our future."

"You're welcome, and I suspect there will be."

"Huh. You just made a verbal contract. Don't mess with Italian attorneys, we never forget." She winked at him and walked toward her car. He waited until she got in her car before heading home.

Her heart skipped a beat when she couldn't get her Honda into gear. It skipped another and nearly exploded when a man dressed in all black tapped on her passenger-side window.

—Chapter 37—

Toni's first instinct was to reach for her phone. But almost before the thought formed, the stranger showed her his gun and motioned for her to open the door. The gun was black with a silver handle. What caught her eye, however, was the long barrel of a silencer. Only killers used silencers. This was not a robbery. Toni had two choices. She could either run for it or let the man in her car. She didn't think he'd shoot her right there on a busy street, so she unlocked the door and turned on the overhead light.

Her thoughts were racing. On Saturday she'd accused Christopher Cromwell of murdering Paula Callaway or of having it done. He couldn't get her out of the office fast enough on Monday. And now here she was with a man who had a gun in her face. *You must be Cromwell's hatchet man,* she thought. And then, suddenly: *Oh, my God, I'm going to die!*

"Turn off the lights," was all he said.

She apparently didn't do it fast enough. He used the butt end of the gun to break it. It wouldn't do to have anyone see them together; he had to get her into his van, shoot her, load her body into a boat and then dump it in Ford Lake. This job would pay a fat bonus, his last. The man in black wanted to take his money and run.

"You are coming with me. Fifty yards behind us is a van, color white. You will walk very calmly to the van and get in. If you do not follow my directions, my partner will do very bad things to your daughter. He might even have some fun with your parents. He is in a car outside your home right now."

She could not know that, in fact, he had no partner.

She tried to buy some time. "Why are you doing this to me? What've I done? Did you kill Paula Callaway? Who are you?"

He spoke slowly and methodically. "All you need know is that I can hurt people when I need to. Please don't make me hurt you. It's time; let's go, Toni."

She was surprised he knew her name, but it fit right in with her suspicions: a stranger just out for the usual mugging wouldn't know his victim's name, but a hitman acting on orders from his boss would. And it certainly fit that that boss could be Cromwell.

Like it did her any good to figure that out now, she thought.

"May I take my purse?" She had pepper spray in her purse, a gift from Papa.

"I don't care what you take, but we're leaving now." The man in black was getting nervous. The longer he sat in the car the less control he had over the situation.

She attempted to get the pepper spray out of her purse, but dropped it on the way out of the car. So much for her plan to spray him as soon as she hit the sidewalk and run past Wheeler Park toward Casey's Pub. She decided instantly that her father could handle any trouble coming his way at home and she had to worry about herself–if she got in that van, she wasn't going to get out alive.

Her assailant put his gun back inside his black leather coat. He saw her bend down to pick up her purse. He was getting agitated, in a hurry to get her shut up in the van. He thought a little physical force might be in order. Just as he started walking toward her, he heard two loud voices coming from somewhere in the dark of Wheeler Park.

"Stop where you are, fella! Don't move! This is the Ann Arbor police."

Toni ducked behind her car as soon as she heard them. Her assailant reacted instantly, firing one shot toward the car, not so much to hit Toni as to make them check on her first. He bolted straight across the street and across the railroad tracks. Having never anticipated this scenario, he panicked for the first time in this whole engagement. He stumbled and then fell, cutting his leg on the jagged edge of a railroad spike. As he had hoped, one cop had stopped to check on Toni, but the other was hitting the street just as he was hitting an eight-foot chain-link fence. He surveyed his options: climb the fence or head west away from the train station in hopes of finding an opening.

Both options were poor ones while his leg was throbbing and bleeding badly. His prior military training kicked in: When in doubt, fire at the enemy and retreat. He positioned himself in the darkness of an old oak tree waiting for his pursuer to give him a clean shot. He could hear the police radio of the officer who was cautiously advancing while waiting for back up. It was now or never. The man in black popped into the open, fired a shot and hit his target.

Waiting only a moment, he ran, hearing a faint cry for help. "Officer down. Officer down, north side of Depot west of the train station."

Salvatore Vincenzo was one of the first to arrive on the scene among the sirens and confusion back at the park. He had wanted to follow her himself, but he'd known that Toni would disown him if he got caught, so he'd trusted his buddies to do the job.

Toni was visibly shaken when Papa got to her. "Are you okay? I knew you shouldn't go out with that doctor."

"How did you know I was in danger?" she gasped. He just smiled and hugged her. She told her story to the detectives who showed up and left her car where it was so the police could collect any forensic evidence that might be in it. It wasn't until they got to Toni's house, that Toni regained her composure and heard the rest of the story.

"I was worried about you. I haven't trusted your doctor friend since he was arrested. I haven't heard good things about him. I was afraid you were in danger. After a lifetime in law enforcement, one just has instincts that cannot be ignored."

"Oh, Papa, trust me. Andrew is a good man. The man who attacked me didn't have anything to do with him, though I think he could've had something to do with the murders."

"What makes you so sure he didn't hire this man to kill for him?"

"Why would Andrew pay a man to kill those women and then have him plant physical evidence that would incriminate himself?"

Papa had no answer for that. "Would you like me to stay here tonight?"

"Thanks Papa, but you go home to Mama."

"Your attacker is still out there." There was no response. "Antionette, did you hear me?"

"Yes, I heard you. I'm a big girl. Now go home." She hugged him and escorted him out the door. She checked every door and window in the house before climbing into bed with Maria.

At the same time, the man in black was nursing his wounds and trying to explain to his boss how things had gotten so screwed up, but the boss was furious. Why hadn't he picked a better place? Why hadn't he popped her at home, like the others? How could he have been so stupid as to put both of them at such risk?

He was a horse's ass and he for sure wasn't getting paid any more money for this kind of screw up.

The following morning, Andrew and Carol went to the airport to pick up Drew. Neither was aware of Toni's attack the night before. Andrew grabbed his copy of the *Ann Arbor News* off the driveway before heading to the airport. While waiting for Drew, he read a brief report about a police incident that occurred right where he and Toni had been the night before.

Drew came running up to his dad, leaving his mom far behind. Andrew gasped as Drew practically tackled him. "Wow, little man! You're not so little anymore, are you?"

"I'm up to ninety pounds. Mom promised that when I get to a hundred I can play football in the Peewee League. I think I'm close enough, don't you?"

Andrew staggered back, put his arm around his son and said, "Oh yeah."

Andrew said nothing to Laura as they waited at the baggage claim. Drew's bags came off first. Laura and Lindsey's bags hadn't circled out and Olivia was fussing by the time Andrew was ready to leave. "We're going to take off," he said. "I know you have a meeting with the DA tomorrow morning; it surely must have been important to be meeting on a Saturday."

She so wanted to rub his nose in her plan, but she couldn't say anything until she'd spoken with Rebecca. "Aren't you going to drive us home?" was the best snipe she could come up with.

"Not bloody likely," he sneered in her ear. Drew hugged his mother and the men left.

They bought a pizza and rented a movie on their way home. As they were sitting around eating the pie, Andrew stopped procrastinating and broached the trial subject. "Do you know what's going on out here?" he asked. Drew nodded tentatively; he didn't really understand it all, but he did know his father was in trouble.

"Well," Andrew explained, "two women were killed in Ann Arbor several months ago. Some people think I did it."

"You wouldn't do that!"

"Ah, thank you. But how do you know that?" He wondered what Laura, or worse yet, Lindsey, had said about his case.

"Because you're my dad, that's how I know."

Unconditional love was just what Andrew needed.

The next morning, Saturday, Andrew wanted to do something normal with Drew, so they went shopping for school clothes with Carol. At the rate Drew was growing, nothing fit him anymore. Later that evening after Drew had succumbed to the jet lag, the phone rang. It was Beverly. Andrew put her on the speakerphone so Carol could hear what she had to say.

"Andrew, I've just heard some alarming news. We have a problem. Laura's role as a key witness for the DA is now very clear."

"Don't tell me she's going to paint me as a bad father, too?"

Beverly had an edge of anger to her tone. "It's worse than that. Laura's going to testify about a fight you had with your father while you were in college. She claims you assaulted him and he ended up in the hospital and you in jail. I've got my researcher looking for the arrest record right now, but it looks legitimate. You *know* Rebecca Bridgeman is going to portray you as a bitter and violent man. Why didn't you tell me about this?"

"Because the courts eventually dropped the charge and it wasn't a big deal. How did you find out what Laura said?"

"She was bragging in the hallway about it. A friend heard it and called me. We need to talk about this as soon as we can. We can be certain this'll come up and be damaging at trial."

"Fine, add it to the list," he said abruptly.

Beverly hung up, perplexed.

Carol, near tears, whispered, "I was afraid this was going to happen. Damn Laura anyway. Why couldn't she have left this alone?"

"Because she's a bitch, that's why," he said with his head in his hands. He looked up and found Carol weeping. "Carol, I don't care how bad this thing gets, we're not talking about that day with anyone. Understood?"

"Andy, we may have no choice. Oh my god, this could ruin me. I thought that day was left in the past."

Andrew walked over and held his sister in his arms. "We do have a choice. Say nothing!"

—Chapter 38—

The next two weeks passed quickly. Andrew and Drew did as much as they could together: played golf, went fishing, hung out at the neighborhood pool, where Drew got a chance to reconnect with his friends before going back to school.

Toni was also busy. She met with Beverly twice, but she wasn't in a position to review any of the material that pertained to the subpoena Beverly got that generated two boxes of QualityCare's files. She did though, tell her story and her suspicions about her post dinner run-in with the man in black. She shared her thoughts and theories about how it all fit together. Beverly took copious notes and they discussed whether to inform Andrew—answer, no.

During the second meeting they discussed specifically how to deal with Laura's testimony about Andrew's assault on his father. They decided that Beverly needed to sit down with Carol and try to get the story out of her. Toni would take a crack at Andrew, though they agreed it was unlikely that either would spill the story: both had already shown significant resistance to shedding any light on the subject.

Toni had talked with Beverly about the research Beverly's paralegal had done on the fight. Since there'd been no trial, the facts were thin. What she could gather made it clear that Andrew had stepped into the middle of an altercation between father and daughter. If he wouldn't talk, then Carol would have to, eventually. Surely she wanted to help her brother.

Andrew introduced Drew to Toni at the pool on a hot and muggy August afternoon. At almost ten, with two mothers and his father's girlfriend behind him, Drew was profoundly unimpressed at meeting another old lady, but was correctly polite to Toni. She saw a nice young man in Drew, much like his father. He stayed around just long enough to cover the civilities and then joined his friends belly-flopping off the diving board and dunking girls in the water.

Toni, ignoring her inauspicious effect on Drew, tried to get Andrew to explain what had happened that day with his father. She leaned close enough to talk in a whisper. "You should tell Beverly what happened with your father, you know. It would really help, I think." She received no response. After a long, silent minute, she said, "Andy, it's important. We're damned lucky to have found out about this before trial."

"Lucky?" he sneered. "Why? In fact, what do you know about it?" Andrew had only talked briefly with Julia about it, and he was damn sure not going to do it again. It was in the past. It was going to stay in the past. Besides, it had nothing whatsoever to do with either his or his sister's life in the here and now, and it certainly didn't have anything to do with this stupid trial.

"I don't have many details, but it's obvious that something provoked you into beating your own father damned near senseless. It will be critical for the jury to see your side of the story, Andy, because if they don't, they'll think you're capable of losing control enough to kill three women you didn't like."

Since he knew the truth, he just couldn't credit that his fight with his father had anything to do with the murder trial so he said, "You know, I didn't ask your advice on this one. Stay out of it. Don't go there."

Exasperated, his refusal to talk just made her wonder and worry more about what happened that day and what he had to hide.

They changed the subject by mutual but unspoken agreement, going on to discuss trivial things like Drew's weight, Andrew's landscaping plans, Toni's résumé. They didn't discuss a possible bad outcome to the trial. Andrew refused to think about living in sixty-four square feet for the rest of his life—or worse yet, not living at all.

Toni said she was considering going back to the political fray in Washington D.C., or, closer to home, Lansing. She had opportunities in health care at the state level. She also thought she could work for a local law firm; she'd already received several inquires—Toni was known as talent worth going after.

She listed her future choices almost absently-mindedly. But this was the first Andrew had heard anything about her leaving, and it shocked him. Maybe from blindness, maybe from necessity, maybe from need, but the thought that she could just dump him scared him to death. "You know you're not allowed to leave Ann Arbor?" was about the best he could come up with to cover his fear of being left.

"Last I checked, I was a big girl capable of making big-girl decisions. But, I admit I'm an Italian family girl who wants Maria to grow up around her Nana and Papa."

"In my opinion, family should get fifty-one percent of the vote."

The rest of the afternoon passed without additional fireworks. Drew appeared to be comfortable around Toni, which pleased Andrew. They called it a day and Andrew took his son back to his ex-wife. He went home and got ready for what would be a long next day.

***

August 26th was the anniversary of Julia's accident and proved to be as difficult a day as he'd expected. He didn't sleep well that night, virtually staying awake for twenty-four hours. He gave up the idea of sleeping, had breakfast, then sat alone in his study and wrote notes in his journal. His thoughts circled around, dived into memories, disappeared into space, came back as resolutions which dissipated into fog, then came back to center and anchor him: friendship. Friendship had always been missing to some degree in his marriage to Laura. He wondered why he had missed the fact that it had not been a strength with Julia. Had the passion and fun masked the facts? He was left with the realization that he had truly never had a partnership with either of the women in his life.

Andrew scribbled madly away in his study. He thought that if he got every conceivable thought about the connection between men and women he'd ever had down on paper it would somehow make his ideas true.

Andrew left for the cemetery with his latest poem and a small cross that he had bought. He stopped to buy some lilies. It was a gloomy day both weather and mood-wise. Andrew took a walk around the cemetery before he stood with his codependent rock. He was looking for the right words.

He wondered what his life would have been like if Julia had lived. He wondered what his four-month-old daughter would have been like. He thought about Toni and how different the two women were. He was almost shocked at himself for thinking about another woman while standing next to Julia's grave. Usually he was totally focused on Julia while he was there. But this day was different.

Julia was gone.

Maybe it was time for him to say good-bye?

He straightened up, rearranged the flowers a little bit, moved backward, stepped forward again. He wanted to leave, but couldn't bring himself to it quite yet. Finally he said, "Julia, I'm not sure why, but we failed each other. I thank God you were a part of my life, but it's time for me to move on."

Andrew left the cemetery and started to drive to Toni's house with the poem he'd written for her, but then he abruptly changed his mind. Writing poems had always been a way for him to discharge pent-up emotions, too sensitive for him to talk about. His poem to Toni was like that, but it suddenly occurred to him that Toni wasn't likely to read it that way. She'd probably tell him he was testing her again . . . and he was, wasn't he?

He wanted to stay in his safety zone, the place he'd carved out to keep the demons at bay, but he'd tried that, and it hadn't worked, the demons had come slashing and frothing at him anyway.

He'd just said good-bye to his dream girl.

It was a good time to say good-bye to his old way of life, too.

He almost laughed, thinking of what he'd just saved Toni from.

—Chapter 39—

Andrew had a barbecue at his house for Team Albright on Labor Day. Carol and her husband came in from Indiana; Carol had decided to stay at Andrew's place through the end of the trial. Beverly McNeil and her husband Travis Washington came. Toni left Maria with her Nana and Papa and joined the meeting in progress.

Beverly set the tone for the afternoon. "We've got some specific concerns that need to addressed here. Besides the obvious things we've talked about and that I'll review shortly, the first thing I want to discuss is jury selection. I want to get your feedback on my thinking. First, I believe we get hurt with a female jury. We want professional men and retired women."

"These victims were all women and the DA is going to paint Andrew as having anger issues with women. The last thing we need is a panel of young female jurors. We also get hurt with anyone who has had or is close to someone who has had a serious illness," Toni said.

"Right," Beverly concurred. "We should also avoid anyone who's got a bias toward doctors in general."

Travis commented, "You need to be careful of the race issue, Bev."

"Why on earth would you suggest that I avoid minorities on the panel? Hell, I can win them over hands down."

"Take a look in the mirror. You're a black female representing a rich white client. How do you think that makes some liberal brothers and sisters feel? I don't think we can ignore the race issues here. You're gonna have to trust me on this one."

"Yes, but how likely is it that they'll be interested in, or make any waves about this trial? Thank you for the reminder, but I don't think we need to worry about them." Beverly went on to the next matter. "I know we've been over this many times, but I remind you, Andrew, Rebecca's job will to establish that you're an angry, bitter man. It will be very personal, and it will hurt. For certain we'll hear from your nurse, Amy, about those 'they should be dead' comments, and we'll hear from Laura about the fight with your father. The DA submitted a long list of possible witnesses, so we'll probably hear from others, back to when you were five years old pulling the neighbor girl's pigtails. And, we need to decide if we're going to put you on the stand."

Andrew jumped in. "Are you nuts? Of course I'm going to testify. The jury needs to see and hear me tell the truth."

Toni immediately disagreed. "The DA will play you like a fiddle. She'll push every button you've got. What'll you say about Laura, the "evil" one? What's your opinion of Lindsey? How about your mother? It wouldn't take much before she got you to admit that you are, in fact, pretty disgusted with the lot of us. And if you get the least bit angry on the stand you'll make the DA's case just that much easier. Besides, what are you going to testify to as your alibi? You were home alone, which of course you were. You get up there and we lose. You lose."

Beverly weighed in. "As your attorney, my advice would be to avoid the stand, but we can weigh the pros and cons again later. I will need to call Carol as a witness early in our defense." She turned to Carol. "You're not only a credible witness but can add some counter-balancing to some of the testimony that Ms. Bridgeman is going to present."

Carol flung a wild looked at Andrew and then looked away and stared at a rose bush like she'd never seen one in her life.

"That's fine, as long as you don't ask her any questions about my father," Andrew said.

"Dr. Albright, I can't defend you if you cut off my avenues to rebut the evidence that the DA presents. I know you know what's at risk here."

"I am only going to say this one more time: That subject is off limits."

Raising her voice, Toni said, "Holy Jesus, Andy, you're going to hear it tomorrow. I'd bet all that I have that the DA's going to mention it in her opening argument."

Travis agreed. "The District Attorney has to pin you down on this. Use your head, man. Get it out of the way up front."

Carol was going to speak when Andrew took her hand and just shook his head no.

Beverly made a mental note to get Carol alone for a one on one. They moved on to the physical evidence. The defense would be simple: Someone else planted it there. The hair was easier to explain than the glass with his fingerprints. Toni's assignment was to work on the glass defense. The last major point of contention was what to do with Drew. Andrew did not want him in the courtroom. The attorneys overruled him. It would be good to have him seen sitting behind his father. Little messages played big in these cases. They discussed Beverly's opening statement and called it a day.

No one slept well that night, particularly Carol, who was tortured with indecision: Should she sacrifice herself to help her brother? If she was certain it would do a bit of good she'd have jumped in immediately, but who knew?

Andrew awoke on the first morning of the trial with a strange feeling of peace. He had reconciled himself to the fact that his fate was in Beverly's hands—it was too late to change that, so he just had to trust that he'd done the right thing by sticking with her even when she'd made it plain that she didn't think she was his best choice.

The trial officially started with the tedious process of jury selection. Team Albright's secret weapon was Travis Washington, whose special gift had always been jury selections. But even with his guidance they didn't seat a favorable panel and had to consider the even split of six women and six men a small victory. The demographics weren't a bit favorable; at least a third of the jury had a family member who had been seriously ill.

Advantage Rebecca.

Beverly expressed her disappointment at the end of the day. "The first battle in every trial is important, and we just got our collective butt kicked. We need an early victory tomorrow." It wasn't quite as bad as she made it, but she wanted to scare either Carol or Andrew into opening the door for a discussion about his father. It had no effect on him.

Just before leaving, Beverly took Toni and Carol aside and said, "Please get him to reconsider. Laura's testimony is going to hurt us in a bad way."

Carol, cringing inside, said, "It won't do any good, I can promise you that." Her brother was protecting her. She just hoped that keeping their secret wouldn't have a negative impact on the outcome of the trial.

That night Carol, Toni, and Andrew had a glass of wine and tried to relax. Andrew was going to spend some time with Drew. Toni and Carol agreed to go through Julia's belongings; Andrew had finally decided to donate her things to charity.

In the basement, Carol asked Toni, "Did you know that I was the matchmaker in Julia and Andy's relationship?"

"No. He doesn't really talk much about her to me. Probably because I don't let him."

Carol was for a moment taken aback. "Why not?"

"The past is the past. What good does it do to go over it and over it? I know that he loved her. I know that he still misses her. But I believe in the here and now, and the here and now is Andy's trial. I can help him with that; there's not a thing I can do or that he can do about Julia's death."

The women came across Julia's wrinkled wedding dress. They both wondered silently why it was so rumpled; neither wanted to think that Andrew had been in the box.

"Well, I hadn't thought about it like that. Andy and I have always commiserated and held each other's hands. I suppose it just got to be the way things were, and I didn't think of it as either good or bad. We both focused ourselves on our careers. Probably at the expense of our personal lives. Julia and I were a lot alike, which made her a good choice to bring Andy out of the dumps about Laura and Drew. Now, I don't know."

"Why?"

"Maybe he needed somebody more like you all along; somebody who wouldn't play into his fears, who maybe had them herself. Someone with more balance in her life. I loved Julia like a sister. I reach for the phone every now and then, thinking about something she'd get a kick out of and then remember she's not here anymore. But she wasn't terribly strong, emotionally, just like Andy."

Carol found Julia's diary in the last box; she knew they couldn't just throw it away. She read a few passages near the end that indicated that Julia thought she was pregnant. Carol gasped. Andrew had never told her about that. In a way she was grateful because it would surely have added fuel to the DA's fire of Andrew's alleged bitterness. "Why don't you keep this? In time, Andrew will want it. Julia shared some of it with me last year; she was a good writer, and it's an interesting read. You should try it."

Toni felt about as awkward as she ever had. She wanted to read the diary and yet she didn't. Keeping it would remind him of her. Did she want that? On the other hand, if he didn't mind if she read it, it might serve as a good test to see if he could let her go. Did she want that? She almost laughed. If she was having this much trouble dealing with a little diary, she had to admit to herself that she was probably falling in love with Andrew.

And, well, why not? He was an intelligent, nice guy. He was honest, as shown by his refusal to take a bribe, and she'd certainly met her share of those who would. He noticed and responded to the people around him. He loved his son and would probably be a good man to have around Maria. He might be moody and she thought he had clung too long to his grief, but on the other hand, that was certainly better than being so callous as to run right out and find another partner as soon as it was socially decent to do so. He was a doctor, he owned a house and he was single. And he seemed to think she was pretty cool, too.

Of course, he was also on trial for murder.

Carol, having no idea where Toni's thoughts had taken her, said, "Keep it, Toni. He's your friend. Julia read some of it to me, so I see no violation of her private thoughts."

They quit the basement, went back upstairs and found Andrew staring out the window.

With a heavy sigh, he said, "How do you explain to your son that people are accusing his dad of killing two women? Both his parents are losers, poor kid."

"Andy, I have the perfect thing for you." Carol disappeared into the guest bedroom. She returned with a yellowed piece of typing paper. "Years ago you wrote me a poem just after my first election run. As you recall, I lost in a landslide. Sit down and close your eyes. Go back to that day. Can you picture it?"

"I can."

"Listen and pay attention to the words." She read them alound:

"The Mirror
You look in the mirror, and see
What it is that you so want to be.
You question who you really are
The answer, however, is never far.

You look away to avoid the reflection.
You run, you hide, you loath the inspection.
You rely on others to accept and approve,
Yet it's only your heart that you need to move.

My friend, do not fear what is in the mirror
For the truth you will find is rarely clearer.
Reality is something we cannot hide;
Though many good people have often tried.

Reach inside and conquer the pain.
Without the effort there is no gain.
When you love the image that you see,
You'll become the person you want to be."

Toni headed for home, Carol for bed, and Andrew for his den. As much as he wanted to escape into the world of peaceful sleep, it would not come that evening.

–Chapter 40–

The courtroom was crowded. Murder cases always packed the house, but this was different. This was one of Ann Arbor's favorite sons versus the world. The reporters took an informal vote: the results split right down the middle. They agreed the verdict would be determined by the skill of the attorneys.

Judge Bennett entered his courtroom. He was short, pudgy, and balding. His bow tie and tiny glasses made him look professorial and grandfatherly. He had a quiet, yet austere, manner and respecting him was easy. He took care of the preliminary procedures and turned the room over to Ms. Bridgeman, who was ready to go with her opening statement. She was, as always, confident that she would prevail.

She looked directly at the men in the jury. She needed to win them over; she thought the trial would hinge on the men. She believed she already had the women. Rebecca was petite, blond and very attractive, which didn't hurt her. She dressed conservatively, without accentuating her figure; she wasn't going to run the risk of annoying the female jurors into disliking her. She knew how to play to a crowd, one of the key reasons she was a rising star in the DA's office. It was also why so many people predicted a successful career climb in her future.

"Ladies and gentlemen of the jury, I am Assistant District

Attorney Rebecca Bridgeman. I will present a case about an embittered man who cannot control his anger. We will establish a pattern to show how Dr. Albright has reacted to the anger-provoking events in his life.

"I will paint a picture for you of a man who's lived through some pretty humiliating and life-changing disasters at the hands of several women. His wife left him for another woman." She paused to allow the male jurors to process the feeling. "She took their son. His fiancée was killed by a female driver just days before they were to be married." She paused again. "This is a man who seriously dislikes women. This is a man who claimed that his sickest female patients should do the world a favor and die. This is a man who once beat his own father senseless.

"We will present evidence that puts the defendant at the scene of the crime. We will establish motive, opportunity, and empirical evidence that Dr. Andrew Albright murdered Paula Callaway. I'm sure that Ms. McNeil will tell you that her client was framed, but the evidence overwhelmingly indicates that Andrew Albright is guilty of murder."

She stayed in front of the jury box for a good thirty seconds before she thanked them and sat down, wanting her thoughts to settle in before Beverly could speak.

Andrew was sweaty and nauseous.

Beverly stood and crossed the room to stand in front of the jury box. "Ladies and gentlemen, I am Beverly McNeil and I represent a fine man, a highly respected physician and a community leader. You have a difficult job as jurors. You must sift out fact from fiction. I encourage you to pay particular attention to *what* is said in this courtroom, not *how* it is said. Some of the facts you will hear are true and some of them are false. It is the ones that are false that clearly show that Andrew Albright is not the person who committed these unspeakable crimes."

Beverly also paused for about tens seconds to give the jury time to anticipate her next words. She had worn a pale yellow suit to convey an aura of friendliness as opposed to the blue, pin-stripe power suit that her opponent wore.

"It is true that Andrew Albright's first wife left him for a woman. It is true that Julia Osborn suffered an untimely death. It is also true that my client loved each of these women. It is true that Dr. Albright was Ms. Callaway's physician. It is also true that my client was at Paula Callaway's house the day she was murdered. It was, however, twelve hours *before* she was murdered. He was delivering her some much-needed medicine because she was unable to go out that day. That's the type of doctor that he is: His patients come first."

Beverly looked at Andrew and then at the jury, playing them for some sympathy.

"Where fiction begins in this case is with the alleged motives that the prosecution will present. Neither anger nor bitterness was the underlying cause of the murders. It was greed. I will paint you a picture of unbridled greed and what happens when it goes unchecked. People are killed over money all the time. I will clearly show that my client was not the greedy party. In fact, he ran from the money. Follow the money, ladies and gentlemen. It's been a standard truth for hundreds of years: Follow the money and you'll find the killers.

"Justice is a funny thing; it is always there in front of you," Beverly continued. "Our collective job is to seek it out. Above all else, justice prevails when we seek the truth. I ask you to read between the lines of Ms. Bridgeman's case and hear what she doesn't say. Thank you for your time and attention."

The District Attorney called Amy Thomas as her first witness. Beverly was a caught off guard with the move. She leaned over to her client and whispered that the DA was looking for a quick kill. She was going to tell the jury right off the bat that Andrew wished his patients dead. As long as the jury believed that fact then the rest would be child's play.

After establishing her background, Rebecca said, "Ms. Thomas, how long have you worked at Partners Medical Group?"

"Twelve years," she said.

"During that time, did you have an opportunity to work with the defendant?"

"Yes, we worked together closely." Amy held no animosity toward Andrew, but Rebecca had convinced her that Andrew was capable of committing murder. Once that door had opened it had been easy to turn her from neutral and protective to truthful.

"Did you ever have an occasion to hear Dr. Albright speak poorly of his severely ill female patients?"

"Yes, I did." Amy had been coached well. She only addressed the questions asked.

"What did he say to you specifically?"

"Dr. Albright told me that he thought that these women should do the world a favor and die."

The jury sat up in unison as if the movie they were watching just got interesting.

"Do you think he meant it?"

Beverly objected, stating that Ms. Thomas couldn't know the defendant's state of mind, but was quashed by the judge after Rebecca explained the long-term working relationship between nurse and doctor.

Amy responded slowly. "It's hard to tell what's in a person's heart, but he said it in the most serious voice."

"Did he indicate why they needed to die?"

"He claimed that they were a burden to all those around them."

Looking into each of jurors' eyes who had ill parents at home, Rebecca said, "Thank you, Ms. Thomas, I know that was difficult."

"Your witness, Ms. McNeil," Judge Bennett said.

"Thank you, your Honor. Ms. Thomas, I have just a few questions. I want to go back to your work history. Is that okay?"

"Of course."

"You testified that you worked with Dr. Albright for twelve years."

"No, that's not quite correct. I said that I worked at the clinic for twelve years."

Even though she'd made the mistake intentionally, Beverly apologized anyway. "Sorry, my mistake. How many years did you work for Dr. Albright?"

"I was his nurse for a little over five years."

"So you worked for multiple physicians during your tenure at PMG?"

"Yes, I did."

"Had you ever heard Dr. Albright make a statement like this before?"

"No, but he was moody."

Beverly interrupted her. "Move to strike?" She wasn't going to let Amy travel beyond where she wanted her to go. Judge Bennett instructed the witness to stick to the questions asked.

Amy answered again. "No, I never heard him say anything like that before that day."

"Could you compare my client's skills and bedside manner with other doctors you've worked for?"

"I'm not sure I know what you mean."

"Was he generally better than, or worse than, the other physicians in his care for his patients?"

"He was average."

This was exactly what Beverly was looking for. She walked over and picked up a document off the table. "Ms. Thomas, I will show you Defense Exhibit One now. Is this a copy of your performance review from last year?"

"It is."

"Can you read for the jury the highlighted section?"

"'Dr. Albright has given me fantastic opportunities to grow. He is one of the most caring, best bosses I have had here at PMG.'"

"Were those your words, Ms. Thomas?"

"Yes, but–" She wanted to explain the difference in Andrew after Julia died.

"Thank you, Ms. Thomas, that's all I have for you today." Beverly knew the art of knowing when to stop. She only needed to plant the seed. Plant enough of them and she would be home free. Go too far and she could blow it.

The DA called her next witness. It was no surprise that it was Laura Donaldson. Rebecca spent ten minutes asking questions regarding how the couple had met and their early-married history. Laura indicated that Andrew was gone much of the time because of medical school and his residency program. Rebecca was successful in getting Laura to expose some of Andrew's insecurities. Then she went after her real reason for putting her on the stand.

"Ms. Donaldson, how did you find your husband's moods?"

Beverly objected on the grounds of relevance, although she knew the Judge would overrule her. He did.

"He was up and down a lot."

"Did you ever fear for your safety?"

"No, not until Andrew went crazy one day and beat up his father."

The jury sat up straighter again, and the gallery buzzed. The judge looked about to rap his gavel for quiet, but the people in the courtroom settled down on their own.

"Can you describe that day?" Rebecca asked.

Laura responded with a faint smile. "We were at his parents' house and Andrew and his father were having a discussion that got heated. I wasn't close enough to hear the exact words. All of a sudden, I heard Andrew yelling something about needing to be punished. He was hitting his father, they fell to the floor, and Andrew was on top of him, beating him. Both his mother and I were screaming for him to stop. Carol was crying hysterically."

Feeling sick, Carol had to leave the courtroom.

Rebecca pressed on. "What happened next?"

"Mrs. Albright called the police. Andrew had stopped before they got there, but he was still in a rage. The police arrested him for assault and battery."

"What became of Mr. Albright?"

"They took him to the hospital with a concussion and a broken jaw."

Rebecca paused before she asked, "Did your husband ever explain why he had done that despicable thing to his own father?"

"He never told me the truth, if that's what you're asking." He'd never told her anything, but it sounded better if she could shade it.

"Thank you, that's precisely what I was asking."

Rebecca introduced photos of the damage Andrew had inflicted on his father. Laura ID'd the photos and then the DA showed them one at a time to the jury.

Although Andrew had been instructed to show no emotion, he hung his head.

Rebecca turned the witness over to Beverly, who took a look at her notes before asking Laura any questions, delaying for affect. She didn't have anything else. The fight had happened and Beverly still didn't know why. She had to call Carol to the stand to undo the damage.

"Ms. Donaldson, you left my client in 'ninety-five, is that correct?"

"Yes."

"Can you describe the circumstances that led to your leaving?"

"I wasn't getting what I needed out of the relationship. I sought comfort elsewhere. I was lonely."

Changing her tone, Beverly probed, "Are you suggesting that my client was the reason for your loneliness?"

"Yes."

"If that were the case, why not develop a relationship with another man?"

"Because, Ms. McNeil, I am a homosexual." Pencils weren't moving, not the response from the jury she wanted.

"Then truth be told, you left your husband because of your own sexual preferences and not out of loneliness or neglect?"

"I guess that would be accurate."

Rebecca cringed; juries distrusted witnesses who gave answers starting with "I guess."

"Did my client ever physically or emotionally abuse you?"

"The only neglect I felt was when he was in medical school. The classroom was his mistress."

"I'll take that as a no. Now, let's be clear here. The specific reason you left Andrew Albright was to pursue a relationship with another woman, right?"

Laura hesitated; she and Rebecca hadn't discussed this. "I would say that's correct."

"Has your ex-husband ever abused your son in any way?"

Laura looked at Drew and smiled. "No."

Beverly had to find out for herself, so she asked, "Did Andrew ever confide in you why he attacked his father?"

"No, he certainly did not. We all wanted to know, even the police," she replied, unwittingly undoing her own earlier testimony.

"I only have a few more questions. Ms. Lindsey Resnick is now your life partner?"

"Yes, she is."

"Do you love her?"

It was Rebecca's turn to object as to relevance.

Judge Bennett intervened. "Ms. McNeil, I'll allow this line of question for a very short period of time. Please give it some direction."

Laura responded without being asked again. "Oh yes, I do love her."

"Is she moody?"

"Do you know a woman who *isn't* moody from time to time?"

The courtroom erupted in chuckles. Even Judge Bennett cracked a smile. He had his gavel in hand to bring order to the courtroom, but he did not have to use it.

"You said that your husband was moody, yes?"

"Yes."

"Would you say more or less moody than Ms. Resnick?"

"I would say a different moody."

"Any chance that you'll leave Ms Resnick because she is moody?"

Rebecca jumped up shouting, "Objection." She didn't even get to start her reason before Beverly withdrew the question.

Laura Donaldson was excused and Judge Bennett called a recess for the evening.

Before going their separate ways, Beverly summed up Day

Two. "We're taking on some water. The DA did a good job of lining up her witnesses. The jury will be thinking all night about you and your father. Andrew, I need to know what happened."

"I thought you did a terrific job on cross," he said slowly while collecting his thoughts. "Our ship is strong, and I doubt the jury is interested in why, and you're not getting it from me."

Toni, annoyed at his stubbornness, couldn't stand it any longer. "Damn you, Andy, you're just being stupid. Get in the game, man! These people are shooting at you. Can I get you a blindfold?"

"I made it clear long ago that this topic was out of bounds. Stay out of it, you two. Get it through your heads: I am *not* going to talk about it."

The two women just looked at each other. Men. Clients. What could you do with them?

Andrew took Drew out to eat. They both picked at their food. Laura would take him home for the night. That was the deal: He could attend the trial but had to spend his nights with Laura. She did not want him living the case twenty-four hours a day. In this situation, she was right.

Toni had dinner with Carol, hoping she would drop a hint about that night so long ago. They discussed just about everything except that fight. If Andrew didn't want Carol to say anything, Carol wanted to say even less. But, she said enough along the way to give Toni some ideas to share with Beverly–most importantly, that there was an undercurrent that Carol was the one who had something to hide, which would explain Andrew's defensiveness.

—Chapter 41—

Day three of the trial started with slightly less fireworks. Rebecca paraded several witnesses in front of the jury to cement Dr. Albright's pattern of hostility. Beverly, of course, was going to parade her own character witnesses, who she believed were stronger than the District Attorney's, when her side was up. Rebecca's first material witness of the day was Christopher Cromwell.

Beverly wondered why she was offering him up so easily. She had to know that part of her defense was going to be pointing the smoking gun his way.

Christopher was poised, dressed in a conservative gray suit, white shirt, and red tie, and ready to go. Although he harbored some feelings of guilt, he hid it well. He commanded respect and the jury gave it to him. Rebecca asked Dr. Cromwell the standard questions, eventually bringing in his role in QualityCare and its success story. He talked with ease about the Board supporting his plan to expand the organization. He expressed sorrow over the deaths, even though they had cost him and his staff considerable time and negative publicity.

"Dr. Cromwell, did you specifically offer Dr. Albright a position at QualityCare after the public offering was complete?"

"I did."

"Can you describe that offer?"

"Arthur Bishop talked to Andrew about eventually becoming QualityCare's CEO."

"I'm sorry, Doctor, but who is Arthur Bishop?"

"Arthur is the CEO of the British Insurance Group. It is his organization that facilitated the processes for our going public on Wall Street. He is now my boss."

"Was the offering successful?"

"Immensely, yes."

"Thank you for that clarification. Now, isn't the CEO job your current position?"

"It is today, but it is probable that I will take a position in London once Mr. Bishop retires."

"What did Dr. Albright say regarding the offer?"

"He never actually commented on it. Instead, he made a clear threat to pull his clinic out of the network if the overall affect on the clinic was negative. He was convinced that he could control the deal."

"How did that make you feel?"

"Honestly, I felt as if I was being blackmailed."

Beverly made a note and circled the word "blackmail" and added "motive?" next to it.

"What happened next?"

"Arthur asked me to take the employment offer off the table, and I did."

"Why take the offer off the table?"

"Because we did not believe that the interest of the new shareholders would be served by having a CEO who was not a hundred percent behind the organization."

"What was Andrew's reaction?"

"He was angry." He answered the next question without Rebecca having to ask it. "He was bitter that we would treat him that way. He felt rejected."

Needing to stop the momentum, Beverly interjected, "Objection. Speculation."

Judge Bennett upheld the objection and admonished Christopher. "Dr. Cromwell, stick with facts, please."

Christopher responded while looking down. "I apologize, your Honor."

Having dispensed with the trivial stuff, Rebecca went for the heavier side. "Dr. Cromwell, did you stand to gain monetarily as part of the public offering?"

"Yes. It is very typical to offer senior management stock options as part of their incentive compensation."

Beverly didn't understand the DA's strategy, and bemoaned again her lack of experience with criminal trials. She knew *something* bad had to be up if Rebecca was serving up a defense witness for slaughter.

Rebecca, on the other hand, was enjoying the moment because she knew she had her opponent confused. She was gaining strategic ground.

"Were these incentives out of line with industry standards?"

"We explicitly worked with our Wall Street consultant to establish something on the conservative side of executive incentives."

"What happened?"

"The QualityCare Board of Directors appropriately rejected the first plan until such time that we could establish a broader stock option plan for all of our employees, not just the executives."

"Did you support that action?"

"Yes, I did."

"Now, Dr. Cromwell, I'm going to ask you some difficult questions that I know this court is interested in." She paused to let the jury settle in. "Doctor, the financial performance of QualityCare was an important factor in the actual public offering price of the stock. Is that correct?"

"Correct. Like the rest of the insurance industry, we needed to improve our bottom line."

"By bottom line you mean profits?"

"Correct."

"What would be the financial impact of the deaths of patients like Paula Callaway on the profits of QualityCare?"

"Anytime a chronically ill member leaves the organization, regardless of the reason, it helps the bottom line."

Rebecca looked at the jury to gauge their body language. She had them where she wanted them, leaning forward in their chairs, engaged and curious as to where she was going.

"Would it be fair to say that the average person might wonder about your own motivation in the deaths of these women?"

Beverly needed to object, even if she was not sure why. "Objection, your Honor. I don't see the relevance of this line of questioning."

Judge Bennett was curious as well. "Well, Ms. Bridgeman, where are we going here? You joining the defense team mid-trial?" The courtroom burst into laughter.

"Your Honor, part of the defense's line of questions will be to cast doubt on Dr. Cromwell's veracity in order to create reasonable doubt. We would like to address that issue proactively."

"Uh-huh. You want to cut the defense off at the knees, right?" The courtroom burst into laughter. "Well, this is a little unusual, but up to your normal less-than-orthodox ways. Proceed, Ms. Bridgeman. Ms. McNeil, there's nothing in the law that says Ms. Bridgeman can't get to your argument first. You'll get your crack at him on cross."

Beverly finally got it. Rebecca was trying to eliminate greed and the IPO as a motive.

Rebecca repeated her question.

"Well, if you are suggesting that I was involved in the murders of these women in any way, it isn't true."

"How did you come to believe someone might think that way?"

"It came to me from someone I have the utmost respect for, Ms. Antoinette Vincenzo."

"Ms. Vincenzo was the corporate attorney for QualityCare?"

"Yes, she was, and in that capacity she sat in my house and accused me of having a stronger reason to kill those women than did Andrew."

"And how did you react?"

"I was upset."

"What did you do?"

"I conferred with my own legal counsel and we decided to take a proactive step in the matter."

"What exactly did you do?"

"I took two lie detector tests." Christopher had been reluctant to do so at first, but Rebecca and Arthur both convinced him that it was in his own as well as BIG's best interest.

Beverly was furiously writing notes attempting to regroup her cross-examination questions.

"Were these tests privately administered through your attorney?"

"No, we went to an objective third party law enforcement agency."

"I assume the results were consistent with your assertion here of zero involvement in the death of Paula Callaway?"

"Both times." Rebecca paused, almost expecting to hear Beverly's voice.

"Thank you, Dr. Cromwell. That is all that I have for you." The results weren't admissible, but the voluntary action made the intended point with the jury.

Beverly got up, still trying to collect her thoughts. She thought of asking for a recess, but she didn't want the jury to have any time to process the fact that they were stealing her defense. She even missed the opportunity to point out to the jury that the polygraph results would never be admitted into the court record, so no one would truly know if Chris were telling the truth.

"Dr. Cromwell, how long have you known my client?"

"I helped recruit him to PMG in 'ninety-two."

"Have you ever known my client to be violent?"

"No, I have never seen him exhibit violence."

"Now, Dr. Cromwell, you testified that my client was bitter about you taking the CEO job off the table. Did I hear that right?"

"Yes, you did."

"Did Andrew Albright ever express an interest in that job?"

"Not directly."

"Okay, did he ever indirectly give you any signal that he desired the job?"

Hesitating, Christopher said, "Well, no, I guess he didn't."

"At any time since you have known my client did he seek employment at QualityCare?"

"No."

"Then why would you think he was bitter when you took the offer off the table?"

Rebecca interjected quickly. "Objection, speculation."

"Sustained." bellowed Judge Bennett.

"My apologies, your Honor. Let me rephrase. Doctor, what do you believe was Dr. Albright's reaction when you took the offer off the table that he did not want in the first place?"

"Objection, leading." Rebecca couldn't let Beverly undermine her offense.

Judge Bennett addressed both women. "Ladies, let's keep this aboveboard. Doctor, please answer the question, but stick to facts."

"I don't know how Andrew felt, but he acted agitated." Not that the agitation had anything to do with the job offer.

"Could you describe what you mean by agitated?"

"He left in a huff."

"Doctor Cromwell, why do you believe that Toni Vincenzo would question your role in this case?"

"Because she's in love with your client and wants to protect him."

"How on earth would you come to that conclusion?"

"Because she told that to my wife, Roxanne."

Beverly had just made a mistake. She wanted to discredit this witness, but anything she said now could be interpreted as badgering. She made a note to talk to Toni about calling Roxanne to the stand later to ask her why she'd say such a thing.

It was standard procedure for attorneys in criminal cases to list every possible name they could think of on a "possible witness" list before a trial, and since Roxanne was on it, the defense could call her to the stand without fighting through the DA.

Beverly closed with, "Doctor, you've known my client for ten years, do you really believe he committed these murders?"

Chris answered truthfully. "I have a difficult time believing that Andrew could do such a thing, but the facts certainly point in that direction, don't they?"

"That's what we're here to decide, Dr. Cromwell."

The judge took a lunch break. Team Albright had lunch brought into the courthouse. Beverly asked Toni about her comments to Roxanne. Toni swore she'd never told Roxanne about any feelings for Andrew. They determined that Roxanne had to spend some time on the stand.

After lunch, Rebecca started in on the physical evidence by calling the pharmacist from PMG. He testified that Dr. Albright had signed out the medication for Paula Callaway, which Rebecca used to establish that Andrew had been at her house that day. The pharmacist also testified that PMG was missing a canister of gas, which turned out to be the same canister that was used to add the deadly toxins that killed Paula Callaway. It had eventually been found in a nearby trash can, just as the plan had called for.

Beverly asked if there was any evidence linking Dr. Albright to the removal of the canister. The answer was no, but again the prosecutor was planting seeds faster than the defense. Beverly grilled him on what Andrew's delivery of needed medication had to do with a murder that took place twelve hours later. She didn't get far with that line; Rebecca popped up and down, calling out "Speculation" at nearly every sentence.

Having established that Andrew was capable of violence, it was time to show how that violence could manifest itself. Rebecca called the Medical Examiner to the stand to present the autopsy results. There were no surprises. Paula was poisoned and the toxins in her body matched those in the oxygen canister. The physical marks on her arms were consistent with being restrained.

Beverly was able to establish on her cross that there was no evidence on the victim that could be traced directly to her client.

Next on the stand was the fingerprint expert, Paul Tanaka. Rebecca was used to bringing the technical and tedious testimony of experts down to the level that the jury could understand. Beverly was not gifted in this area. While Rebecca had the witness talking about the swirls and curves of the human fingerprint, Beverly got lost in the details of the side-by-side posters of the fingerprints on the glass and those of her client, taken during his jail intake process. There was no doubt that the fingerprints on the glass belonged to Dr. Andrew Albright.

Beverly's only saving grace came in her last line of rebuttal question. "Mr. Tanaka, you claim the fingerprints on this glass found at Ms Callaway's home belong to my client, correct?"

"Yes."

"Then tell me, Mr. Tanaka, is it possible that the fingerprints could have been left at an earlier point in time?"

"That, Ms. McNeil, is not my area of expertise. I'll leave that one for the detectives." Beverly made a mental note to grill Detective Schmeidekamp on the matter.

"Let me make this easier for you. Technically speaking, with all your skill and tools available, you cannot tell this court when the fingerprints were left on the glass. Am I correct?"

"That is correct," he said as he shot the DA a quick glance. Beverly thanked him and took her own seat with a boost of new confidence.

The DNA expert went much the same way. The hair samples found at the scene of the crime matched Dr. Albright's. Beverly made no progress on this witness other than to reinforce her theory that the evidence against Dr. Albright had been planted there by someone else.

Rebecca's last witness of the day was Charles Schmeidekamp. The DA went through his testimony slowly. She wanted to use up as much of the remaining time as possible, leaving the jury with a complete picture of the evidence, and leave no time for Beverly to make any other points. If she could tie up Friday just as effectively, she would have the jury right where she wanted them, mentally, over the weekend.

Schmidy described the crime scene as well as the investigation that led him to Andrew Albright. He shared with the jury that Andrew had no viable alibi. He had dinner with his son that evening, but the murder happened at 3:00 in the morning. He focused specifically on the collection and custody of the evidence to avoid any possibility of a mix-up or tampering. His testimony was routine but effective. Most importantly, it ended at 4:35. As Rebecca finished, Beverly stood to begin her attack.

"Ms. McNeil, you can take your seat. I think starting your cross at this late hour would not be prudent. We will recess until tomorrow morning at nine a.m. sharp," the judge announced.

—Chapter 42—

Beverly returned to the courtroom Friday morning wondering if she had the ability to salvage her case and save her client.

She and Toni had spent the better part of the previous evening discussing their strategy with Travis. First they wanted Schmidy to admit that it was possible that the hair strands and fingerprint evidence had been planted. The second goal loomed more difficult: They needed to get Schmidy to discuss several other suspicious deaths of QualityCare members for which Andrew was not a suspect. This would support their "greed" theory.

Judge Bennett began the day by announcing that he planned to adjourn at 2:30. It was an autumn-summer Friday and many people, including him, were headed to the lake for the weekend. The judge called Schmidy back to the stand, and passed him off to Beverly for her cross-examination.

"Detective, you testified yesterday that you have twenty years of experience in law enforcement. During that time, how many murder cases have you investigated?"

He answered while twisting his moustache. "I'm not really sure."

"Have you ever testified in court before?"

"Of course." He was still playing with his moustache. Andrew thought he looked nervous and wondered why.

"Have you ever been asked that question before?"

"Of course."

"Would it surprise you if I told you that you testified just a month ago to having investigated over a hundred and fifty murders in that twenty years?" Beverly didn't expect Schmidy to be a difficult witness, but she also didn't expect him to help her prove her client's innocence. She'd settle for a small gain.

"That sounds about right."

Beverly looked at the jury to emphasize the point. "In that time, have you ever run into a case where the physical evidence had been left at the scene of the crime by someone else?"

"I'm not familiar with a similar case where multiple pieces of evidence were planted, if that's what you're asking. It's hard to keep that many cases straight."

"Let's get more specific, shall we?" She glanced down at a file she held in her hands. "Two years ago you investigated a case involving the murder of an attorney by a coworker. The case took place at another law firm here in town. Do you remember that case?"

"Vaguely," he said knowing it had been one of the most publicized cases in the last ten years. Beverly presented a court reporter's transcript of his testimony during the trial in question. She had highlighted several passages and allowed him a couple of minutes to read the transcript.

When he made eye contact she asked, "Detective, can you give the court a brief summary of what happened in that case?" She walked over and stood in front of the jury box.

"The deceased was allegedly killed by his law partner. They were feuding over money in the partnership. The physical evidence put him at the scene of the crime. We discovered that the crime had actually been committed by the deceased man's wife."

"And how did the physical evidence of the law partner show up at the crime scene?"

"It was placed there by the wife."

"Why would she do such a thing?"

"I can't speculate on why she did that."

"Is it possible she did it to frame someone else?"

"That is one possibility."

"Are there any others?"

"Can't say."

Beverly noticed several jurors taking notes. "Let's come back to our case here today. Is it possible that the physical evidence linking my client to these murders was planted in a similar fashion?"

"I don't believe that to be the case."

"That's not what I asked you."

"My professional experience tells me that the facts do not yield that conclusion."

"Judge Bennett, would you instruct Mr. Schmeidekamp to answer the question asked?"

"Detective, you've done this before. You know the drill. Answer the questions asked of you. Counselor, remind the witness what the question was so there's no confusion."

Beverly repeated, "Is it possible that the physical evidence at the scene of the crime was planted there by someone else?"

Schmidy looked over at Andrew and said, "Yes, it's possible."

Beverly did a mental hand-spring. She might finally be regaining some ground. "Now, Detective, I want to ask you about several other suspicious deaths you're working on."

Rebecca jumped up and objected. Both she and the judge knew where she was going with this line of questions. Judge Bennett was going to get to the bottom of this one immediately. "We'll take a thirty-minute recess. Bailiff, please escort the jury to the jury room. I will see both attorneys in my chambers. Now ladies." He filed into his adjacent office and they followed like suckling puppies.

"Ms. McNeil, your client is not on trial for those crimes. Why bring them up here?"

"It is our understanding, your Honor, that there have been two other recent deaths of catastrophically ill QualityCare members. One premature baby and one car accident victim on life support. While my client has not been questioned or accused in these cases, we believe that they fit the pattern of murder for money. Call it Wall Street greed if you like."

Rebecca weighed in. "Your Honor, this is the worst case of a fishing expedition I've ever seen. Dr. Albright is only on trial here for the murder of Paula Callaway. Can't we stick to that? This diversion tactic is straight out of first year law."

The judge thought for a moment and then ruled. "Ms. McNeil, unless you have some tangible evidence that allows you to connect the dots here, I'm not allowing this line of questions."

"But you're eliminating a valuable piece of our defense."

"Find another angle, Counselor; this one is out." He turned and asked Rebecca, "Ms. Bridgeman, how many more witnesses do you intend to call?"

"Actually, I'm done. We'll rest our case after Detective Schmeidekamp is excused."

"Fine. When we finish with this witness, we'll adjourn for the weekend so Ms. McNeil can get her defense case squared away."

Beverly pleaded, "Judge, I'd prefer to start my defense right after lunch. I have the witnesses on hand and ready to be called before we wrap for the day."

Everyone in the room knew that she needed some time to earn points before the jury had the entire weekend to stew over what they'd heard, but the judge wasn't inclined to care.

"The jury has plenty to chew on over the weekend. We will adjourn when you're done with this witness," he reiterated.

When court reconvened, Judge Bennett explained to the jury that they were to disregard the previous question asked by defense counsel. Beverly decided to take a calculated risk. She was going to call Paula's boyfriend as her first defense witness Monday morning, and now was the time to set up his testimony.

"Detective, I understand from your testimony that you discovered that Ms. Callaway called Dr. Albright's home phone number at three-twelve a.m. the morning she died?"

"That is correct."

"Why do you think she did that?" She was asking him to speculate, but Rebecca didn't object–she thought it played right into her hands.

"We believe she was trying to signal who the killer was. Otherwise, she would have called nine-one-one."

"Is it possible she was calling Dr. Albright because she was instructed to do so?"

"Makes no sense to me."

"Did you interview Paula's boyfriend, Reggie Ryan?"

"Of course we did. He was the first person on the scene."

"Mr. Ryan had just returned from Grand Rapids?"

"Correct."

"Did Mr. Ryan tell you that in his absence he instructed Paula to call Dr. Albright if she was having any problems?"

"I do not recall him saying that." The truth was that he had not asked.

"Thank you, Detective, I have no other questions right now."

Rebecca rested, pleased with the status of her case.

Beverly and Toni spent the better part of Saturday morning going over what had become "their" defense. Toni had spent so much time working with Beverly, she was an honorary, if not official, member of the firm. They argued over what to do about

Carol; they needed her to talk about the events surrounding Andrew's fight with his father, but Toni doubted they'd get much out of her. Beverly decided to put her on the stand anyway. They discussed the timing for putting Roxanne Cromwell on the stand, and when and if Toni herself should be called.

Andrew's spent the time with Drew on the golf course. Drew played well, though Andrew merely went through the motions. He wondered how long he might be able to play golf with his son.

Toni had dinner with Andrew on Sunday night. They hadn't spent a lot of time alone recently. He had already prepared dinner when she came over. They batted around more ideas about the trial and the witnesses when Toni innocently asked, "Do you know that Carol asked me to hang on to Julia's diary?"

"No, I didn't know that, but it's okay. In fact, read it if you want. It might help you understand Julia."

"Too private," she said.

"Trust me, it's not all that private."

"You've read it?" It was not that she was shocked as much as he had never mentioned it before.

"Yes, I read most of it last New Year's Eve. I was going through her stuff. I was lost and wanted to be closer to her. I don't remember anything specific in it. Too painful."

"I don't know, I still don't think I should read it."

"Do what you want, either way it's no big deal."

While finishing the dishes together Andrew asked her the question that had been nagging at him. "*Did* you tell Roxanne that you loved me?"

Toni continued drying the pan she had in her hands, but the question threw her. She had the answer to the actual question, of course, it was the unasked one that she was thinking about. "No, I didn't; I don't even think your name came up that night. If it had, though, I think I probably would've told her that I do care about you, because I do. Time will tell where we go from here. For now, let's concentrate on winning this trial. Agreed?"

"Absolutely. I think that's the right way to go."

"Listen, I need to go home and put Maria to bed. Please try to get some sleep; you're looking dreadful, no offense."

He walked her to her car and kissed her lightly on the lips, thinking that it was a good thing that Toni didn't love him because he was headed for prison if Beverly couldn't pull a rabbit out of a hat.

Toni apologized to Maria for being gone so much. It was no problem for her. She enjoyed being with Nana and Papa because they spoiled her. Toni read her two stories that night and then tapped her daughter on the head three times. Maria tapped her mother three times on the cheek to say that she loved her as well.

Toni made herself comfortable on the couch. She stared at Julia's diary for a long time before she started to read it. She didn't get very far. Given her own emerging feelings, she felt as if she was cheating on a dead woman. She knew it was silly, but the feeling surrounded her and she succumbed to it, putting the book in her backpack and heading off to bed.

—Chapter 43—

Monday morning came and Beverly had to get back to planting the seeds of doubt about where the physical evidence had come from. So she called Reggie Ryan to the stand first.

Reggie told the jury that he and Paula had been together for six years. He was very clear that Paula was a fighter. He knew from the first second that this hadn't been a suicide. After dispensing with the preliminaries and building the credibility of their relationship, Beverly went after what she wanted. "Mr. Ryan, can you tell the court where you were the night Paula died?"

"I was in Grand Rapids, visiting my father; he's pretty sick."

"Do you travel often?"

"I'd say that between work and family I'm gone at least one day a week and sometimes two."

"What was your role in Paula Callaway's care?"

"I played two roles; first, I was her morale coach." Reggie paused and choked back the tears that were forming. "The second was to make sure she got the right medications and home treatments."

"What were Paula's instructions in case of an emergency while you were gone and neither you or the home healthcare nurse were with her?"

"Under any set of circumstances involving her health, she was to first contact Dr. Albright or the doctor on call. Then she was supposed to call me. I bought this pager for exactly that purpose."

"Why not have her call nine-one-one?"

"To be honest, Paula panicked several times early in her illness. She called nine-one-one only to have them instruct her under similar circumstances to call her doctor. This procedure was actually started by Dr. Bruce Meyers, Dr. Albright's partner."

The weekend had obviously done some damage to the jury's attention. Beverly had hoped for intense interest; instead, they simply looked bored, other thoughts still lingering from the break. She feared they had already made up their minds.

"Mr. Ryan, do you believe that Paula was following those instructions when she dialed Dr. Albright's phone number that night?"

"Without a doubt. We'd talked about this a hundred times," he said, looking right at the jury.

"Do you think Dr. Albright was in Paula's bedroom that night?"

"Objection," Rebecca shouted. "Speculation."

"Overruled. Continue, Ms. McNeil. "

"Your Honor, I–" Rebecca was getting geared up for a fight when she was cut off.

"Ms. Bridgeman, is there something about being overruled you don't understand?"

"No sir."

"Then let's continue, please."

"Reggie, was Dr. Albright in her room that night?"

"Absolutely not," he said, still looking at the jury.

"Do you think Andrew Albright killed Paula Callaway?"

"I do not."

"Why not?"

"He treated her with considerable care. I'll never believe that he killed her. I wouldn't think he was capable of such a thing."

"Thank you. I have nothing further for this witness."

Rebecca was thrilled with the direction Beverly had taken. She had anticipated it and was ready for it. In fact, she had a series of questions she was sure the jury would get tired of hearing. "Mr. Ryan, is it safe to assume that you know the defendant, Dr. Albright, relatively well?"

"Well enough."

The answer satisfied Rebecca. "Did you know that Dr. Albright told his nurse that some of his patients deserved to die?"

"No."

"Did you know that he physically assaulted his own father to the extent that the man needed to be hospitalized?"

"No."

"Given that we know both of those events happened, does it not seem possible that Dr. Albright might be capable of things that many people would deem improbable?"

"I still don't think he killed Paula."

"Mr. Ryan, do you allow for any possibility that he may have committed this murder?"

"No."

"Thank you, Mr. Ryan. That is all I have for you today."

Beverly then called a series of character witnesses who all testified that Andrew was an excellent, caring physician and a loving father. Each testified that these allegations were far outside of his character. The testimony was persuasive in each case.

Rebecca, however, came back each time with her two-pronged attack: was it also outside of his character to have threatened the life of his patients, and was it further outside his character to have sent his father to the hospital? Rebecca made the point clear: Andrew might appear on the outside as a well-adjusted, considerate, caring doctor, but on the inside he was a smoldering volcano, ready to blow.

Beverly was losing ground and didn't have enough criminal trial experience to counteract this strategy. She spent the better part of the morning treading water, while Rebecca tossed bricks at her. She needed something positive on her side before the jury left for the day. She couldn't afford to play catch-up on Tuesday. She next called Dr. Carl Ludding, an expert psychological profiler, highly respected in his field and in the courts. He testified that Andrew didn't fit the profile of a murderer. He did an adequate job of justifying the abnormal behavior exhibited by the decorated doctor, but in the end he too fell to the DA's two-pronged attack. It was one more brick added to Beverly's burden. This one hurt bad. This had been her professional witness. She immediately decided that she had to abandon any additional witnesses in this line of defense. Arthur Bishop was next on her list of witnesses, but she instead made a snap decision to bypass him in lieu of bringing Carol Sheffield to the stand. It was clearly a desperate move for salvation.

Carol's lone job was to testify as to what had happened between Andrew and his father, which of course she didn't want to talk about at all. It started out badly and only got worse. She answered even the preliminary questions with short, terse answers. Andrew got visibly upset and his sister looked ashen on the witness stand.

"Ms. Sheffield, I want to talk to you about the night my client attacked your father. Can we talk about that?"

She did not answer at first. After a lengthy pause and a prod by the judge, she said, "If we must."

"Were you there that night?"

"Yes, I was."

"Did you witness the event?"

"I did. I did . . . I did," she cried, suddenly falling apart and burying her face in her hands. "I caused the whole thing; it was my fault," she cried, tears flowing down her cheeks.

Caught by surprise, Beverly was slow to proceed. "I am sorry, Carol. How did you cause or provoke this?"

Carol sat there, trance-like. Andrew glared at his attorney, and waved for her to come over to the table, which she ignored. Carol started to speak three different times, but couldn't get the words out.

Beverly walked up to the witness stand and said quietly, "It's okay, Carol, take your time and simply tell the court what happened. Everything will be fine." No response. "Carol?"

Carol looked at the jury and then looked at the judge. "I can't do this." She believed if she told the truth her career and marriage would be ruined. She was crying so hard by now she was having trouble catching her breath.

Andrew decided he'd had enough. He stood up and shouted, "Leave her alone! She does not understand what happened that day!"

Judge Bennett looked at Andrew and scolded him. "Dr. Albright, I am going to have to ask you to please sit down. This is unacceptable behavior."

Andrew responded even more loudly, while moving toward the witness stand. "What is unacceptable is putting my sister in this position in the first place!"

"Ms. McNeil, you have two seconds to get a grip on your client or I'll have him removed from the courtroom."

Beverly grabbed his arm and whispered, "Andrew, stop. You don't want the jury to see you do this. Stop it."

He rushed past her and Judge Bennett jumped up, calling out, "Bailiff, remove the defendant immediately." Andrew was taken forcibly from the courtroom. Judge Bennett called a recess until the following morning. Before he left the bench, he called Beverly to step up and see him.

"Beverly, your client is shooting himself in the foot. This was the exact behavior you were trying to convince the jury he wasn't capable of. You realize that I'll have to cite him with contempt. My thinking is that it may do more harm than good being in the courtroom tomorrow if you plan on continuing to question Ms. Sheffield."

"Your Honor, I can't proceed with Ms Sheffield. It was my plan to put Dr. Albright on the stand tomorrow." She clearly didn't know what else to do. What would Travis do? she asked herself. Was running away an option? She was scared for her client.

"That's your call. Given what we saw today, he'll have to earn an Academy Award for good behavior to be helpful. I'll hold off on the contempt charge pending tomorrow's activity."

Beverly had never considered a plea bargain with the DA. Maybe now would be a good time. Then again, what motivation would Rebecca Bridgeman have to go that route now? She was ahead on points and the clock was certainly in her favor.

—Chapter 44—

Andrew was ashamed of what he'd done, primarily because his son was in the courtroom to witness it.

Beverly told Andrew to meet her in her office at 7:30 that evening, when she got right to it. "Andrew, we have no choice but to put you on the stand and hope you can convince the jury that you're not what they saw today. We have to pull out all the stops, including your telling the jury what happened with your father. We're going to be here all night if that's what it takes to get you ready. I know we've rehearsed twice before, but this is a new ball game, now."

"I'll spend as much time as you like in a coaching session. But I just can't talk about the fight with my father."

"Listen, I'm going to ask you the damn questions and you're going to answer them! This is *not* a debate. You asked me to help you and now you get to thank me by helping yourself. Do you understand me?"

"As well as you understand me!" Andrew knew things weren't looking good for him; he had no intention of taking Carol down with him when he went.

Beverly pushed herself away from her desk and stood up. She paced the room for a couple of minutes, obviously fighting for control of her temper. "Okay, okay, let's calm down and focus on what we can agree on to convince the jury that you did not kill Paula Callaway."

"Okay, let's go. Let's start with my alibi."

"What alibi? You said you were home alone all night. You said you had dinner with Drew and then headed home."

"Exactly. Drew is my alibi." Andrew had convinced himself that Drew was a plausible out.

"What time did you finish dinner with Drew?"

"Nine-ish."

"The time of death, the phone call, was at three o'clock in the morning. How does Drew fit that picture?"

Andrew didn't respond, but still insisted that he wanted to get on the stand to tell his story. Beverly prepped him as best she could. Around two in the morning they called it quits. She went to bed thinking that she needed to stall for time somehow. Putting Andrew on the stand wasn't going to work.

Toni, too, was up all night. She alternated between reading the diary and making notes about it. At 4:00 AM, the diary screamed at her. She read the passage three times. She knew then that Beverly had to put her on the stand. She wrote a whole page of notes that she planned on giving Beverly in the morning. She was tempted to call her right then, but it was better that Beverly at least be fresh; she doubted she herself would be.

In fact, she almost missed the show. She finally closed her eyes at 5:00 in the morning. If it hadn't been for Maria, she would likely have slept through the morning session of the trial. She got ready in record time and tried to call Beverly on her way to the courthouse. Beverly, who was busy lecturing Andrew about his behavior, didn't answer her cell phone, so Toni left her a message.

Beverly finally checked her messages on her cell phone, one

from her husband wishing her luck, and another from Toni with a rushed message. "Call me as your first witness. I have a list of notes and questions for you. I'll explain as soon as I can get there." Beverly was not the least bit sure what the message meant but this was certainly a better tactic than starting the day with Andrew Albright.

The judge came into the courtroom before Toni got there. Beverly asked if she could have a ten-minute delay to confer with her first witness who hadn't yet arrived.

Judge Bennett turned to the DA. "Ms. Bridgeman, any objection?"

"No sir." She figured she could afford to be magnaminous. She had the case won.

A few minutes later Toni came running toward the courthouse. Beverly was waiting for her outside.

Gasping for air, Toni said, "No time to talk. Just ask me the questions I've outlined here. I'll address the father issue as well as build the foundation you'll need to call one more witness."

"Are you sure? You know you'll be viewed as a subjective witness. Rebecca will toast you and then eat you for breakfast."

"If I'm right, what kind of witness I am will be the last thing on her mind. If I'm wrong, we're screwed." They walked into the courtroom.

Judge Bennett reconvened the session and instructed Beverly to call her first witness of the day.

"I call Toni Vincenzo."

Rebecca sat up straight, surprised. Beverly was putting a witness on the stand who was plainly open to attack. Why?

Beverly went through Toni's background, her employment at QualityCare, and asked about her performance review. Toni had wanted this on the record so it wouldn't look like she'd been fired, which would give her a reason to be a biased toward Christopher or QualityCare's management.

Beverly switched subjects. “Ms. Vincenzo, can you tell the court what happened on the night Dr. Albright attacked his father?”

“Yes, I–”

Rebecca was up before Toni could finish. “Objection, your Honor, this has to be hearsay; she certainly wasn’t a witness to the events that day.”

“Your Honor,” Beverly said, reading her notes, “Ms. Vincenzo has not only discussed this with Carol Sheffield, but she’s got written corroboration from Julia Osborn’s diary. Ms. Osborn was Dr. Albright’s fiancée.”

“Let’s take this discussion into my chambers.” Judges hate surprises and this was evidence not recorded elsewhere and certainly hadn’t been reviewed by the DA.

As soon as they walked through the door, Judge Bennett turned and sternly inquired, “Ms. McNeil, this looks a little desperate to me.”

Beverly swallowed hard and responded, “Your Honor, I believe the diary represents crucial evidence that pertains to this case. If Ms. Bridgeman wishes to review the diary and call rebuttal witnesses to the testimony, she’s welcome to it.”

“Wait a second, Judge, I haven’t reviewed the diary and couldn’t possibly cross-examine this witness on this subject.”

The judge pondered his decision for a moment, then looked up from the desk blotter and rendered it: “Rebecca, I’m going to allow the testimony, but with a very short string. If you don’t believe the facts Ms. McNeil elicits come from a first-person account, then you can argue that in front of the jury. Do your cross on the testimony given and you’ll have every right to review the full document and have all the time you need to prepare for more cross-examination. Ms. McNeil, are you planning any more surprises?”

"No sir," she said lacking confidence in her response. "I do, however, intend to call Roxanne Cromwell after lunch."

Judge Bennett rose, saying, "Bailiff, please make sure that Mrs. Cromwell is in the courtroom after lunch. Let's go ladies, and play nice. I don't want a circus out there. Yesterday was bad enough."

Beverly went back to the defense table and leaned over Andrew. "No matter how bad you feel about whatever you're about to hear, keep your mouth shut and your head up. Got it?"

"I told you I didn't want that damn argument to get into this trial! Why the hell are you letting it?"

"Because if I don't, you're going to be convicted of murder and spend the rest of your life in prison, that's why."

The judge signaled Beverly to get back to the business at hand and repeat the question for the witness, which she did.

"I had a conversation with Carol Sheffield about this some two weeks ago at dinner. While she didn't say much, she did make it clear that the fight was her fault. It wasn't until I read some passages in Julia Osborn's diary–she and Andrew had taken a vacation to London together, and he told her the story–that I put it together."

"For the record, Ms. Bridgeman introduced Ms. Osborn in her opening statement as Dr. Albright's deceased fiancée, correct?"

"That is correct."

"How did you come upon this diary?"

"I was asked to hold it for Dr. Albright. When I informed him that I had it, he gave me permission to read it."

"What did you conclude about the event in question regarding Dr. Albright's scuffle with his father?"

Carol and Andrew stared sadly at each other.

"Andrew was a medical student in Florida and had come

home for winter break. Apparently Carol's father had come home early that day and caught his daughter in bed with a man and had thrown the guy out of the house. Then he began verbally abusing Carol. When Andrew walked in, Mr. Albright told his son that his sister was a whore. He was ranting and raving about her behavior. Carol was crying and yelling as well. Andrew tried to separate the two, but Mr. Albright had been out drinking and was just out of control. Then Carol started in on her dad about how unfair it was for a drunken man to call his daughter a whore. Then he hit her. That wasn't what provoked Andrew's attack, though; it was what Carol said next."

"What did Carol say?"

The jury was watching Carol, who was weeping.

Slowly, Toni said, "She told her brother that she was, in fact, a prostitute. Two weeks earlier the escort service she worked for had set up a 'date' for her at a posh local hotel. The man who showed up at the door of the hotel was her father, Mr. Albright. Apparently he'd been consorting with hookers for a long time. Andrew started screaming at his father for being a hypocrite. Then Mr. Albright went after Carol Sheffield and Dr. Albright stepped in to protect her and the fight started."

Looking at her notes, Beverly asked the next question. "In your opinion, why wouldn't Carol Sheffield tell us anything about the fight?"

Rebecca was up immediately. "Objection, speculation."

"Your Honor, we're only offering facts in evidence."

"Fine, but rephrase your question."

"Ms. Vincenzo, can you describe Ms. Sheffield's current life situation? I mean, what is her occupation?"

"Carol Sheffield is a respected state senator in Indiana. She is running for a seat in the United States House of Representatives in November. Her family, friends, and political supporters don't know about her past, and I can only imagine what this kind of information will do to her fall campaign, or life, for that matter. Andrew was protecting her, of course."

Rebecca furiously scribbled some notes. Sympathy wasn't something she wanted the jury to give to Andrew.

Beverly picked up the glass found in Paula Callaway's home. "Ms. Vincenzo, this is state's evidence exhibit four. As you know, it has Dr. Albright's fingerprints on it. Do you recognize this glass?"

"Yes, I've seen a glass just like this one before."

Toni's notes said: Ask me where but don't ask me why.

Beverly followed the path laid out for her. "Where have you seen this glass before?"

"It looks exactly like one at Christopher Cromwell's house. I had a drink there, out of a glass just like that one."

Rebecca wasn't worried. Rather than object, she'd handle the issue on cross. Plenty of people could have glasses just like that one.

"One more question, Ms. Vincenzo. I've highlighted a section of Ms. Osborn's diary; would you please read it for me?"

Rebecca objected. Cutting her off, the judge reminded her of their meeting in chambers. "We covered this and you agreed to my ruling. Objection overruled."

"Julia made the following entry on April twentieth, nineteen ninety-nine: 'I had the most wonderful trip to Florida with Andrew. We've set a date for our wedding and my special man is taking me to Ireland and Scotland for a pre-wedding honeymoon. He thinks Scotland rocks, but wait until he gets to Ireland. I'll show him what rocks. Today was our last day in Florida and I partnered with Roxanne Cromwell in our golf outing. What a bitch. She had the nerve to tell me that her daddy cut her off from her money stream and her husband was just going to have to keep her living in the style and manner to which she was accustomed. How shallow can one be? She made some bizarre reference to having a contingency plan; something about a savior in a black hat, not a white one. It gave me the creeps.'"

Beverly looked down at her notes, "What is the relevance of this?"

"About a week after I accused Christopher of having the motive and means to kill Paula Callaway, I was attacked by a man wearing nothing but black clothes."

"Objection, relevance."

"Sustained. Counselor, we covered this issue before. Move on."

It seemed just as well to Beverly that she move on–until she could talk with Toni, she didn't know where she was supposed to go with her questions. "That's all I have for this witness, your Honor."

"Your witness, Ms. Bridgeman."

Until she had a chance to read what else was in the diary, Rebecca didn't have much to cross with except Toni and Andrew's relationship. She wanted to show Toni as a protective lover.

"Ms. Vincenzo, can you tell the court what your relationship is with the defendant?"

"We are friends."

"Good friends?"

"The best, I hope," she said, smiling at Andrew, who was smiled back.

"Do you dine together?"

"Of course."

"Has Dr. Albright kissed you?"

"Yes."

"Are you sleeping together?"

Beverly addressed the judge. "Please, your Honor?"

"You knew this was coming. She's gonna have to answer."

"No, we are not sleeping together," Toni said, looking directly at the jury.

"Did you ever tell Mrs. Cromwell that you were in love with the defendant?"

"I told her no such thing."

"So, you don't love him."

"If I told you that I loved him, but I am not in love with him, would you understand the difference?"

"No. Regardless of your definition, do you love him enough to protect him?"

"Absolutely."

Rebecca attacked. "Does that include perjury?"

"No. I am an officer of the court, just as you are. I take my oath seriously, just like you. I can assure this court that no person on earth could cause me to violate that oath."

"It has been known to happen."

Beverly objected once again.

Judge Bennett interrupted. "Ms. Bridgeman, stick to asking questions and save your opinions for your closing argument."

Rebecca continued. "Fine, now let's go back to the glass, shall we?"

"Be happy to," Toni said.

"What makes you believe this glass came from the Cromwell home?"

"The etched C reminded me of some of the glasses at their house."

"Don't you think there are thousands of glasses in this city that bear the owners' last initial?"

"Yes, I do. But there's something else."

"What would that be, Ms. Vincenzo?"

"Roxanne Cromwell made a big deal out of the maker's mark

on the bottom of the glass and these particular ones are only made in London, England. She told me they were a gift from Arthur Bishop. Go ahead and look; you'll find that mark on the glass."

Rebecca resisted the temptation. She didn't know if she could keep her face straight if the mark was there. "That doesn't mean Paula Callaway didn't have a set of glasses from London, does it?"

"Well, I can't answer that, but maybe Mr. Ryan can."

Surprised at her own mistake–she didn't usually set traps for herself–Rebecca figured she'd better get Toni off the stand before she did more damage to the state's case. "That's all I have for you now, but I reserve the right to recall you after I've reviewed the diary."

Judge Bennett called a recess for lunch, after which Roxanne would be called. The DA was worried that Chris was going to come under suspicion again. She called his office and told him to meet her for lunch.

Toni and Beverly had a chance to catch their collective breath. Toni finally told Andrew about the night she'd been attacked. They drilled Andrew over lunch for everything he knew about Roxanne, which wasn't much, but he did remember some of what Julia had told him after their trip to Florida.

Just before they returned to the courtroom, Beverly's curiosity made her ask, "What made you read the diary last night?"

"Fate. Who would have known that Julia held the keys of truth here? Let's rock Mrs. Cromwell's world and find out what she knows. I suggest that you rough her up a bit."

Roxanne Cromwell moved smoothly up the courtroom aisle after being called. Knowing every eye was on her, she made the best of it. She took her time settling into the witness chair, turned and smiled at the judge, who she knew through several fund-raising dinners and parties, then turned, smiled at the jurors, then nodded her head at the bailiff, giving her permission to be sworn in.

Amused despite herself, Beverly asked Roxanne a few light-weight questions instead of digging in immediately as she'd planned. Finally, once she was sure Roxanne felt totally in control of the room and full of her own self-importance, she started with the tougher questions. "Mrs. Cromwell, do you know anything about the murder of Paula Callaway?"

"Absolutely not. These are terrible things that happened. I only know what I read in the papers and what Chris has told me."

"Did you know that your husband was a suspect in these murders?"

Rebecca objected and was rejected with the wave of a hand and a single word response by Judge Bennett.

"I know he felt that he had to take a lie-detector test to protect himself."

"Good enough, we will come back to this in a minute, but can you tell us how you met Dr. Cromwell?"

"Christopher and I met while he was cardiologist at the HMO clinic in Boston. We've been married twenty-two years."

"Do you have children?"

"We do not."

"Objection, how is this relevant to anything going on here?"

"Your Honor, I need a little leeway here to establish the foundation for some crucial questions coming up."

Roxanne's pulse began racing with the word "crucial."

"Go ahead, but go quickly."

"Mrs. Cromwell, is there any particular reason you and your husband have not had children?"

Roxanne responded without a hint of remorse. "I was unable."

"Did you ever tell Julia Osborn that you didn't have children because they didn't fit into your plans?"

"I don't recall having said that," she said, a little defensive now.

"Can you tell the court what your father does?"

"He and my brother are both radiologists. Today they hold the patents on several radiological products that they've designed and developed."

"At one point in your life, were you to join them in their business after getting out of medical school?"

"That was the plan."

"What happened?"

"I never completed medical school."

"Never completed or got kicked out?"

The DA didn't know where this was going, but took notes, trying to make the mental connection.

"Never completed."

"In fact, if I checked with the medical school, wouldn't they tell me you were dismissed for cheating on a final exam?"

Now Rebecca knew where this was going. It wasn't good. The judge knew as well and he was poised to reject the objection that was forthcoming. His glare in Rebecca's direction had its intended impact. She kept silent.

"You may be correct."

The jury made a note. Jurors love to have liars caught in the act. Attorneys, depending on which side they're on, love it less.

"Let's go back to the family business. Was there a time when your father gave you a percentage of the profits from the business?"

"Yes."

Looking at the jury, Beverly asked her, "How much, on average, per year?"

"I don't recall."

"Was it more than a hundred-fifty thousand?" Beverly was guessing.

"Yes, but I really don't know how much more."

"Does he provide that money today?"

"No."

"Why not?"

Rebecca shot up. "Objection!"

"Denied!" Judge Bennett motioned for her to sit down.

Getting flustered, Roxanne responded crisply. "You will have to ask my father." Beverly wrote a note just to give the jury the impression that she *would* follow it up.

"Mrs. Cromwell, before lunch, Ms. Vincenzo read a passage out of Julia Osborn's diary. I am going to have the court reporter read it back. I will also show you the highlighted section in the diary."

The judge instructed the court reporter to read the statement. Beverly gave Roxanne a minute to stew on the fact that she was expecting Christopher to make up for her daddy stiffing her.

"Did you make this statement?" Beverly asked.

"No, I did not make that bloody statement," she snapped, as if Beverly were being impertinent for even entertaining such a thought.

It was Rebecca's turn to dodge the bricks flying her way: Beverly was close to establishing motive.

"Mrs. Cromwell, are you not well known in the social circles of Ann Arbor for saying that your husband is well trained to keep you living in the manner in which you are accustomed? In fact, are you not proud that he is willing to do so?"

Rebecca had convinced Christopher Cromwell to come to court during his wife's testimony. The man tried for a nonchalant grin at the question, but it clearly threw him.

"I may have said something similar to that to some of my friends. We're always joking around," she said, perspiration starting to show on her forehead.

"Let's change subjects."

Roxanne had to physically restrain herself from sighing with relief, she was so glad to get that one behind her. Since she'd never been considered material to the case, Rebecca hadn't prepared her for what it was like to be on the witness stand, and it hadn't occurred to her to prepare herself for anything beyond her entrance.

"This glass is state's exhibit four. It was found at Paula Callaway's home with Dr. Albright's fingerprints. Do you recognize the glass?"

"No, I'm sorry, why would I?"

Guessing, but thinking it was a worthwhile guess, Beverly asked, "Mrs. Cromwell, if I asked Mr. Arthur Bishop to come testify as to whether he ever gave you and your husband a gift of glasses just like this one, what would he say?"

"Objection, speculation," Rebecca said, just for the sake of doing something.

"Sustained. Rephrase, Counselor," imparted Judge Bennett.

"Have you ever received a gift of tumblers just like this?"

The seed was there. Roxanne worried the problem around like a squirrel over a nut. Arthur *could* identify the glasses. She waffled a bit. "We may have, I don't recall."

"Do you have any glasses at home that look like this?"

"I'm sorry, but I don't recall." Just like that, Roxanne lost her credibility and also the jury.

"But you might?"

"Yes, we might."

Christopher was getting downright nervous. He wondered what the hell was going on here. He had received daily reports and the last he'd heard Rebecca had been destroying the defense.

"If Dr. Albright was a visitor in your house, would you offer him a drink?"

"What? Well, I suppose so."

"Did he come over to your house often?"

"Uh, not often. From time to time, of course."

"Did he usually stay long enough to have a drink if it was offered to him?"

"Yes, usually."

"So, you could have had his fingerprints on your glasses, right? Is there any chance you put the evidence there, Mrs. Cromwell? You certainly had the opportunity, didn't you?"

"Absolutely not. I did not put any evidence in Paula Callaway's house," she said truthfully.

Beverly pressed forward. "You had a financial motive to make sure your husband did well in QualityCare's public offering, did you not?"

"I always support my husband's endeavors."

"But this was important, was it not?"

Roxanne fidgeted in her chair. "No more so than for his overall career development."

"You had motive and opportunity to put false evidence at Paula Callaway's house, isn't that correct?"

"Damn it, I had nothing to do with the glasses, his hair, or the shoes being at that woman's house! I already told you that!"

Beverly almost dropped her notes. "Hair? You had samples of his hair? And shoe prints? What shoe prints?"

Roxanne's mind froze; she couldn't think of any reason why she'd know about the shoes. She'd screwed up. "Uh, the ones I read about in the paper," she finally lied.

"Can you remember what paper or who wrote the article?"

"No, of course not. But it was there."

"No, Mrs. Cromwell, that little bit of evidence was never

reported–the police always keep back some information, and in this case, that was it. Mrs. Cromwell, did you kill Paula Callaway?"

"No."

"Do you know who did?"

"No," she lied, looking at Christopher.

She was trapped. She couldn't give them the name of the real killer without admitting that she'd hired him.

"Roxanne, are you aware that Ms. Vincenzo was attacked by a man just days after she was at your home talking about the death of Paula Callaway with you and your husband?

"No. Why would I?"

"You sent your man after her to shut her up, didn't you? A man dressed all in black, a man you'd call a 'hero,' right?"

"I did not do it. Tell them, Christopher, tell them I did not do it," she called out to her husband, almost frantic to turn the spotlight off herself.

"Did Andrew Albright kill these women?"

"Yes, yes, yes, of course he did!" Reinforce the lie; use anything to turn the tide away.

Beverly changed the question. "Roxanne, *why* did you kill those women?"

"I didn't kill them, I tell you! I didn't do it," she repeated, almost in a whisper, almost giving up.

"But you know who did, don't you?"

Roxanne broke. "I am so sorry. I am so sorry. I can't believe this. Christopher, I'm so sorry. I wanted it all for you." Still hedging her bet. Still lying, even in defeat.

Beverly immediately moved for dismissal.

Judge Bennett asked that the jury be escorted out of the room. He looked at Roxanne, who was rocking in the witness seat, tears flowing unstopped down her cheeks, repeating over and over that she didn't mean it, didn't mean it, didn't mean it.

He asked that she be removed from his courtroom, and taken into custody. She had a right to consult her own attorney, but he didn't have to wait for that attorney to show up.

Twenty minutes later, after formal arguments from both attorneys, Judge Bennett asked the jury to return. "Ladies and gentleman of the jury, the State of Michigan wishes to inform you that it has dropped the charges against Dr. Andrew Albright. This concludes your service. The State appreciates your time and attention." He raised his gavel and claimed the case dismissed.

—Chapter 45—

Andrew hugged everyone in sight, beginning with Drew. Beverly insisted on having a celebration in her offices in one hour. Carol, Andrew and Toni sat outside the courthouse, shocked by the swift reversal in their fortunes.

He said it more than once. "Who would've thought Julia's diary had the answer all along? Who would've thought, huh?" He turned to Drew. "Little man, I am so glad you were here today. And I apologize for what happened yesterday."

"You were just protecting Aunt Carol. That was pretty cool."

Andrew was afraid it wasn't; he was afraid Carol was going to be an unintended casualty of the battle now that her secret had gone public. She would later comment in private that she was glad that it was in the open. She was confident that her marriage would withstand the storm, and if it cost her votes in an election, so be it.

When Laura arrived to pick up Drew, she'd already heard the news on the television; she hugged her ex-husband and congratulated him. Andrew wasn't sure how sincere she was, but then again, he really didn't care.

After Drew had left, Christopher quietly walked up to Andrew and planted a hand on his shoulder. "I cannot believe this Andrew. I am so sorry. I had no idea and I don't have the words. I'm shocked and mortified."

"There will be time later for us to talk. You don't need to apologize for something you didn't do or know about. It was damn decent of you to say it, though. For now, you should tend to your wife. I'm off to celebrate." Maybe out of sheer exuberance, Andrew took Christopher's hand in his and shook it, washing away one more layer of anger.

An hour later everyone involved in the victory was celebrating in Harris, Steele, and Washington's conference room. Beverly took delivery of a package, which contained a basket of wine, cheese, crackers and fruit. The card said "Congratulations on a great defense. Rebecca."

Both Toni and Beverly commented aloud that this was a woman *definitely* running for political office.

Several partners from the clinic came by. It was turning into a real party. Pretty quickly, Rebecca's wine and the law firm's celebratory bottles of champagne were bone dry, but not before there'd been a few toasts.

Andrew started them. "First, I want to thank all of you for believing in me. Secondly, I want to thank you ladies for the great job you did. It didn't look too good there for awhile, did it?" Everybody groaned, but laughed, because the low points were behind them. "But you kept plugging, thank God. Lastly, I hope I will *never* need your services again."

Beverly went next. "I want to thank Andrew for insisting I take up his defense. I think I'm switching to criminal law, now." She laughed at the astonished looks around the room. "Not. Never. I couldn't stand the strain of that every day."

Travis Washington commented. "Andrew, I want to thank you for paying some bills around here; we'll now be able to keep the lights on for awhile." The room broke out in giddy laughter–at this point, even the lamest of jokes were hilarious. "Okay, and next, Toni, I am hereby authorized on behalf of the partners here at HSW, to offer you a position in our law firm as an associate partner." People started to laugh. He waggled his hands in a calm-down motion. "No, no, this is completely serious. That was outstanding legal work you saw out there."

After a brief pause, everybody applauded Toni.

"I'll have my agent give you a call in the next day or two." Then she laughed. "Yeah, *right*. In all sincerity, thank you. I'll look forward to discussing it with you," she said, knowing full well she'd take the offer, whatever it was.

"Stop by my office before you leave, I have a packet of information for you." Travis shook her hand and patted her on the back.

When the last toast had been given and everybody was again mingling, Beverly came up to Toni, who was seated next to Andrew.

"Toni, I have to know."

"Know what?"

"You took a very big risk today. You could not have known that Roxanne would fold. In fact, had you failed, it would have been the proverbial nail in Andrew's coffin. Why did you do it?"

"Don't know or plead the fifth. You choose."

"I'm not buying that for a minute. Tell us why you did it."

"Because it was the right thing to do. Beyond that, I still plead the fifth." She put her hand on top of Andrew's.

He felt it, but he was looking at Beverly at the time. He turned his attention back to Toni when he felt it again; tap, tap, tap, with her fingers.

While the crowd was buzzing around them, Andrew leaned over and whispered, "Me too."